A Lie for a Lie

Emilie Richards

BERKLEY PRIME CRIME, NEW YORK

THE BERKLEY PUBLISHING GROUP
Published by the Penguin Group
Penguin Group (USA) Inc.
375 Hudson Street, New York, New York 10014, USA
Penguin Group (Canada), 90 Eglinton Avenue East, Suite 700, Toronto, Ontario M4P 2Y3, Canada
(a division of Pearson Penguin Canada Inc.)
Penguin Books Ltd., 80 Strand, London WC2R 0RL, England
Penguin Group Ireland, 25 St. Stephen's Green, Dublin 2, Ireland (a division of Penguin Books Ltd.)
Penguin Group (Australia), 250 Camberwell Road, Camberwell, Victoria 3124, Australia
(a division of Pearson Australia Group Pty. Ltd.)
Penguin Books India Pvt. Ltd., 11 Community Centre, Panchsheel Park, New Delhi—110 017, India
Penguin Group (NZ), 67 Apollo Drive, Rosedale, North Shore 0632, New Zealand
(a division of Pearson New Zealand Ltd.)
Penguin Books (South Africa) (Pty.) Ltd., 24 Sturdee Avenue, Rosebank, Johannesburg 2196,
South Africa

Penguin Books Ltd., Registered Offices: 80 Strand, London WC2R 0RL, England

This is a work of fiction. Names, characters, places, and incidents either are the product of the author's imagination or are used fictitiously, and any resemblance to actual persons, living or dead, business establishments, events, or locales is entirely coincidental. The publisher does not have any control over and does not assume any responsibility for author or third-party websites or their content.

A LIE FOR A LIE

A Berkley Prime Crime Book / published by arrangement with the author

PRINTING HISTORY
Berkley Prime Crime mass-market edition / February 2009

Copyright © 2009 by Emilie McGee.
Cover illustration by Ben Perini.
Cover design by Annette Fiore Defex.
Interior text design by Stacy Irwin.

ISBN: 978-0-425-22664-3

BERKLEY® PRIME CRIME
Berkley Prime Crime Books are published by The Berkley Publishing Group,
a division of Penguin Group (USA) Inc.
375 Hudson Street, New York, New York 10014.
BERKLEY® PRIME CRIME and the PRIME CRIME logo are trademarks of Penguin Group (USA) Inc.

PRINTED IN THE UNITED STATES OF AMERICA

10 9 8 7 6 5 4 3 2 1

1

The last time I saw a circus parade, I was only four years old. That sunlit summer afternoon is still absolutely clear to me. Vendors with pushcarts hawked sky blue cotton candy in paper cones. Clowns in pumpkin-colored wigs flapped giant shoes over cobblestones as they presented children with plastic pinwheels and monkeys on sticks. As the entourage drew closer my handsome young father lifted me in his arms and told me how Hannibal, his personal hero, had driven elephants, just like the ones coming toward us, across the Alps from Carthage to bring Rome to its knees. Thoughts of any powerful government falling prey to the "little guy" still bring tears to Ray Sloan's eyes, and I'm sure that the day the circus came was no exception.

I know those memories of sunshine and the loving embrace of my father aren't figments of my thirty-seven-year-old imagination. Nor is my memory of Ray slugging a greasepaint glutton of a clown who tried to chuck me under my chin. Then there's my final memory, the two of us dodging toddlers and shrieking old ladies as Ray raced helter-skelter from the police who had been charged with escorting the parade, along with the cages of lions and tigers and bears.

Oh, my.

To this day, Ray is not a fan of chin chuckers. To this day I'm still a fan of circuses. I'm also a fan of Ray's, although extra careful with what I choose to report in our letters and phone calls. These days Ray lives in an Indiana survivalist compound with a dozen other Vietnam vets, preparing for the moment when he, like Hannibal, might be called to send Rome, the ATF, or the CIA packing.

The good news is that so far, nobody seems interested in asking Ray for help.

I'm not sure where we happened to be living when that last circus strutted into my memories. I do know where I live now. Emerald Springs, Ohio, my home for nearly three years. Today, if a clown chucked me on the chin, I would be forced to smile and treat him with understanding, maybe gently suggesting a short course on good touch/bad touch. These days I am the wife of the minister of one of our town's most historic churches. It will not do to slug anybody. Unless, of course, they're trying to kill me, which has happened more times since my arrival in town than I care to think about.

Having Ray Sloan for a father, spending childhood summers marching and orienteering and flipping men twice my size, had its positive side. Thanks largely to Ray's survival training I am still alive, even well. I'm hoping to stay this way for years to come. Like my daddy, I'm planning to survive.

"Aggie, what on earth are you thinking about? You're waving your finger in the air."

I glanced at my best friend, Lucy Jacobs, who was sitting in the driver's seat beside me. Luce was trying to find a place to park her cherry red Chrysler, and it was no surprise she wasn't having any luck since, for half a mile behind us, both sides of dusty Horseshoe Bend Road were lined with cars.

Clearly we weren't the only good citizens of Emerald Springs who knew we were about to be invaded. In a town like ours, news travels as fast as butter melting on pierogies. There's a certain collective osmosis here. I'm not sure words are necessary. Like lemmings with larger brains and better survival instincts, the entire population of Emerald Springs probably stepped across their thresholds half an hour ago and headed for their cars. Hopefully no one is going to end this simultaneous migration by throwing themselves under the wheels of the battered RVs turning in to the acreage ahead of us. But stranger things have happened.

I carefully curled the waving finger back into my fist. "You wouldn't believe the places my mind can go."

Lucy lifted one perfectly penciled eyebrow. "You're kidding, right? We work side by side. I helped you solve three murders. Next to Ed, nobody's seen your mind twirling into outer space more often than I have."

"And yet, from somewhere deep inside, you still find enough goodwill to let me ride in your car."

"What *were* you thinking about?"

"The day I was four and watched a circus arrive with my father."

"That sounds like a perfectly normal thing to do." She spared me a doubtful glance, wrinkling her perky little nose. "You did *normal* things together?"

"Ray has his normal moments. When the girls and I visited last week, he acted like any contented grandfather."

"Oh, really? He's taken up bridge? Golf?"

"No reason to. He has his food dehydrator, his weekly paintball skirmishes, his obstacle courses. He and his comrades are building a wall so massive it's guaranteed to keep out any tank battalion making a wrong turn into rural Indiana. Better yet, if we're all lucky, it'll keep the guys in."

"I can't believe you take the girls with you."

Okay, Lucy knows too much about me. My family background does sound like a screwy sequel to *Apocalypse Now* or *Hair*. My father is a burned-out survivalist, and my mother, the much-married flower child Junie Bluebird, traveled the craft festival circuit through my childhood and adolescence with my sisters and me in tow. But nowadays, except for Ray, our little family can almost pass for normal—if no one looks too closely. My sisters, Vel and Sid, are happy and productive, and they visit as often as they can. Junie has settled down right here in Emerald Springs, where she opened her own quilt shop, and joined the Chamber of Commerce. She even—I hope—pays taxes.

I tried to explain our little Indiana getaway. "Deena's gotten so good on the rifle range, she could keep us in wild game—if we weren't vegetarians. And considering she's now officially a teenager, the self-defense tricks Ray taught us will come in handy. Teddy can stalk wild asparagus and make a sourdough bread starter pretty much out of thin air." I left out the part where Ray had taken one good look and started me on a physical fitness program designed to make sure I can qualify for some underground version of the Army Rangers.

"I'm always surprised when you come back in one piece."

"For the most part, the guys at the compound are harmless. They aren't amassing weapons." I paused. "At least not that I could see."

Although the off-limits underground bunkers do worry me a tad.

Lucy spotted a space on the other side of the road that was not large enough that a normal person would consider it. She fishtailed between two oncoming cars, and slid into it at an angle, stopping just inches from the trash-strewn drainage ditch. I had to give her credit. The back bumper of her Concorde had neatly cleared the road. I doubt she was on the right side of legal, but I also doubted anybody in authority would care. The cops were probably more concerned with crowd control up ahead.

Lucy flipped off the ignition. "Well, speaking of misfits . . ."

I was glad to change the subject. "I can't believe a circus bought the old Weilly farm. I *can* believe you made the sale. The other realtors in Emerald Springs must despise you."

Lucy smiled like a cat. "Oh, they do, they do. And it's not a circus. I keep telling you. The new owners call themselves Sister Nora's Inspirational Tent Show. They don't just entertain, they bring people to the Lord."

Somebody should have taught Sister Nora about acronyms, a lesson she apparently hadn't learned at Tent Revival University. I said it out loud and managed not to smile. "SNITS. Which is what the city council is having, I bet. We have an ordinance against setting a mousetrap without a hunting license, but there's nothing in place to keep exotic animals off this property? Or a religious cult?"

"Ohio doesn't have any laws against owning exotic animals. The farm is just outside the city limits, and Sadler Township has rules about pigs and cows, but not elephants." Lucy shook back her copper curls, then decided that wasn't good enough. She fished for an elastic band in her purse and scrunched her hair into a springy ponytail. I could relate. We were about to launch ourselves into the heat. Outside the safety and security of the Concorde's efficient air-conditioner, the sun was unrelenting. June in central Ohio can be hot and humid, but this June was setting records. And nobody was sure where the humidity came from, since it hadn't rained in Emerald Springs for almost three months.

Before leaving home I'd done the ponytail thing myself, although the majority of my dark hair had already slipped out and was waving limply against my cheeks and nape. Chastened by Lucy's good example, I tried for renewed order.

"I can't believe the girls aren't here to go with us," I said. My daughters, Deena and Teddy, were off with my mother camping in Junie's motor home. With her new quilt shop doing a tidy business, Junie has finally found assistants capable of keeping things going for a few days when she's away. As soon as we'd gotten back from Indiana, she and my girls had gone off for a fling to a nearby lake. Before I'd had time to unpack my own stuff, Lucy had kidnapped me to bring me here.

"Just remember all the details, so you'll have a great story to tell them," Lucy said. "And quit stalling."

I opened my door and nearly succumbed to the first fiery burst. The air was as still as a meditating monk. Maybe a breeze would have been cooling, or maybe it would simply have swept more heat in our direction. Having accompanied Junie through deserts and swamps during my checkered childhood, I'd certainly experienced worse. But despite Ray's exercise plan, I was still too soft these days, unrepentantly opposed to sunstroke and heat prostration.

I caught up with Lucy, who looked comfortable enough, even though sun plays havoc with the complexions of green-eyed redheads. I decided a new freckle or two wouldn't be amiss. Lucy's cute enough to turn the head of every male who comes within ten yards of her. Extra freckles might weed out the ne'er-do-wells from the potential husbands.

Marrying off Lucy is something of a change of pace for me, but in the last year I've realized I need a *new* avocation, since my old one—solving murders—comes with a nasty downside of potential victimhood. Now, to stay busy, I'm planning to find Lucy an acceptable man, so I can become godmother to red-haired bouncing babies. Of course Lucy's Jewish, so I'm not sure about the godmother thing, but there has to be something equivalent.

Of course I have, as yet, not mentioned this to her.

We weren't the only ones hiking down the road to see Emerald Springs's latest sideshow. With zombielike determination, family groups, teenagers, old couples arm in arm were staggering toward the acres that were slowly filling with tractor trailers, RVs sprouting satellite dishes, and cages on flatbed trucks.

I caught up to Lucy. "Don't the animal rights folks make a fuss about the way these animals are transported?"

"I've done a little research. Sister Nora's fielded a few crackpot complaints, professional grousers who don't think any animals, even well-cared-for ones, should be in captivity. No circuses, zoos, rodeos. Nada. But it seems to me those complaints have been more public relations than serious lawsuits. No authority has ever cited the show. When they were still a circus, they had a sterling reputation."

Sterling seemed like the wrong word. Nothing about the procession of dilapidated vehicles looked shiny or valuable. Battered cutlery was more like it. The kind you toss in the picnic basket because it doesn't matter if somebody throws away a knife or a spoon with the chicken bones. The circus—whoops, the inspirational tent show—looked like it was subsisting on its last dime. I wondered how Sister Nora could afford to feed the two elephants waving their trunks in the distance. And meat for the big cats? I shuddered. Did they intend to raise it here?

"How on earth did they afford this land?" I asked Lucy. "There must be what, eighty acres?"

"Ninety, but after the owner died, the place was abandoned for most of a year. The heirs didn't want to work with a realtor, so every once in a while they advertised it for way too much, with no takers. The land's okay, but the house is so run-down I wouldn't even consider it for one of our flips."

Lucy and I flip houses as a team. She finds likely prospects that don't need extensive renovation, and together we do the work. So far we've managed three. Now we're looking for a fourth project, something fast and easy to sink our not-so-massive profits into. So far neither of us had been thrilled with the possibilities. Or maybe the prospect of scraping and prying and carrying out truckloads of garbage when the temperatures are so fierce is the roadblock.

"I'm not sure a farmhouse would be a good flip anyway," I said as we drew closer. "Any farmer worth his salt would pay less and do the repairs himself. And nobody would want this place for a summer cottage. Horseshoe Bend isn't the prettiest country road I've ever seen. More Heartbreak Hollow than East Hampton."

"Which is perfect for Sister Nora, since none of the neighbors are going to have the cash to kick her off her land or the clout to get the authorities to do it. They'll leave her alone. If an animal gets out and bothers somebody, they'll shoot it."

I winced.

We were nearing the gate into the property now, which was wide-open for the trucks and RVs. Lucy kept moving.

"As to how they paid for it?" Lucy smiled at me and wiggled her brows. "Aren't you glad you know me?"

Actually I was. Thrilled, in fact, since my friendship and partnership with Lucy was one of the reasons I had come to terms with living in a town where "change" was something you threw in the Salvation Army bucket at Christmas.

"How did they pay?" I prompted.

"She converted a multimillionaire."

"She? Sister Nora?"

"The one and only. He paid for the farm in cash. A little, wizened dude named Henry Cinch. We might spot him. Look for the old guy with the bald head."

"That's pretty general."

"No, his bald head is counterintuitive. He has all his hair on top, and none around the edges. Anyway Henry made his money in Texas. Apparently a lot of it. Now he's getting rid of it as fast as he can."

"Most likely it's that New Testament teaching about rich men, heaven, and the eye of a needle. I mean, if he thinks his end is near enough, he'll want to spend his ill-gotten gains on good things pretty quickly."

"Does it work that way? You can live any way you want, then repent at the last minute?"

I ignored the theological challenge, since answering big questions is my husband's bailiwick. "It sounds like he's doing more than repent. He's divesting. I wonder if they'll use some of his money to fix up the house."

"They'll sure have the labor to do it."

About that, Lucy was right. Even if none of the RVs held tiny, munchkin families sleeping six to a bed, enough vehicles had gone through the gate to indicate that at least a hundred people were connected to SNITS. Probably a good many more.

The crowd was gathering just outside the gate. There was no chance of a riot. Midwesterners are far too polite, too orderly, to push their way onto private property. We're not, however, too polite to gather and stare. We're also, as a species, prone to keen interest in anything that smacks of the strange or illicit. I wasn't sure which category Sister Nora and her crew might fall into, but I was anxious to find out.

Lucy walked around the edges of the gathering mob, waited for another truck to pass, then minced her way across the cattle guard that ran parallel to the fence. With an apologetic glance at the people who were watching us, I followed just in front of an approaching RV, nearly sprawling head-first when I caught a toe between steel pipes.

I caught up to her. "Luce, if we were going in, why didn't we just drive? Why all the parking nonsense?"

"Because I figured we'd make better time on foot than lining up with the other vehicles. I have a couple of documents for Sister Nora."

I grasped her shoulder and held her in place. "Lucy?"

She shrugged it off. "Okay, just Welcome Wagon stuff and information about county trash pickup. But I wanted to see this up close, didn't you?"

We walked farther into the melee, and there was, indeed, a lot to see. Scruffy men clad—at most—in tank tops and cutoffs were directing the vehicles into roped-off areas. Ten yards from where we stopped, a bare-chested giant with a narrow head and stevedore shoulders was pounding metal stakes into the ground with a sledgehammer. A much smaller sidekick walked along beside him carrying the stakes. Four muscular women just beyond us were unloading a van filled with picnic tables that had to weigh several hundred pounds each. Two men on the ground were setting them into some kind of frame on wheels and carting them in the direction of the man with the stakes.

"Cookhouse," one of the men said as he passed, nodding in that direction.

He had answered my unspoken question. No one seemed annoyed we were staring. One of the Amazon women hefting picnic tables even flashed me a warm smile. Everybody seemed to know exactly what to do and how to do it. And from the little I'd seen so far, nobody seemed to mind.

"They seem happy," I told Lucy. "For what might be a cult."

"If they offer you Kool-Aid, opt for bottled spring water."

We continued on our way, past circling wagons and RVs that were cranking up awnings and setting out barbecues. We passed children spilling happily from cars into the unrelenting sunshine; men erecting what looked like a temporary corral for the horses; and horse trailers that smelled pungent and earthy, but not abundantly so.

"They take particularly good care of the horses. As a girl Sister Nora starred in the equestrian act," Lucy said. "This is what remains of the Nelson–Zimboni Circus."

"You did all this—you *learned* all this—while I was in Indiana?"

"Well, I had to do something, didn't I? Other than grieve your absence?"

I poked her in the arm. "Doesn't it seem, *um*, precipitous to you? I leave for a week, I come back, and we're watching an inspirational circus move in."

"Actually, they've been looking in our area for a long time. Just a few realtors knew, and we were sworn to secrecy. Then I heard about this place, realized it would be perfect, and talked the owners into listing with me. When Sister Nora saw it, she wanted it fast. I gave her fast. The place was deserted. The tent show had the cash. It was something of a coup, if I do say so myself."

The roar of a lion lifted me off my feet and deposited me a few inches farther from Lucy.

"Horses were only part of the show," she continued, as if

she was already used to the presence of man-eating beasts so close to our fair town. "Nelson–Zimboni is generations old, but it was never large like Ringling Brothers or Clyde Beatty. Instead they were known for quality, and they had a huge following in small towns like this one. The equestrian act was one of the biggest draws. Gorgeous horses, gorgeous women, death-defying feats. From what I've had time to unearth, Nora's whole family starred in it. She doesn't talk about that now, though. That's all in the past."

"The horses don't seem to be." I pointed to the trailers. "And neither do the lions."

"The Nelson wing of the circus created and maintained the animal acts. I guess they started at a time when zoos were just for city folk, and circuses filled the gap everywhere else. Little Beau and Baby Bubba only got to see tigers and lions under the big top."

"I'll be interested to see how Sister Nora uses them in her evangelism. Anybody who doesn't agree with her preaching gets a trip into their cage of choice?"

We moved out of the route of a tractor trailer and started up toward the house that sat in a grove of listless, dehydrating maples.

"I don't know how Emerald Springs is going to take to all this," Lucy said. "The animals, the revival meetings."

Not to mention a lot of talk about heaven and hell. We'd been used to talking about hell when I lived in Northern Virginia. That close to the White House, everybody was sure that whoever happened to be residing there was courting the devil, so it came naturally. But here?

"People in Emerald Springs want to think about the Cleveland Indians or the Cincinnati Bengals," I said. "They want to discuss whether little Jennifer is going to make it to the finals of the Emerald Springs Idyll, not whether she's going to make it to heaven. Which reminds me, I've got to be back by four."

"Tell me again why you got corralled on that committee?"

The fund-raising committee Lucy referred to, the reason I had to be back in town, had been foisted on me by several powerful members of our church. Our task was to make sure that the Idyll, an overinflated talent show, ran smoothly and raised as much money as possible. It was exactly the kind of committee I hated most.

I listed reasons that didn't make me sound like a wimp. "It's important. You and I are between flips, and I need something to do this summer besides drive Teddy to swimming lessons and Deena to the stables."

"And because Sally Berrigan twisted your arm."

"That was only part of it." The other parts were Dolly Purcell and Esther, our organist. All three were members of our church.

"Is this in some minister's wife handbook? Caving in to people who can make your husband's life miserable?"

"Chapter one, second page, third paragraph. But really?" I slowed, because although I'm in relatively good shape after forced marches and chin-ups last week, I was feeling winded from the heat. "It is a good cause, Luce. A new pediatric wing for Emerald Springs Hospital feels pretty personal. Suites where parents can stay comfortably with sick children, a four-bed pediatric intensive care unit, a play area. How could I say no? If I can do anything to make it happen, I need to."

Lucy didn't even try to argue. In fact her real estate agency had pledged a whopping sum to the new pediatric unit, and I was pretty sure a fair piece of it would come right out of Lucy's pocket.

"I see Sister Nora." Lucy nodded to the porch of the old farmhouse just yards away now.

The sunshine was a bright smear, and without conspicuously shading my eyes, I couldn't view anything clearly. I made out at least three figures to one side of the house, under the deep shade of a sagging roof, but not much more. I lowered my voice to a whisper. "Do we genuflect? I'm about as familiar with how to do that as you are. Which knee do we go down on?"

"You're going to like her." Lucy broke into a smile and started up the steps.

I was halfway up before the glare lessened and I could see a small cluster of people on a porch that was badly in need of paint. A middle-aged woman broke away from the others, who continued to converse in hushed tones, and started toward us. She was reed slender, almost emaciated, and her skin was the seasoned tan of my leather sandals. Both attributes made her enormous, pale blue eyes nearly pop out of her head. She wore a blue work shirt that hung limply on her thin frame, and jeans that were probably a "minus two." She was average height, and if she hadn't been so gaunt, she would have been pretty. The blonde hair piled on top of her head and twisted in place with a barrette was probably a few shades lighter than the good Lord had intended, and threads of silver were making it more so. All in all, though, she was striking, a woman who would be hard to forget.

I guess that's a good thing in Nora's line of work.

"Lucy." Sister Nora extended her hand and grasped Lucy's. Her smile was warm and genuine, not one bit fake television preacher.

Lucy returned the smile. "I brought you a packet of information. And I wanted to see if you needed anything while you're moving in."

How Lucy could say that with a straight face intrigued me. Sister Nora needed a lot of things. Barbed wire around the perimeter, for starters.

Lucy turned to me as Sister Nora did and made the introduction. Sister Nora grasped my hand and squeezed. For a drinking straw of a woman, she had a grip like the governor of Kah-li-foan-ia.

"Quite the commotion, yes? I'm sure your little town is wondering what we're all about." Sister Nora spoke with absolutely no accent. But that made sense for somebody born into a traveling circus. Growing up on the craft show circuit did the same for me.

"We don't get a lot of excitement here," I admitted. "This is about a year's worth, all at once."

"I hope you'll assure your friends and neighbors we mean no harm."

"Aggie's husband is the minister of a church on the Emerald Springs Oval," Lucy said. "You'll probably want to get to know him."

Sister Nora nodded, as if she was taking that to heart. "Everyone will be welcome here, sinners and saints alike."

I wondered where Ed would put himself on that continuum. The Consolidated Community Church is a liberal church. Of course we're fond of saints while not so fond of sin, but we're also prone to thinking there's a middle awash in multiple shades of gray.

"I'll be sure to tell Ed," I promised. Ed was going to find that conversation fascinating. In my future I could look forward to scintillating lectures on the role of the traveling evangelist in nineteenth-century America.

"We're looking forward to meeting everybody in the community." Nora's irises were like star sapphires, a deep blue with the oddest twinkle of light beaming straight from the pupil. "We have a message for the people of Emerald Springs."

I knew better than to ask what it was. I *knew* better. But here I was, my curiosity mixing with perspiration and oozing out every pore. I glanced at Lucy, who didn't seem to know what Nora had meant by a message, either. Apparently the "message" had gotten lost in negotiations for the farm. Offers and counteroffers and roof inspectors will do that.

"Is this a message you'd like me to pass on?" I asked at last, knowing I shouldn't, but incapable of stopping myself.

"It is," Sister Nora said, with a nod. She still looked pleasant. She still looked completely comfortable with our conversation. Neither prepared me.

"The world is coming to an end very soon," she said in her husky, everyday voice, as if she were talking about a favorite series she was watching on television. "We are destroying the environment and the result will be a catastrophe. I've negotiated with God because I firmly believe the world's a better place than He does. So he's giving us one more chance. And the people of Emerald Springs have been chosen to provide Him with proof. We're here to teach you what you have to know to protect and save God's handiwork. And if all else fails, we will preserve whatever we can."

I had no idea how to answer that. Beside me I could sense Lucy shifting her weight uneasily. All I could do was clear my throat and release the first thought that came to mind.

"It's going to take elephants?" I asked.

Sister Nora smiled gently. "It's going to take all of us."

2

"Elephants? That was the best you could do? You thought elephants were the crux of the matter?"

I turned up every vent near my seat so the Concorde's air-conditioning was hitting me directly in the face. Getting back to Lucy's car had taken longer than we'd expected. We'd had to avoid a string of poodles prancing on their hind legs, two cages of black bears, and three children riding the most beautiful white horses I'd ever seen. Bareback.

"I don't remember *you* saying much of anything," I answered, once the air-conditioners were at full tilt. "Did you really think discussing whether to have the closing at your office or the title company was more relevant than how she's going to save the world?"

Lucy slowed for a group of girls just a little older than my thirteen-year-old Deena. In bright shorts and capris the girls were like roses blooming in the midst of the desert, lush and sweet and a welcome contrast to the dust-coated foliage lining Horseshoe Bend Road. If Sister Nora was right, they might not live long enough to drop even a single petal.

She was silent until most of the onlookers were well behind us, then she sounded faintly chagrined. "I honestly didn't know they were *that* kind of religion."

"Sister Nora never said anything to you about the end of the world?"

"Well, no. She seemed like your typical circus evangelist to me, Aggie. I see so many of them!"

I tried to imagine how this entire scenario was going

to go over in our conservative little town. Which part of the following would be most discussed? The lions, elephants, and tigers—and yes, there were tigers, as we'd discovered on our way out. The presence of maybe a hundred new citizens, many of whom looked as if Sister Nora had converted them as they exited county jails and state prisons? The tent revivals? The impending end of life as we knew it?

"At least she isn't preaching hellfire and brimstone. She's all about global warming." I paused. "Or maybe it's the same thing, just her interpretation. Satan spewing coal dust into the air. Satan producing gas-guzzlers faster and faster until the glaciers disappear. I wonder if she knows the exact time line?"

"You should have asked her. I'm sure she would have been only too happy to tell you."

"That's what I was afraid of." I glanced at Lucy. "There's just the slightest chance, Luce, that your popularity index is going to take a dive in the next weeks. No matter how important the message, Sister Nora's delivery system's going to be controversial. You'll be the realtor who sold the Weilly farm to the biggest kooks in Emerald Springs history."

She sounded faintly glum. "Nobody expects less of me. Not after being seen so often with you."

I suppose that was true. I had garnered a certain reputation in town, which had probably rubbed off on my friend. In a way, it was surprising that the ladies in charge of the Emerald Springs Idyll had agreed to have me on their exalted committee. I could just imagine the arguments that had ensued. I needed at least one more year of quiet good works, no murders, and a leash on my tongue in order to restore confidence in my ability to be just one of the other moms in town.

"So what are you going to tell people?" I asked. "About Sister Nora and SNITS."

"It would be helpful if you didn't abbreviate, okay? Maybe nobody else will figure that out."

"It could be worse. She could have called it Nora's Up-lifting Tent Show. NUTS."

"Your brain works in mysterious ways."

"Nora's Universal Tent Salvation."

"You can stop anytime."

"What are you going to tell people about her?"

Lucy turned on the main road that would take us straight into town. In a way it was frightening how fast we had gotten here, considering that in deference to the people sight-seeing on Horseshoe Bend Road, we had been traveling about as fast as a well-fed lion in summer.

"As little as possible," Lucy said. "Even less."

"The news will travel fast. I don't think Sister Nora intends to keep this revelation to herself."

"I kind of think I'll be the least of it, don't you?"

We could only hope.

One thing about Lucy—she can locate any piece of property in the county with only a clue or two. Homeowner. Landscaping details. Architectural style. I had no chance of delaying my arrival at the Idyll meeting any longer. The moment I'd told Lucy it was at the home of Veronica and Farley Hayworth, I'd sealed my doom. Farley Hayworth owned one of the two most successful realties in town, and Lucy was an agent for the other. So not only did she know exactly where to find the Hayworths' house, she knew how much they paid for it eight years ago when they'd felt the need for seven bedrooms as opposed to the four the childless couple had formerly shared.

Now as we traveled in silence I envisioned white-aproned maids readying a different bedroom each night. The Monday bedroom. The Tuesday bedroom. Or maybe Veronica and Farley started at opposite ends of the house and moved inexorably toward the middle bedroom for a one-night rendezvous each week. Never having been rich, I'm not sure how it's done. Ed and I share a bed every night, but he tells me I won't share the blankets.

We crossed the magic line into Emerald Estates, our lit-

tle town's answer to Grosse Pointe and Beverly Hills. From
what I can tell, the primary criterion for building a house in
Emerald Estates is the use of as many types of building
materials as possible. Stucco and brick are considered just
okay. Stucco, brick, wood siding, and stone slabs? Ooh la
la. Size is a consideration, too. Too large to find one's way
from the family room to the master bedroom without a
map? The ultimate.

We passed ostentatious takeoffs on Greek Revival,
Second Empire, and Tudor architecture. The Tudor had been
the scene of one of the murders I'd been caught up in. I
looked away, just in case the house remembered and blew a
raspberry in our direction.

"Here we are." Lucy slowed and stopped in front of the
largest home on the block, sitting on at least three outsized
lots and trying with some small success to put its neighbors
to shame.

"One of the first homes to go up in Emerald Estates," she
recited. "The home of Veronica and Farley Hayworth is a
modern interpretation of the Italianate period, in vogue during the latter part of the nineteenth century. You'll note the
low-pitched roof, the elaborate brackets under the eaves,
and the soaring arched windows. That cute little tower at the
top is called a campanile."

"You forgot the double columns."

"And the double columns," Lucy finished up. "I was a
guide on a house tour for the Junior Women's Club a couple
of years ago, and that was my spiel. Of course a good wind
would blow this masterpiece away. You'd be amazed at
the problems these homeowners have. Too much attention
to appearance and not nearly enough to substance. Rumor is
the Hayworths spent more than they paid just to bring it up
to code."

"I hear the snickers of the little people now." Truly,
though, the whole concept behind Emerald Estates always
gives me pause. There are some lovely homes in our town
that have seen centuries of use and still stand tall, with

ageless grace. Too often they've been divided into cheap
apartments, or converted into law or medical offices. While
those homes yearned for dignity and a few bucks to make
necessary improvements, the developers of Emerald Estates were busily building froufrou copies and selling them
for the moon.

Still, a residence in Emerald Estates automatically comes
with a country club membership and some unspecified number of Jacuzzis. Plus a chance to live among rich or richer
neighbors. It isn't about architecture at all.

Lucy made a shooing motion. "Scoot now. Go and see
how the other 1 percent lives and remember every detail so
you can describe it to me. I hear Veronica Hayworth redec-
orates every two years, whether the economy needs it or
not. You have a ride home?"

"Sally Berrigan will give me one."

"Are you going to tell people why you're"—Lucy
checked her watch—"ten minutes late? I've got to warn you,
I've been on committees with Veronica, and she's known for
being at least ten minutes early to every meeting. She's not
going to look kindly at you for walking in late."

"I'm sure she'll forgive me if I tell her I was hobnob-
bing with a prophet, right? Even people in Emerald Estates
understand that the end of the world is worth being a few
minutes behind on my schedule."

Lucy narrowed her eyes.

"No," I promised. "I won't breathe a word. But I bet
Farley Hayworth and every other realtor in town is spread-
ing the news."

I slammed the door and Lucy took off. I looked down at
my gray cotton pants and hoped that there were no unspeak-
able splatters from the old Weilly farm. Eau de tiger poop. I
straightened my cotton shirt, but that did little to keep it from
clinging to my damp skin and C-cup breasts. I was afraid
the maid would tell me to use the rear entrance.

The porch was surprisingly narrow, not a comfortable
place for the Hayworths to sit and enjoy their reign as the

unofficial king and queen of Emerald Estates. There was a plant stand with pots of blooming annuals in one remote corner, and a grouping of palms and rubber plants closer to me, but no furniture within yards of the door. Perhaps the point was to keep we-of-the-riffraff standing straight and tall while we waited for someone to answer the doorbell's summons.

Testing my theory, I pressed the button and heard the opening bars of Bach's Minuet in G chiming in the entryway. I'm not much of a musician since, if I admitted to such a thing, I would forever be called on to direct choirs or accompany hymns. Still, I do know a bit. One of Junie's boyfriends was a classical pianist. That was the year we hauled a trailer with a Chickering upright behind our RV from one coast to the other, a small price to pay for music lessons.

Just as I'd guessed, my knees were ready to buckle into a sedate curtsy by the time a woman in a double-breasted navy dress arrived. The outfit was completed by a headband of the same color and fabric, piped in white to match the dress's collar and cuffs. I supposed this was an update on the frilly little triangular hat of another era. The headband successfully held back every strand of naturally blonde hair, but unfortunately the Hayworths' maid had a wide, high forehead marred with a constellation of lines. I wondered if the headband had been chosen by the mistress of the house to highlight this flaw, in case Mr. Hayworth liked to dally with the help.

"I'm here for the Emerald Springs Idyll meeting," I explained. "Agate Sloan-Wilcox?"

"It's already begun," she said, standing firmly between me and the entry hall.

"They're expecting me."

She sighed. "I was polishing the silver."

I saw the problem. She had allotted the time between three fifty and four for arrivals, for showing committee members to the room where the meeting would be held, for offering tea or coffee, even sherry. She would have been happier if I hadn't come at all.

"I apologize."

She didn't sigh again, at least not audibly. But her nostrils flared. Then she stepped aside and allowed me entrance. The floor was a rusty red marble, probably Italian, and the towering chandelier was fine leaded crystal. A curved staircase, a rosewood masterpiece, swept up to the next floor.

I had no time to admire the views or the antique table replete with a florist's arrangement of roses, irises, and Canterbury bells. "Please follow me," the maid said, turning toward a hall leading left. I wondered if the strict attention to schedule was her invention, or if it had been foisted on her by Veronica Hayworth.

"They're in the conservatory," she said.

"With the lead pipe and Colonel Mustard."

She pivoted, frowning, and I saw how some of the lines in her forehead had gotten their start.

"Clue," I explained, in apology. "The board game. I've played a million rounds of it with my daughters."

And could that explain my unnatural interest in solving murders? Maybe it really was that simple.

When the lines didn't smooth, I tried my friendliest smile, digging deeply for my dimples. "I don't want to keep you from the silver a minute longer than necessary."

She turned on her heel again and stomped into the hall.

We walked so fast I wasn't able to grasp many details. Lots of gilt-framed mirrors. Walls in dark, earthy tones. Renaissance art with the requisite somber religious themes, then farther along—to lighten the mood—oil portraits of dogs from different historical periods. We passed many different living areas, most likely each with a different title. Parlor, den, family room, formal living room with a gorgeous grand piano, throne room. All were decorated with unique and tasteful flair.

About the time I thought we needed to call for rescue, we turned a corner into a supersized sunroom. The stone floor was sprinkled with tribal rugs, and the furniture looked like it had been hand-carved in some South American rain forest before it was smothered in bright prints and poufy pillows. Shrubs and trees, including what amounted to a citrus grove, were clustered in groups next to a bubbling fountain. Orchids and bromeliads bloomed in profusion, and orange blossoms scented the air.

"Mrs. Wilcox has arrived," the maid announced from the doorway. Then she led me toward the group of women sitting at a glass table near the fountain.

Talk at the table ceased the moment I appeared. I felt eight pairs of eyes sizing me up. The only pair that looked familiar were the pale blue ones belonging to Sally Berrigan, the no-nonsense chairperson of our church Women's Society. Sally is involved in every worthwhile charitable cause in Emerald Springs and runs a good portion of them. Midsixties, military bearing, silver hair styled in a short bob that probably takes ten seconds a day to care for, Sally focuses on getting things done. I'd stood no chance once she caught me in her sights. Sally had decided I needed a new focus for my life, and here I was.

I am a wimp.

The other women were a complete contrast. Sally has a solid retirement income, a shipshape brick Colonial landscaped with native plants and trees, and a Prius. If she had millions, she would dress and live exactly the same way. My first impression of the other women was that they would deny their aging parents shelter and their suckling babes nourishment if it meant climbing another rung up the social ladder.

Okay, that was *so* not fair. But I had never seen that many diamonds twinkling around necks and wrists, not to mention fingers, in my life. And this was not a crowd that would resort to cubic zirconias, because this was also a crowd that could spot them in a heartbeat.

"My apologies for being late," I said. Then, because I couldn't help myself, I added: "It's a real circus out there."

The woman at the head of the table rose gracefully and held out a long-fingered hand. She had dark hair drawn back in a knot from a sharp-featured face perfectly suited to the hairstyle. Her figure was willowy and tastefully garbed in a black spandex shirt adorned by a wide, gold chain belt. She didn't have to tell me who she was.

"Veronica Hayworth, Aggie. And we're glad you could make it. We know young mothers have trouble getting away. We're just glad you could join us."

Her grip was reassuringly firm, her smile wide enough over large, perfect teeth. Despite this, when her brown eyes didn't light along with it, I knew I had gotten off on the wrong foot and would have to do major tap dancing to get back in rhythm.

Veronica introduced the other women, and although I tried, I remembered only a few by the time she'd finished. There was a Bitsy or Mitzi, a Diana, a Camille. They ranged in age from Veronica's mid- to late forties all the way to retirees like Sally. I murmured greetings and took the only empty seat, hoping that I could simply disappear now, while knowing full well I would never disappear among these women. I was a chunk of agate surrounded by large-carat gems.

"We'd really only just begun," Veronica said, with another toothy smile. "Most of us know each other already, but for fun we picked a question out of the bowl and answered it by way of introduction." She reached for a lovely handblown fishbowl and held it out to me. There was, of course, only one folded slip of paper inside.

I wondered if this was my punishment. The expressions at the table ranged from bored to expectant. Gamely I thrust my hand inside, unfolded the paper, and read the question out loud, glad I hadn't suggested that Teddy do anything remotely similar last month at her eighth birthday party.

"If you were an instrument in the Cleveland Orchestra, which instrument would you be?"

I smiled, as if I thought the question were intriguing, even fun. "I'd be a sarrusophone."

There was a long silence. Finally a blonde at the end of the table smiled dismissively. "Oh, you mean *sousaphone*."

I called on that summer of music history. "No, a sarrusophone's a wind instrument, something like the contrabassoon. It's made of metal, so it's louder. But you can see why being one would be appealing?"

They couldn't.

"They're almost never used," I explained. "I would rarely be called on to perform."

The room was silent, and in seconds I realized why. I'd as much as announced I was not a worker bee. I hastened to improve the situation.

"Not that I'm lazy, of course. I just don't like the limelight."

Veronica gave a throaty laugh. "Well, we won't have to worry about a conflict of interest with Aggie, girls. She won't be trying out for the Idyll, will she?"

Everybody else laughed, too, although the ripple was strained. I was now on probation.

"Aggie, you must have worked on a number of committees," Veronica said. "Being a pastor's wife."

I tried my most winning smile. "Not so many. I make a point of not going head-to-head with the people who issue Ed's paycheck. I worry—"

"Aggie is our historian and a tireless worker," Sally interrupted, vouching for me.

"Well, nobody here is issuing anybody's paycheck." Veronica paused. "Except Grady Barber's."

"Which still concerns me," Sally said, leaning forward, her hands clasped earnestly on the table. "The size of that paycheck, I mean. We're paying that man twenty thousand dollars to judge this show! That's twenty thousand that could go toward the new pediatric wing."

Veronica's voice was soft, but her tone was as hard as, well, a sarrusophone's.

"Sally, without a celebrity judge, the only people that will come to see the Emerald Springs Idyll are the family and friends of the participants. And then only reluctantly. It's all about the judges, don't you see? With Grady sitting at the side of the stage, everybody's going to come. They'll all want to hear what he has to say. They'll buy tickets for every single night. Advertisers are fighting to put ads in the programs and to be announced as sponsors. We'll make money hand over fist."

"But twenty thousand dollars? It's extravagant."

"It's cheap! It's well below his normal fee. He's an Emerald Springs boy; he's famous, and he's only doing it at that rate as a special favor to me. Besides, we've solicited personal donations from the hospital board to cover most of it."

There was a silence as they both regrouped and drew deep breaths. And into the breach I leapt.

"Grady Barber?"

Every head turned; every eye stared at me again.

Tropical birds were singing from airy bamboo cages behind Veronica's chair. I'd missed this on my initial view of the conservatory. I squelched an urge to spring to my feet and throw open cage doors as a distraction.

"If Aggie doesn't know who he is, what about all the twentysomethings? The teenagers?" Sally demanded.

"Aggie, you're not from Emerald Springs?" Veronica asked.

I shook my head, although an answer was unnecessary. Had I been, they would have known better than to ask me to serve beside them.

"You've heard of *Wayfarers of the Ark*?"

I scrambled for the right answer. I'd heard of *Raiders of the Lost Ark*. The Ark of the Covenant. Geometric arcs. The Arc de Triomphe. Archetypes. Noah's ark. Then I realized where this was going. I heard a snatch of a song in my head, a high, sweet tenor voice singing . . .

Sailing toward a rainbow . . . stretching overhead . . .

"The movie," I said. "I remember the theme song, from my childhood."

"Exactly. And the artist who performed it was our very own Grady Barber, who played Idan, Noah's grandson. He's also the same Grady Barber who had a big hit last year with 'Remember Me in April.' " She smiled, as if I couldn't possibly have overlooked this—which, of course, I had.

Veronica finished on a note of triumph. "He's agreed to come to Emerald Springs and be our judge. At quite a reduced fee, may I stress again. But after all, *this* is where he got his start."

"I know it's too late to reconsider," Sally said. "The tryouts are almost upon us, and I'm aware the contracts have all been signed—"

"It's certainly official."

"And there's truth to what you say about better attendance with a celebrity. But there are ways to lighten our financial load," Sally went on. "Since we're also responsible for all his expenses, let me suggest we make sure he has as few as possible. We can give quiet dinner parties so he doesn't run up extravagant restaurant bills, stock his room with quality snacks and drinks. We can chauffeur him everywhere he needs to go, so he doesn't call a limo service or rent a Porsche."

Sally was definitely reaching to make her point. To my knowledge Emerald Springs has one shoestring limo service, and anybody who needs to rent a car usually does it in Columbus or Cleveland and chugs into town under Chevy power.

"We've booked him the best suite at the Emerald Springs Hotel." Veronica's tone was noticeably frostier.

Sally smiled. "Of course we have. I wasn't going to suggest a room in my attic."

The tension eased a little. Some of the other women entered into the conversation, volunteering to host a dinner at their homes or assume chauffeur duty for a day. One volunteered to make baskets of local snacks and baked goods to be delivered to his room. Another agreed to stock the suite's refrigerator with carefully chosen drinks. A curly haired brunette said that her husband's dry cleaning service would wash or clean Grady's clothes for free.

My gaze flitted back to the cages. I wondered how I could help with this phase of the committee's work. Volunteer Ed to preach a sermon while Grady had his breakfast? Ask Teddy, my serious eight-year-old, to do tempera portraits of Noah's animals to adorn the suite? Ask Junie to tuck Grady in every night with one of her prizewinning quilts?

"And that's on top of your other assignments, right, girls?" Veronica asked. "We're all going to be busy-busy."

I've never believed you can actually feel a person's gaze. I was sure that was only a plot device used in Gothic novels. But I'd been admiring the birds—cockatiels and maybe small parrots of some variety—when I suddenly felt the hair on my arms and nape begin to sizzle. I refocused and realized that indeed, a number of previously maligned Gothic authors were having the last laugh. I *was* being watched. Times eight.

I had missed something.

Unfortunately, I wasn't that lucky. I hadn't missed anything yet. What I'd felt was only anticipation. Theirs.

"So that brings us to you, Aggie," Veronica said, neatly stacking an inch-thick pile of papers in front of her. "Everybody's plate is heaped to the brim. Logistics. Promotion. Coordination with the college for use of parking space and room rentals. Our big party for the hospital board and largest donors. Tours of the present pediatric wing so people will know why this is so important—"

"I'd be happy to help with that." Suddenly, a job I could fit in between summer dentist appointments and soccer games. It might be a stretch, but surely I could manage a tour or two.

"We have that covered, thanks," Veronica said. "That and nearly everything else."

Nearly is not a good word. I know what nearly means. Nearly, as in: *We're nearly finished giving out all the prizes except the booby prize . . .*

I steeled myself. "What did you save for me?" I smiled like a team player. Like a hard worker. Like a practical woman with no choice other than slinking out of town with her tail between her legs.

"We need a liaison between Grady's personal assistant and this committee. Somebody who knows the town and local resources. Somebody who can get things done, fix little problems, run interference if needed with the hotel or the production staff or anybody else. Somebody who thinks quickly on her feet. Sally says that's what you're known for. And besides, you're a vegetarian, and nobody else is."

"I'm sorry . . . ?"

"Grady's a vegetarian. He lives in Southern California, after all," she said, as if that explained everything. "And one of the conditions of his coming was that we have somebody check the menus and snacks he'll be eating to be sure there's no meat, dairy, preservatives. You'll understand."

I didn't, but I tried to. "Kind of like a poison taster."

Nobody laughed. I fumbled for an excuse. "Um, that sounds like a big job, and unfortunately I do have—"

"Oh, yes, indeed it is," Veronica said, before I could go on. "But luckily, it's only one job, not the multiple the rest of us are carrying. We didn't want your first time on this committee to be too difficult."

I weeded out seven pairs of eyes and went for Sally's. She had been waiting and took up the hard sell. "The busiest part will be the first week he's in town, Aggie. And that's religious education camp at church, so the girls will be occupied all day anyway. I know you were planning to help with camp activities, but May tells me if *we* need you more, she'll be glad to give you a pass."

I wished I could get my friend May Frankel, who was chairing camp this year, in a dark alley. Of course, May and Sally were simply trying to be helpful. Both of them were sure that working on this committee would be good for me, that I'd meet new people, experience a little vicarious limelight. And now that I no longer seemed to be stumbling over dead bodies, I might establish an identity apart from the church and the police department.

Veronica must have timed my hesitation so she'd know the precise moment to leap in for the kill. She leaned forward. "I know this cause is dear to your heart. Sally tells me your younger daughter had a friend who nearly died a few weeks ago, before they could move her to a pediatric ICU in Columbus. Isn't that right? It must have been particularly upsetting for a young mother with children of her own. The way things are now, all young mothers of Emerald Springs walk so very close to the edge."

I was in the sights of a crack shot. My father could put Veronica's talents to good use. No, what was I thinking? Veronica would round up my father and his cohorts, make them shave and change out of camouflage. Then she would find them nine to five jobs drilling ROTC units or working as instructors for the local agricultural extension office.

"Of course I'll do it," I said, as if I hadn't just flashed through every possible way of wiggling out of it. "Just let me know what's expected, and I'll take care of it."

Veronica's smile stretched all the way to her wisdom teeth. She picked up the stack of papers she had so carefully straightened and held it out to me.

"It's all right here. Phone numbers, contacts, schedules, Grady's diet, Grady's requirements for his suite, Grady's contract. Thank you, Aggie. We were all so sure we could count on you."

3

Ed looks great in a tux, but even for a fancy reception in Grady Barber's honor, getting him into one isn't worth the hassle. Since Ed debated his way through prep school in a coat and tie, if he can't wear a disintegrating Harvard T-shirt, he's most comfortable falling back on old habits. Knowing what I was up against, I had asked him to choose his best white shirt, and any tie his mother hadn't given him for Christmas. Now, in the mirror, I could see he was waiting for inspiration and wearing the T-shirt in the meantime.

"You look good," he said, coming up behind me as I tried for the third time to fasten the clasp on an agate-and-moonstone necklace. Every Christmas of *my* life my mother has given me something handmade and beautiful.

Ed took the necklace and fastened it. "In fact you look so great I hate to see you walk out that door. The kids are going to be gone soon, we'll have the house to ourselves."

"Nice try, Romeo." I stopped his hands from sliding lower. "I have to be there, and *you* are required to go to this party, too, so don't try to get out of it." I faced him. "Shall we count the events I've been required to attend since your ordination?"

"If it will take up the rest of the evening."

"This is your chance to meet a movie star."

"It's my chance to practice the self-control I preach and not punch Grady Barber in the nose."

I understood where Ed was coming from. In the three weeks since Veronica Hayworth shamed me into taking on

the job of "gofer" for the Emerald Springs Idyll, Ed had
been on the verge of filing a missing person's report. And
the chances the local cops could find me? Not good. These
days, from the moment I got up, I ran from one errand to
another. Even I didn't know where I was half the time. The
days were a blur, the checklists longer and harder to complete. I had dreams where I'm tethered to a chariot with a
toga-clad Veronica cracking the whip behind me.

"Has my snook'ums missed me?" I leaned over and
kissed his patrician nose. Ed looks like the Anglo-Saxon
royalty that supposedly lifted a leg against the trunk of
his family tree centuries ago. Reddish blond hair, dark
blue eyes, a princely set to his wide shoulders. For a moment his plans for our evening sounded a lot more fun
than mine.

"I don't mind you being gone. I do mind you being unhappy," he said.

"Actually . . ." I rested my hands on his shoulders. "I
seem to be good at solving problems. That's something."

"And tonight's the payoff?"

"I wish. With Grady in town, it's going to be a lot more
work for me. But I can see the end. And I'll feel so good
when they break ground for the new pediatric wing."

The doorbell rang, and before I could start downstairs to
answer it, Lucy—who has our house key but can also pick
the lock if she's so inclined—slammed the front door and
called up the stairs. "Ready, Ag?"

"You're coming?" I asked Ed. "You're not going to stand
me up?"

"Unless we have an emergency."

"Researching your next sermon is not an emergency.
Watching old episodes of *Masterpiece Theatre* is not an
emergency."

"I'll see you in an hour. Or I could trade you one absence at any meeting of your choice. Quid pro quo."

"One hour."

Lucy, hair tamed into an aura of corkscrew curls, was

standing by an open window panting and fanning herself when I got downstairs. "Your air-conditioning is broken."

"You're standing by our air-conditioner." Of course she knew this already.

"Can't you get the church to do something?"

Our old Dutch Colonial parsonage is spacious, even charming, but unfortunately the parsonage committee is most interested in historical preservation. "They've been promising a new kitchen floor for almost two years. It would take a committee of six just to choose a window fan."

"How do you sleep at night?"

I gathered my beaded purse, another Junie gift. "These days by the time my head hits the pillow, I'm so exhausted, a little sweat is soothing."

Lucy was wearing a slinky black cocktail dress and sandals with heels so spiked I'm not sure why she didn't tilt forward forty-five degrees. Until that moment I hadn't realized I wanted some, too. Badly.

Teddy, my eight-year-old, trudged down the steps struggling under the weight of a backpack stuffed with all the clothes and games she'd need for a night with her friend Hillary Frankel. Her glasses were slipping down her nose; her new Dutch boy bob swung forward and temporarily hid her freckled face. I was afraid if the heat didn't break soon, Teddy was going to insist on lopping off even more of her pale red hair.

"I'll see you tomorrow morning," I said, corralling her for a kiss after she went to Lucy for a hug and hello.

"If you're home." This was said matter-of-factly, simply a reminder that I wasn't around as much as I used to be.

"I intend to be. And if I have errands, you can come with me."

Deena followed her sister's path, stopping for a hello to Lucy, as well. In addition to a backpack, she had a sleeping bag. Luckily for me the Frankels have two daughters, and Maddie Frankel and Deena are good friends, too.

In fact, they are such good friends, Deena, Maddie, and

three of their other friends had given me the shock of my life.

"You're sure you don't want to come?" I asked, ruffling Deena's hair—still long despite the heat, and still strawberry blonde although we'd gone round and round about that recently.

"No chance, and besides, everybody's coming over and we're going to practice."

I said a short, silent prayer for May and Simon, Maddie and Hillary's mom and dad. A horn honked outside and both girls took off for the front door, calling good-byes behind them.

We waited for the door to slam and the furor to quiet, then Lucy and I followed in their wake.

By the time we got in her car, Lucy had already told me my green linen sundress was a shade informal, although my necklace was perfect. Oh, and I should think about getting a few reddish highlights to match the rest of the family. Lucy fills in when my sisters aren't around.

"You've as much as disappeared for three weeks," she said, pulling into what passes for traffic in our little town. "Go ahead and gripe. I know you want to."

"You're sure?"

"I'll turn the floor over to you until we arrive at the Hayworths'. What have you done?"

"Done? What haven't I done?" I launched in, talking a mile a minute but skipping the basics, which Lucy already knew. After that first meeting, I had been made the assistant and resident errand girl for Grady Barber's assistant, Fred Handlemann. And while, on the surface, being the assistant to an assistant doesn't sound that tough, the difficulty has come in the form of one Grady Barber, whose years in Hollywood seem to have removed him so completely from the reality of Emerald Springs, that he believed his wish is our command. He had only to suggest something, and it would be so.

I gulped in more air and tried to finish my list. I was already on the third round of fingers, and not sure I had enough without starting over again. "No pillow top on the hotel mattress. It has to be firm, but not hard, preferably brand new, and he wants six-hundred-thread-count Egyptian cotton sheets. Oh, in a neutral color, since anything too dark or too bright will keep him awake—"

"He sleeps with the lights on?"

"No, he just lies awake and thinks about them, I guess. But he *does* require a certain kind of night-light, an expensive one with a motion detector. If he gets up to go to the bathroom, he wants to be able to see."

"He doesn't travel with this stuff?"

"Of course not. We're supposed to get it ahead of time and have it in the room. Maybe we'll auction everything as collector's items after he leaves. But nothing he wants is cheap."

I could hear my voice rising, but I went on because Lucy is a good audience, and Ed is heartily sick of my rant. "Then I'm supposed to go over the menu for every single meal he eats. We've arranged dinners and parties. I've had to talk to every person who's cooking for him, and go over a list as long as my arm. No meat, and that means no lard in any of the baked goods, and no trans fat to replace it, only canola, soy, or olive oils, and then, only cold-pressed. His personal trainer has advised against dairy, but Grady's going to be liberal while he's here and allow about a cup of nonfat milk in his diet each day. It's my job to add up every drop in any guise to be sure he doesn't get more."

I glanced at Lucy, who was trying not to smile. "You think I'm kidding, don't you? I am not kidding. I have a list of ten vegetables—locally grown without pesticides or chemical fertilizers—that he likes to cycle through each week. I'm supposed to be sure he gets them in a certain order."

I couldn't seem to stop, although I doubted Lucy would ever ask me a question again. My personal favorite request—although that changed from day to day—was the list of

requirements for the massage therapist who would be at
Grady's beck and call during his time in town. It seems
Grady was particularly fond of Ayurvedic Abhyanga massage, in which herbal oils are used to unblock the whatsit
from the whosit. Sometimes the therapist hangs from the
ceiling, in order to apply extra pressure with his or her
tootsies. This, I would not mind witnessing.

"You have no idea how much the manager of the Emerald Springs Hotel and Spa is learning to hate me," I finished.

"Very shortly we'll hold a one-day seminar during which
you practice saying no. Over and over again."

"That's just the personal stuff. Somehow my job's spilled
over to making him happy at the auditorium, too. Finding
the right chair, the right variety of spring water, organic fruit
for snacks, making certain the temperature is exactly right
and no vents are blowing on him, making certain no lights
are shining in his eyes. He has to be completely comfortable
so he can make our contestants as uncomfortable as possible."

"I can't believe you've stuck it out."

Despite her words Lucy knew why I was putting up with
this. Not just because I was learning that I'm good at taking care of details. Not just because I am determined to
make sure Emerald Springs can offer the kind of pediatric
care a town like ours needs. But because suddenly, my own
daughter is involved in the Emerald Springs Idyll.

"Deena," I said.

She nodded. "I know. I have days when I look at your
girls and wish I had kids, too. Then there are days when
I'm glad I don't."

I had been completely taken by surprise that my daughter wanted to try out for the Idyll, much less that she would
be "good" enough to make it to the next round. Deena has
a host of talents, none of which is best displayed on a
stage. Still, without warning me, one week ago she and
four of her best friends showed up at the first round of au-

ditions, garbed in the trademark outrageous and far-too-provocative clothing of the Spice Girls. They had chosen the Spice Girls hit "Wannabe," which was popular about the time Deena was learning to talk. Unfortunately somebody else's mother had listened to AM radio. A lot. Probably to help survive the terrible twos.

Luckily Deena had snatched the role of Sporty, and though her tank top was tight and way too short, at least the sweatpants hid most of the rest of her developing body. The same could not be said of Carlene O'Grady, known these days as Ginger, whose spangled dress was shorter than her panties. Make that thong.

Thongs!

"I tell myself failure will be good for her," I said. "I assure myself Grady Barber will let the girls down easily. And I did refuse to let her dye her hair brown like the real Sporty's, so hopefully there won't be any lasting traumas."

Lucy was nodding sympathetically. "I saw Deena at the swimming pool with her friends. She told me she tried out for fun, that they were just dressing up and fooling around at somebody's sleepover and decided to see what happened."

Now this is the thing about honorary aunts. They learn all the secrets mothers are never privy to. But I had suspected the "Price" Girls—as the group calls itself—had come about like this, much the way many of the others who'd tried out had put together their acts. With little thought and lots of moxie.

During the first round of tryouts I'd been in and out of the high school auditorium, consulting with Veronica and the committee, and wheedling favors from the adolescent stagehands. This had been the round that winnowed the wheat from the chaff, using the judging talents of an Emerald College professor, a choral director from the next county, and the proprietor of a Columbus dinner theater.

The first round had seen some amazing performances. A worker from the county pound had arrived with three mutts who sat on the stage barking dutifully at his off-key rendition of "How Much Is That Doggie in the Window?" The barking had been the high point, although all three dogs had been quickly adopted.

We'd seen acrobats whose cartwheels looked like they were on a harrowing trip down a mountainside. Magicians with bunnies that could not be found in top hats or anywhere else on stage. Tap dancers who couldn't tell heel from sole, and ballerinas with double-jointed toes. When Deena and her friends arrived, bright-eyed, giggly, and occasionally in sync as they spun, swung their arms, and pointed their fingers, the judges had perked up. Deena's flip over her friend Tara's back had probably won the day. The fact that only a few of the girls could belt out anything approximating a tune hadn't fazed anybody.

"She got the role of Sporty Price because she was the only girl who could do a flip. The others said they would lose without her," Lucy finished.

"I wonder what else she'll do in the coming years because somebody else tells her how important she is?"

"You don't really want an answer to that, do you?"

I didn't. "They were invited to attend the party tonight, but luckily they decided it was for old fogeys like me."

Lucy parked her Concorde in a narrow space on the street that nobody else had been foolish enough to take. "In the years ahead I'll be here for you, Ag. I promise."

The party wasn't starting for another half hour. Maybe I was just developing Veronica's habit of showing up early for meetings and other events, so I could be firmly in control when they started, but I really did have to check with the caterer one last time. I also had to check all the floral arrangements to be sure there were no lilies. Lilies make Grady sneeze. Lucy had agreed to help with that and with making sure the French black olives with herbs that are Grady's favorites sat in bowls on the bar where he could easily spot them. I draw the line at dropping them into his mouth.

Veronica's maid answered the door, dressed the way she had every time I'd been here. Not being familiar with maids, I had wondered if there was a cocktail party uniform, something frillier and lower cut. I was disappointed.

"Hi, Winona," I said. "Are you ready for the onslaught?"

Either Winona is not an affectionate soul, or she's afraid Veronica will fire her if she's seen smiling on the security cameras. Last week she did tell me her first name, which was like prying a pearl out of an oyster, but she still refuses to call me by mine. She opened the door wider and ushered us inside, but I actually saw her glance at the guest list first.

I introduced Lucy, and Winona gave the slightest of nods. "Shall I take you in, or do you want to find your own way?"

"We'll follow the noise. Good luck with everything."

Her nostrils flared. I figured that was answer enough.

I headed for the kitchen. Veronica's house always looks like it's ready for a formal dinner for fifty, but today I could see the subtle differences. More flowers. Shinier surfaces. Even the dust was dusted.

Men and women in bow ties and stylish vests bustled by. Caterer's staff, perhaps, or bartenders, or even the valets who would park cars in a church lot half a mile away. Veronica is a member of that particular church. I'd had more than one occasion in the last weeks to say prayers of thanksgiving that she isn't a member of ours.

We turned a corner and Veronica was there, giving credence to my growing feeling that she, like most versions of the Almighty, can be everywhere at once.

"I am so glad you've arrived. I was beginning to worry." She glanced at Lucy, then back at me. "And you brought a helper. How nice to see you, Lucy."

Since Lucy and Veronica's husband are rivals, I waited for teeth to be bared, but both women behaved. Veronica clearly knew Lucy's broker and all the agents were giving a large donation to the hospital—which was why Lucy was on the guest list.

"Lucy's going to do some last-minute checks for me," I explained.

"And you'll do one more check with the caterer?"

Veronica was resplendent in a long, red Asian cheongsam that set off her black hair and high cheekbones. Her husband, in addition to having a successful realty, had been the only child of millionaires who had already departed this life. That inheritance showed tonight, in the imported embroidered silk as well as everything around us.

"I have a new list of forbidden foods." I'd gotten it from my purse and now I waved it at her.

"But it's too late to change the menu."

"I know, but I can make sure he isn't served the things that aren't on his diet."

"Grady was always such a picky eater." She smiled fondly. "The school cafeteria was a horror for him. He rarely ate lunch. Oh, we are so lucky to have him back here. After all his success. After everything he's done and become. I'm still just so amazed he agreed."

Even though I'm a minister's wife, there is little I wouldn't do to make the kind of money we're paying for a small outlay of Grady Barber's time. But I knew better than to say so. This was Veronica's night. She was Lady Bountiful and Mother Teresa rolled into one, the savior of our town's children, the woman who was giving us a new pediatric wing, as well as something fun to think about during the hottest, driest summer on record.

"Well, let me go and do my part to make sure everything's perfect," I said.

"I'm sure it will be." She dazzled us with her smile. "It had better be . . ."

Was this meant as a threat? Could a threat be delivered after such an extravagant display of pearly whites? I really didn't know what Veronica could do to me if a mistake had been made. But not feeling inclined to find out, I smiled, too, and bolted for the kitchen, leaving Lucy to patrol for lilies.

The kitchen was simmering with activity. The caterer, a young woman named Joan, who'd probably cursed her career choice a hundred times since winning this contract, nodded in my direction. Her assistant—equally young and fresh-faced—rolled his eyes as I strode in with the new list.

"Before you say a word," I warned, "I'll read this latest fax, then we'll figure out what not to serve Grady. You don't have to change a thing. We just have to warn the servers."

"How could anybody's diet change this radically from day to day?" Joan asked.

"Passive aggressive behavior," the assistant muttered.

I tried to be charitable. "Grady's used to having his way. He's just out of the habit of being sensible."

"A narcissist. Or a sociopath."

"Studying psychology, are we?"

"It doesn't take a degree."

Since I'd had the same thoughts, I shot him a smile and unfurled my list. "No shallots." I looked up and saw no reaction. This might go better than I'd feared. "No porcini mushrooms . . ."

Five minutes later I was on my way. The servers would be warned not to present the stuffed mushrooms to the guest of honor, and the spinach dip would go home with Joan. Veronica hadn't paid for a spinach dip bodyguard, and putting a Grady Beware sign beside it might detract from the carefully orchestrated atmosphere.

Lucy was rearranging flowers in the dining room, and she glanced up. "Three stinky stargazers and half a dozen tiger lilies, which don't smell, but who am I to make those decisions? I took them all outside and trashed them so even the garbage is lily free."

"You're a saint. Are there Jewish saints?"

"Try the apostles. Last I heard they were Jewish."

"Ed would have remembered that. Or Sister Nora."

In the weeks since I watched the circus arrive, I'd only heard wild, unsubstantiated rumors about Sister Nora. Lucy hadn't been around to discuss what she knew, and I hadn't had time to follow up. I'd been too busy making certain the Emerald Springs Hotel stocks Grady Barber's bathroom with Renova toilet paper—which costs the moon and comes in three bright colors and black, which, for reasons I prefer not to think about, was Grady's hue of choice.

I paused. Now was not the time to dig for info, but I couldn't help myself. "How is she, by the way?"

"Despite all the committees forming to evict her and her band of merry men?"

"More likely evict the lions and tigers."

"Those, especially. She's fine, under the circumstances."

I wondered which circumstances Lucy meant. Hostile townspeople, a flurry of media interest, or lightning bolts from above? Or maybe just the diminishing ozone layer.

"She's really managing okay? She's getting through this? I hear there have been picketers along with CNN."

"For a God-fearing town that prides itself on the Constitution and family values, there are a lot of people upset she's bringing a different spin on religion."

"Is it true she's working her revelations about global warming around lion taming and death-defying feats on the tightrope? That could distract."

"I haven't been to a revival meeting. It's not exactly my style."

I lowered my voice. "Veronica's furious. She says the tent show is distracting people from the Idyll."

"She's furious because my realty sold Sister Nora the farm and her husband's didn't."

I wanted to continue, but the clock was ticking. "I have to check with the string quartet. I'm told Grady doesn't like Bach, Beethoven, or Brahms."

"This time you're joking."

I punched her lightly on the arm. "I just want to be sure they know to time their breaks with Veronica's announcements."

"I'll be wherever the olives are."

When I found the musicians they were gaping at petite,

blonde Camille Beauregard, the only member of our illustrious committee besides Sally who I've developed any fondness for. Camille has a sense of humor, a sharp tongue, and a mania for staying fit. She and her surgeon husband begin each morning with an hour of aerobic exercise, and that's her warm-up. Tonight her arms, in a sleeveless lamé cocktail dress, rippled with muscle as she single-handedly heaved chairs and music stands into a niche beside the sofa and across from the Steinway grand. The wide-eyed musicians were clutching their instruments, as if they were afraid they might be next.

"Veronica wants them out of traffic," she explained as she heaved and tossed.

I picked up a chair and dragged it to the newly assigned place, ignoring the musicians the way she had. "Did you ask for their schedule so Veronica can work around it?"

"Veronica, work around something?" She laughed and flung the last chair into place. "They've promised to stop playing on cue. They know the score." She laughed again. "Get it? Know the score. Save me from myself, Aggie. The freaking party hasn't even started."

"There's no hope for any of us." I left as she lifted the sofa with one hand and smoothed the Persian carpet under it with the other.

Guests began to arrive at the stroke of eight. By then Lucy, Camille, and I were safely ensconced in a corner, me with a really good cabernet, Lucy and Camille with mixed drinks. Lucy was drinking a redheaded slut, and when she asked for it, I thought she was just introducing herself to the bartender, who was at least ten years too young. I'd been all prepared to have a frank talk about self-esteem and steer her toward someone more suitable. I still had my eyes open.

"Deena really would have hated this," Lucy said.

I tried to imagine my daughter with all the well-dressed and well-heeled people sifting into the room. The arrivals were laughing self-consciously and looking for places to hide out or be seen, depending on personality type. Deena would have bolted for the door.

I didn't conjure my daughter, but another familiar teenager walked into the room.

"Madison Sargent." I set my glass on the table beside me. "Is she a finalist?" Since Madison's only sixteen, I was certain she wasn't one of the big givers.

"She is. You know her?" Camille, in charge of the first round of tryouts, had been forced to hear every single act. She'd survived only because she's in such superior physical condition.

"She and her mother go to our church," I said. "What did she do? Sing? Dance?"

"Sing. She was a big hit."

I knew this didn't count for much, since the Price Girls had been a hit, as well. In fact from what I could tell, any act without an animal, trampoline, or stilts had been a hit.

"Will you hover over my wine? I'm going to say hi to her." I wound my way across the room and reached Madison just as her mother, Tammy, joined us.

The Sargents look more like sisters than mother and daughter. Tammy was a teenager when Madison was born, and Madison's father has apparently never been in the picture. Both women are tall and willowy, with dark blond hair. Tammy's is cut in layers to her shoulders and Madison's falls straight down to her shoulder blades, but they have the same smoky green eyes. Tammy helps out with the church youth group, although Ed has always been careful to have other parents helping as well. Ed's afraid Tammy is more inclined to be one of the gang than to help the gang make responsible, mature choices.

I greeted them. "I hear you made the finals, Madison. Congratulations."

Madison looked pleased. "It's really exciting. And it's so cool to be here."

I couldn't help but be excited for her. Madison's eyes shone, and clearly she was impressed with Veronica's house.

If we could make the Idyll fun for the contestants and the audience, the whole hullabaloo might be worth it.

"Madison wants to meet Grady Barber." Tammy has a low, sultry voice, and she uses it to great advantage. I wondered if she had ever yearned for time on the stage herself.

I glanced at my watch. "He's not here yet, but if everything goes the way it's supposed to, he should be here pretty soon."

I looked back up to see Veronica signaling me from the doorway.

"I've got to take care of some details, but I hope you enjoy yourself." I smiled my way past them and headed for Veronica, not even taking the brief detour to my wineglass, although I regretted that when I saw a server scoop it off the table and carry it away before Lucy could tackle him.

"Fred just arrived," Veronica said when I reached her. "He's frantic, and he's asking for you."

I wondered if I could slip out through the kitchen, intercept Ed, and take him up on his offer of a night in paradise. I'd had enough phone calls with Grady's assistant to know that he took things personally. "Where?"

A minute later I found Fred Handlemann pacing back and forth in Farley Hayworth's country squire study. The room was one stuffed pheasant short of Balmoral Castle.

"Aggie Sloan-Wilcox," I said, holding out my hand. Fred's hand was soft in mine, but then, everything about Fred looked soft. He wasn't overweight, but I could swear somebody had injected him with an extra layer of fat. I flashed on the Pillsbury Doughboy and knew that at every subsequent meeting, I would have to fight an impulse not to poke him to see how fast his flesh rebounded. Or to make him giggle. Clearly he needed a good giggle now. He looked distraught.

"Please tell me there's no new crisis," I said.

Fred was halfway to being bald, and he rubbed his head as if it were a powerful totem. Then he adjusted thick, tinted glasses and rubbed his head once more. He might as well have worn a blinking neon sign advertising stress for sale.

"You've done just the best job here. The best." Head rub, glasses readjusted. He managed a sickly smile. "But Grady isn't quite happy with his room."

How many ways could I tell Grady to carefully place his head where the sun never shines? I guess that particular pleasure was eliminated the day I married a seminary student, but I'm ashamed to say the urge still resides deep inside me.

Instead I sounded pleasant, even friendly. "So, what's the problem? Shall we ask the management to dynamite the hotel and start over?"

"The elevator's too slow."

"There are stairs. Can we tell him walking up one flight is better than a gym?"

"The stairs are on the opposite end of the hallway from his room."

"How lucky he is that he'll get even more exercise."

"I guess you're saying there is no hope of moving him?"

"It's the nicest suite in the building, Fred. Warren Harding slept there."

"Warren Harding was a crook and a loser."

"And your point would be?"

This smile was real, and he was instantly transformed into someone far more appealing.

"We can move him," I said, "but he'll like the alternative even less. Stick with this. It's the best we can do."

"The fluorescent bulb over the bathroom mirror washes the color from his cheeks."

"He does know it's not permanent, right? That when he steps out of the bathroom, voila, color's back?" I saw Fred's smile fading. "I'll go to the hardware store and get a full-spectrum bulb to replace it tomorrow. Will that help?"

He looked relieved. "Immeasurably."

"There's just nothing in the whole wide world we wouldn't do for Grady Barber."

"I can imagine a few things you'd like to do." He lowered his voice. "He's not usually this bad, Aggie. Something about coming home, I guess. Bear with him, okay?"

"I can if you can."

We stepped out of the study and passed into the entryway. Winona was just answering the door, and our mayor, Brownie Kefauver, and our chief of police, Grayson Adams, stepped in. Brownie's eyes widened when he caught sight of me. Unfortunately Brownie's wife, Hazel, dropped dead at my feet last spring, and he begged me to find her murderer. Now that the killer is old news, Brownie doesn't like our encounters, since I'm a reminder that for a brief moment in his life, he was a murder suspect himself.

Knowing this, I made a point of saying hello and extending my hand. The police chief and I have never been formally introduced, but I'm well acquainted with one of his detectives, Kirkor Roussos. As Brownie had no choice but to shake, Adams, who is as tall and muscular as Brownie is short and puny, held out his hand and pumped mine, too.

"Nice to see you again," he said. "How's the family?"

I suspected I could make up sextuplets and a husband who had abandoned me. The chief wouldn't know the difference. But I just smiled and said, "Fine, thanks for asking."

A noise behind us cut short this fascinating exchange. A man was trying to push past Winona, who had her arms out to each side gripping the doorframe.

The chief whirled and advanced, a maneuver so deftly done it would have won him a boost to the next round in the Idyll. "What's going on?"

Since the man was still pushing, Winona grunted most of her answer.

"He . . . doesn't have an invitation!"

"Hey, stop that right now." The chief whipped out his badge and flashed it. "If she says you can't come in, you can't come in. Got it?"

I had a quick impression of a man my age or perhaps a bit older, dark haired, ordinary enough. His eyes flicked to the badge, then he stepped back. I could hear Winona's *whoosh* of relief.

Adams took another step forward and blocked most of my view. "Just what are you doing here?"

The man in the doorway stepped back to the edge of the porch and was lost to me, except for his voice. "I forgot my invitation. I tried to tell her."

"If I were you, I'd go home and get it. If you can't find it, don't come back. If you *do* find it, don't come back. If we have to escort you off the property, we will."

"I'm going."

Apparently he did, because the chief relaxed and turned back to us.

"That happens a lot," Fred said from behind me. "Party crashers who want to meet Grady face-to-face."

I glanced at him, but if it did happen a lot, Fred still wasn't used to it. He looked even more worried than he had at the start of our conversation.

I didn't have time to consider this. Several members of the church were approaching, including Sally and Dolly—who had gotten me into this mess—so I stayed in the hallway and somehow managed not to throttle the life out of them. Before I could head back to get more wine, I saw Ed in another group coming up the walkway. Once he was inside I snatched him by his jacket sleeve and led him where all the fun was supposed to be happening.

"Great tie," I said. "Eat anything you want, it's all vegetarian. Eat all the stuffed mushrooms because Grady can't, and they look scrumptious. Oh, after we sneak out of here, I have to go to the hardware store to buy him a grow light."

"Why? Is he going to raise vegetables at the hotel?"

I explained about full-spectrum bulbs, how much better they were for plants as well as for narcissistic actors who needed constant affirmation.

Then I continued. "A guy tried to sneak in; Grady's upset that the Emerald Springs Hotel elevators are slow—"

"He's on the second floor."

"He's too important for those extra seconds."

He closed his eyes. "Is there a bar?"

"You have a two-drink maximum. No matter what else Grady does, remember that."

We were in a long line to get more of the luscious cabernet, when there was a stir at the door. A dumpy-looking woman in a flowing lavender caftan swept into the room, smiling and nodding at the assembled dignitaries. I recognized her as the accompanist who had played for the first round of tryouts, although I couldn't remember her name. She made her way to the piano and sat. Somebody had silenced the quartet, who were now scurrying to join us at the bar. The room fell silent, too. The woman lifted her hands, and waved them ceremoniously. Then she played a few graceful arpeggios to get the attention of the few groups that hadn't caught on.

"I'm Lisa Lee," she said. "And I think everybody here knows this song."

She began to play in earnest. I recognized the introduction to Grady's signature, "Sailing toward a Rainbow." Then, right on cue, in strolled the star himself, in an Italian suit and a shirt that could only be silk, and he began to sing.

Sailing toward a rainbow
Stretching overhead
Colors flaming in the sky
Violet, gold, and red
Symbol of a better day
Vowing a new start
But I have lost the ones I loved
Empty arms and broken heart.

Grady stopped and grinned. The grin was puckish and endearing and somehow out of place on the face of a man in his forties. But the assembled crowd didn't think so. He had them in the palm of his hand, and the applause began as a roar.

He waited, nodding graciously, smiling the little-boy smile. When the applause finally died, he lifted his hand and turned. Veronica was right there, surprisingly demure and clearly flattered, and he motioned her forward.

"I can't believe I'm home," Grady said. "And I wouldn't be, if it weren't for my old friend. Veronica, come and accept a round of applause yourself."

Veronica shook her head and laughed, but Grady reached for her hand and drew her to stand next to him. Then he held her there and invited all who were present to join him in the chorus.

They say a brand-new world awaits
A promise has been made
But who'll be here to greet us
When the rainbow starts to fade?

He continued alone, while Veronica blushed prettily beside him, and Lisa Lee swayed back and forth over the keys.

I'll confess, right after I was conned into becoming Fred's assistant, I borrowed the DVD of *Wayfarers of the Ark* from the library and corralled the girls to watch it with me. Until then I had forgotten how lovely this theme song was when sung by the teenaged Grady. Now I was happy to find that his voice was still sweet, clear, and effective, and the song that much more moving because of it.

Grady might be twenty-five years older than the teenaged Idan pining for the world before the flood, but his boyish good looks had held. He was a man now, with broader shoulders and a more substantial build. Silver threaded through the golden hair, artfully, of course, almost as if Mother Nature had gotten help scattering it in the right places. But the changes only added a hint of power to his stage presence. He looked warm, approachable, more Bing Crosby in *The Bells of St. Mary* than Anthony Hopkins in *Silence of the Lambs*. If I hadn't spent three weeks poring over a list of ridiculous demands, I might have fallen under his spell. At least I could still admire his acting ability.

He finished, and the crowd went wild again. He released Veronica, gave a short, humble bow, and held his hand out to Lisa Lee. "Where did you find such an extraordinary pianist?" he asked.

I happened to be looking at Lisa and wishing, not for the first time, that Junie hadn't dumped her pianist lover until I'd had a few more lessons. Lisa was smiling, but I thought her eyes weren't quite as friendly.

"Oh, I've just been hanging around Emerald Springs hoping you would come back so I could play for you," she said sweetly.

Everybody applauded again, then people began to move forward to crowd around Grady for a chance to speak to him.

"Well, that went well," a familiar voice said.

I turned and saw that Fred had come up behind me. I introduced him to Ed, who managed to be polite. "Glad our superstar made it," I said. "And he really does have a wonderful voice."

"He must have come in through the back. I'll introduce you when the crowd thins."

Since I'd have to meet Grady sooner or later, I nodded. By the time we finally got our wine, Fred came back to take us over to his boss. Ed, who by that point was deeply involved in a conversation with a councilman about parking near the church, declined. I figured that meeting Grady couldn't be worse than broken meters and restricted zones.

We waited at the edge of the crowd for our turn, and finally Fred drew me forward. "Grady, I want you to meet Aggie Sloan-Wilcox, who's taken care of so many of the arrangements to make you comfortable while you're here."

Grady turned a warm smile in my direction, and I held out my hand. "We're honored to have you working with us," I said.

"The pleasure is mine. And I realize how much you're doing to make this easier. All my traveling is a real drain, so I appreciate every extra comfort."

He had a lot to appreciate, then, but I didn't say so. He turned to Fred, and the smile died. "Where in the hell were you, Fred? I got here and you weren't anywhere to be found."

Fred shot me a quick glance and gave a slight shake of his head, but Grady didn't pay attention. The tone of his voice dropped fifteen degrees. "You know I want you within reach at all times."

"Something came up, and I had to take care of it."

"Take care of things on your own time, not when you're supposed to be watching out for me."

Fred touched his head, his glasses, and he swallowed hard. I bristled self-righteously for the pathetic wuss, but what could I say? I didn't know where Fred had been or how much of a pattern this was. Maybe Grady had a right to be annoyed.

Grady turned on the charm once more and aimed it at me. "Fred's so nearly perfect at what he does that any lapse is all too obvious. Fred, be a good boy and get me a drink, would you?" Fred shot off to the bar and left me alone with the great one.

I was trying to make sense of this split personality when the mood swung once more. One of the caterer's staff arrived with a tray of gorgeously arranged appetizers. He held them in front of Grady, offering a napkin with his other hand.

Grady shook his head. The young man didn't see the signal and moved a little closer.

"No," Grady said sharply. Then, when the young man didn't move back quickly enough, Grady shoved the tray, nearly upending it on Veronica's priceless carpet. This was unnecessary rudeness, the action of a man who expected everything to happen exactly when he wanted it to. Unfortunately two cheese puffs made the dive and landed just in front of him.

I debated cleaning up the mess, but darned if I was going to kneel at this man's feet after that misplaced display of temper. I needn't have debated. Winona, who had been ushering in a new wave of guests, saw what had happened, strode over, grabbed a napkin from the server who was now a good four feet away, and squatted to remove the evidence.

She stood and gazed at Grady for a long moment, then she squared her shoulders, turned, and left.

Everything had happened so quickly, not a ripple swept the room. But I felt the entire episode right down to the marrow of my bones. I had more than a week ahead to deal with Grady Barber. I wondered if I knew anybody in a foreign country who would take me in for the duration.

4

Every time I walk into Junie's quilt shop, I'm amazed at the way she's transformed the space Lucy and I renovated for her. Feeling Quilty was once a run-down Stick Victorian, hidden by overgrown shrubs and pottery gnomes. Lucy and I had seen the potential for a quick flip. Brighter paint, a little plumbing, a few swipes of the old chain saw and voila, instant sale.

We'd expected to be in and out quickly, but Junie had seen the house and fallen in love. Suddenly the house on Bunting Street had become a long-term project. Now the Victorian is a mellow mauve, with accents of rose, spruce green, black, and cream. The oak floors glow; the walls are a variety of soft pastels that won't detract from the vibrant bolts of fabric nestled floor to ceiling. Notions reside in baskets and vintage boxes in what was once a gentleman's study. Books and patterns live happily where meals were once prepared. The walkout basement has been turned into two bright classrooms, and the second floor is Junie's apartment, all sunshine, splashes of brilliance, and welcoming open spaces.

My mother defies description. Although she's been married five times, she never took a husband's name. Nor did she keep the one—Kowalski—that her parents bequeathed her. Sometime before I was old enough to know better, she became Junie Bluebird. And although she claims that at least one of the reasons she took the name was because she wanted to be the bluebird of happiness, I'm not sure she's joking. Few people dislike Junie, and they are all suspect.

She is some multigenerational amalgam of apple-cheeked grandma, all-knowing earth mother, and free-spirited nature child.

Junie is happy anywhere she goes. The craft show circuit was an endless source of pleasure, new people, new towns, new husbands. In a matter of hours she could take the dumpiest apartment and make it feel like home. But even though she genuinely loved traveling across the country, I think she's thrilled to be settled at last in Emerald Springs where she can watch her granddaughters grow, share her love of quilting, and make friends who will still be here when she wakes up every morning.

And she seems to be making a lot of those.

"I do like those fabrics together, Sue," my mother was saying from behind the island in the center of what was once a living room. A woman with springy gray curls had bolts of blue and green fabrics piled in front of her waiting to be cut, but she was clearly concerned about one of her choices.

"However, for your inside border I think you might consider this one." Junie reached behind her and grabbed a bolt shuddering with wildly colored polka dots.

"Ooooh, yes!" Sue grabbed the new fabric, as if somebody might dive in and take off with it.

"I think you're set," Junie said. "It's going to be magnificent. Miss Emma?"

Emma Beale, one of Junie's two helpers, stopped straightening bolts surrounding the fireplace and toddled over to cut the fabric. Miss Emma is approximately a hundred years old, and she's been quilting for ninety-nine of them. She moves as rapidly as a shallow creek during a deep freeze, but she can answer any question and nobody's ever in a hurry to leave Feeling Quilty anyway. There's a coffee urn, cookies from a bakery that just opened in another house down the street, and comfortable chairs on the porch to sit and chat about projects and classes in progress.

Junie greeted three other women by name before she made it to Teddy and me. She gave Teddy a big, grandmotherly hug and agreed that my orderly daughter could straighten the notions and make sure everything was in its proper place. This had become Teddy's Saturday job, and she took it seriously.

Once Teddy had skipped off to the notions room, Junie slipped her arm around my shoulders and steered me toward the kitchen and freedom. We didn't speak until we were sitting in deck chairs on a stretch of grass that will one day be a lovely patio. When the time comes, Junie won't have to pay very much to have the grass removed. The bluegrass is now browngrass and looks as if it wants to be put out of its misery. The Japanese magnolias and forsythia we'd planted to screen out the parking lot are only just holding their own. I know for a fact Junie plugs up the bathtub when she takes her daily shower and hauls the water to her trees and shrubs at night when nobody is watching. There's a strict watering schedule in effect, and Junie's determined her trees are not going to die.

"I almost didn't recognize you, precious. It seems like weeks since I've seen you."

I'm told this is something mothers often say, but Junie wasn't trying to shame me. This was simply fact.

I inched my chair to one side to take advantage of what shade the magnolias produced. "Every day I tell myself this nightmare will be behind me soon."

"Do you ask yourself how you got so involved and whether you should set limits?"

Junie sounded genuinely curious. As a girl I was never reprimanded, only questioned like this. There were times a good whack on the fanny would have been kinder.

"Teddy's little friend came this close to dying of meningitis . . ." I held my thumb and index finger just far enough apart for a hair to pass between them. "And at least partly because the pediatric wing at the hospital is so out-of-date, and there's no pediatric ICU here. What if that had been one of my girls?"

"I know it's an issue dear to your heart. And you feel better equipped to handle all these details than to ask others to help you."

There was a question there, as well. I was raised on subtext, so I know. "Everybody's working hard. But as silly as it is, I like being good at something and doing it well."

Junie was silent long enough to let me know I'd caught her by surprise. "What aren't you good at?" she asked in a tone also appropriate for "You say you're leaving the girls in Ed's care and joining the Hare Krishnas?"

Believe it or not it's a big responsibility to have somebody in your life who thinks you're nearly perfect. Luckily Ed has no delusions, but he loves me anyway.

"Junie"—my sisters and I have always called our mother Junie, and none of us can remember why—"this self-esteem thing is a common problem among the mothers of school-age children and the wives of ministers. I know I'm darned good at the first and passing fair at the second—when I remember not to say everything I'm thinking. I'm pretty good at flipping houses, although the housing slump means we aren't making much money doing it. And I seem to have a talent for finding murderers."

Of course, I nearly died a couple of times practicing that particular skill. So that's not great for my self-esteem, but I didn't go into that. "I guess I just need something else. And right now the Idyll is it."

"I'm looking for another assistant."

I closed my eyes. "Come on, in a month this place would be history. Remember the costume I made for Deena's third Halloween?" Deena's Cinderella ball gown, my first real sewing project as an adult, had turned out so badly that Ed and I had smeared ashes on her cheeks and told everybody she was Cinderella before her fairy godmother showed up. We'd made certain no photos survived.

"It was certainly one of a kind," Junie said.

"I don't need a job. Lucy and I will get back to flipping.

Right now I just need to prove I'm a nice, normal person who's also intelligent, efficient, and able to stay out of trouble. And speaking of that . . ."

I launched into a description of last night's party, which had ended—no surprise—with Grady singing "Remember Me in April," the hit song which had brought him back into the limelight last year, and the one which some people say fanned the embers of his career back to flame.

"When he's singing, he seems like the nicest guy in the world. When he's talking to somebody important, he does, too. But Grady Barber's got it in for all the little guys in the world. I shudder to think what the next round of the Idyll will be like."

"The movie where he got his start. What's it called?"

"Wayfarers of the Ark." I could see this wasn't familiar to Junie, who'd never been much for movies. I explained. "It's the story of Noah's ark, only it's about the members of Noah's family, how they feel about getting in a boat with all those animals just because Noah tells them to, how they feel about leaving friends and family behind, knowing they'll drown. Grady played Idan, Noah's grandson. In the movie there's a young girl he's in love with. The two of them try desperately to find a female unicorn as a mate for Idan's own unicorn. In the end the girl finds a female but can't get back in time to board the ark. Idan is forced to sail without her."

"You say this is a children's movie?" Junie was irate. "This is a message we want children to hear?"

I patted her hand. "We can't protect them from the Old Testament. It's everywhere. Anyway, forget the story. What's most important is that to promote the movie, the producers launched a big talent search to find fresh new talent for Idan and the girl, Dalia. It was a public relations stunt. Anyway, Grady was a senior at the high school here. The talent scouts were visiting small cities and towns, and for some reason Emerald Springs was on their route. Grady tried out, singing an original song he'd written for the audition called 'Sailing toward a Rainbow.' They loved him; they loved the song. The rest is history."

"And success turned him into a monster."

"I don't know, maybe he was a monster before he got famous."

I was tired of thinking about Grady Barber, so I turned the conversation to the shop. We chatted about new fabric she was expecting, a class she was planning, about Teddy's swimming lessons. Finally Miss Emma ambled out to say that several customers needed Junie's advice. I glanced at my watch and realized I'd stayed longer than I had planned. I still had a long list to finish before Monday evening, when the second round of the Idyll began. And before then, I fully expected a few frantic calls from Fred. I'd seen him this morning when I popped over to the hotel to replace the bulb in Grady's bathroom while the great one was off having breakfast. Fred had looked even doughier, a man who wasn't getting enough sleep or exercise.

I stood to go. "Why don't you come for dinner after the shop closes?"

"I can't. Miss Emma and I are going out to see Nora."

I almost passed over this. After all, my mother has her own life here, and I can't know all her friends. There are far too many. Then I froze.

"Tell me you don't mean Sister Nora of the tent show."

Junie stood, too, and tugged a Feeling Quilty T-shirt over her substantial hips. "Exactly who I mean."

"You're calling her Nora. You won't drop the *Miss* in Miss Emma, but you're dropping the *Sister* in Sister Nora."

She waved that away. "Sister is only a title. And Miss Emma is Southern, and she's been called Miss Emma since she was fifteen. She can't remember to answer to anything else."

I didn't let a discussion of titles and regional customs sidetrack me. "You've been there before? To the tent show?"

"It's quite a wonderful way to spend an evening. Miss

Emma is fond of the lion tamer. She once had an affair with the zookeeper at the Atlanta zoo."

This was a vision I did not want in my head. The Miss Emma I know weighs about sixteen pounds, less than an ounce of which is hair and teeth. One day she'll die reaching for a bolt of fabric, and hours will pass before anybody notices the subtle difference.

"How many times have you gone?" I stepped closer, because I know my mother too well. "Tell me you're not going to join up."

"I think you'd better come along tonight to see what it's really about. Nora has as deep a concern for the environment as anyone I've ever met. She genuinely loves those animals and takes extraordinarily good care of them. And her faith is strong. There's nothing there to frighten anybody."

"It can't be that simple," I said. "Where's the part where she tries to convince you to give up all your worldly goods— to her—and go live in a circus trailer?"

"Nora believes she speaks with God. That's why she's going to build a biosphere on her new acreage. God's told her this is where it has to go. But she hasn't asked me or anybody else for a cent to make it happen. She says God will provide the funds."

"Biosphere? Here in Emerald Springs?"

Junie didn't seem to think that was strange. "What better place, precious. You and I are here to help, aren't we?"

+ + +

In the heyday of circuses, running away to join one was considered romantic, adventurous. High-spirited teenagers and wives in need of more excitement than plucking chickens and pickling beets probably thought the circus and the life it promised were visions from God. Those who loved the runaways and wanted them to stay home probably thought the circus was an enticement of the devil.

As I parked my minivan on Horseshoe Bend Road, I won-

dered which side of that coin Sister Nora's Inspirational
Tent Show would come down on. Even though it was seven
o'clock, and the sun was moving steadily toward the horizon,
I felt more like I was in hell than heaven. I'd had a full day
working on preparations for the Idyll, including a closed-
door meeting with the doleful manager of the Emerald Springs
Hotel who, after less than twenty-four hours of Grady's presence, had come far too close to blubbering. I wanted an evening at home with my husband, daughters, and an electric
fan. But I know my mother. In those olden, golden days
Junie would never have settled for chickens and beets. I
wanted to make sure that when and if Sister Nora leaves
Emerald Springs, she didn't take my happy-go-lucky mother
with her.

As I jumped down to open the sliding door, Lucy got
down from the passenger seat. I had called her in a panic,
and she had agreed to come, although she'd pointed out
that after a night of arranging olives and tossing out perfectly lovely lilies, this was a bit much.

I found Junie and Miss Emma happily ensconced in the
rear captain's chairs, playing with the air vents. Sometimes
my mother is easily pleased.

"You're sure you want to do this tonight?" I asked them,
gesturing toward the sinking sun. "It's not cooling off. And
it's going to be even hotter inside that tent. We could go
home and rent a movie. *Trapeze*? *The Greatest Show on
Earth*?"

Junie, who never misses a chance to go anywhere in
costume, was wearing baggy pants and a polka-dotted shirt
with an orange-striped bow tie. A very, very large bow tie.
Feeling Quilty was probably missing an entire bolt of
orange-striped fabric. I'd picked her up a little early, and
there hadn't been time for greasepaint or a bulbous red
nose, which had not been a miscalculation on my part.

"Saturday night is the full show," she said as she hopped
down. "I can't wait to see it."

I wondered if I should have brought my girls. But the

Price Girls had scheduled an emergency rehearsal, and Teddy would have asked for the theological implications in every act. I'd thought I'd better check out the tent show in person first, particularly if there were picketers—who luckily appeared to be home cooling their heels tonight. The show was old news now, and the media had gone away.

I held out a hand to Miss Emma, who was surprisingly nimble, if slow. She wore faded jeans and a babydoll eyelet blouse that showed every crevice and liver spot. There were other cars parked up and down the road, but not as many as I remembered from my first visit. The thrill had probably worn off, and caution had set in. Not only were there wild beasts in the tent show, there was a message, and it wasn't being served up with air-conditioning.

We walked down the roadside, slapping at the occasional mosquito. Miss Emma whistled "Entrance of the Gladiators," which is the classic circus theme song. I'd done some homework that afternoon, trying to find out whatever I could about Nora and the others.

I shared my sudden wealth. "Circuses originally came from England. Did you know that? When they started they were small, the original dog-and-pony shows, and they weren't able to travel very far because they had to build seats and rings everywhere they went. Once they went under the big top, they could travel faster and farther. Eventually they were transported by rail, long, long trains. Some of the shows took up as much as thirty acres once they set up."

"You've been reading again," Lucy said. "I've warned you about that, Ag."

"Yes, well . . ." I sneaked in the rest of it. "Some historians believe the circus was really important for changing attitudes and broadening horizons. Women were stars and highly valued in their acts. People of different races and cultures were visible in places they'd never been seen before."

"Like in sideshows? Freak shows?" Lucy said. "This was a good thing?"

"Well, not by our standards, of course, but for some people the sideshows were a way to earn a decent living instead of living off charity. And the circus was a place where they could be accepted as part of a community."

"Are we going to sing a hymn before we even get through the gates?"

I swatted her with the notebook I'd pulled from my purse to fan myself. "I couldn't find much about Nelson–Zimboni, though."

"I bet you didn't look on the Internet, did you?"

The computer and I—all right, the entire technological universe—do not see eye to eye. Sometimes late at night when everybody else is asleep, I can hear Ed's laughing maniacally from the study.

"I like my information to come from reliable sources," I said airily.

Miss Emma stopped whistling. "They didn't have sideshows. I can tell you that much. No hoochie-coochie dancers, either. Not Nelson–Zimboni. Class acts, all the way. I saw them, you know, when they were still all one circus. Watching Caprice Zimboni on a tightrope was like watching Pavlova dance *Swan Lake*."

I'd never heard Miss Emma put more than five words together in under a minute. "What else do you remember?"

"Caprice Zimboni, she was slender, tall, dark haired. She was ice, but Nora Nelson was fire. Nora was all pale skin and golden hair, womanly, not thin like Caprice. She rode a white stallion, bareback, too, and when he was racing around the ring so fast he was nothing more than a blur, she'd stand up and hold out her arms and twirl and leap and do flips, and she never faltered. They'd leap through hoops of fire together, her and that horse of hers. I remember there wasn't a sound under that tent when she performed, just the beating of hooves, the hiss of flames."

"Wow." I was impressed by the speech, Miss Emma's memory, and the information.

Lucy was impressed, too. "Now that's an act I'd like to see."

"I remember when they split up, the Nelsons going one way, the Zimbonis another. Nobody ever said why, either. I guess times were hard for circuses. No call for a medium-sized one. Too small for Madison Square Garden and too big for all those little Madison Counties stretching across America. I guess it was just easier to split up then to try and expand. Too many big circuses ahead of them."

I wanted to know more, but why? I had an overactive imagination and enough curiosity to kill every big cat in Nora's show. And for what reason? I was thinking the way I used to think when I was trying to find a murderer. I reminded myself that curiosity had proved to be bad for my health.

We reached the open gate into the farm. On either side there were clowns in rainbow wigs making balloon animals to greet us. They clapped as Junie passed inside, and she obligingly squeaked a vintage bicycle horn one offered her. I was given what looked like a balloon dachshund to tote around with me. At least it didn't weigh anything.

"We're early." I'd been afraid we might have to park half a mile away, and at the speed Miss Emma walked, I had worried we'd miss the show.

"We could see the animals. They're in a separate tent," Junie said.

I wasn't sure that was a great idea. Junie believes a number of things about which the rest of us are skeptical. One, she thinks she's psychic, which couldn't be further from the truth. Two, she believes that when she talks to animals, they know exactly what she's saying, and she understands their responses telepathically. She's been known to converse for long periods with our family cat, Moonpie, and once she insisted I change our brand of cat food because Moonpie had seen a television commercial for one he liked better. Oddly enough, Moonpie's appetite improved greatly after that, but I refuse to consider that proof.

Right now, I didn't want to risk learning that Leo the Lion was ready for a short stroll around the grounds and all Junie had to do was turn the key to make it so.

"Let's not," Lucy said, before I could. "It'll be hot and putrid. Let's walk up to the house and see if they've made any progress fixing it up."

There were lots of people milling around. Some were clearly part of the show, and the rest were townspeople like us, gawking and pointing. If Nora's mission was to save the world, she'd picked a strange place to do it. I didn't see any sign of religious fervor in the vicinity. I saw people moving the way swamp dwellers probably do. Slowly, with great effort, their bodies glistening from sweat, their shoulders hunched against the humidity.

Once we were past the gate and the initial crowd, I could see the big top glowing on a slight rise in the nearest field. In the fading sunlight it looked like a huge, perfect pearl, and from that same direction, I could hear the music of a brass band. Not circus tunes, exactly, but music that was upbeat and energetic and totally unfamiliar to me.

"Lucy? Junie?"

We turned as one body and stared in the direction of the woman's voice. Before anyone said her name I recognized Sister Nora. She was dressed all in white—the preferred garb for prophets, I suppose—white jeans, white spangled tank top, white leather boots. Her blonde head was bare but she wore white riding gloves.

"I'm so glad you came," she said, when she was close enough. "We have a new show. Tonight's the premier performance."

I had heard that SNITS did interesting if peculiar reenactments of Old Testament stories. Daniel in the lion's den was an obvious choice, of course, performed by an excellent lion tamer and all the big cats. I'd heard a rumor that the new show was a retelling of Moses and the Israelites

escaping from Egypt. I was hoping this wasn't true. I
didn't want to see the ten plagues in living color under a
circus tent.

"Miss Emma and I can hardly wait," Junie said. She in-
troduced her assistant, and Sister Nora greeted her warmly.
Then she turned to Lucy and me. "You're Aggie," she said.
"I remember you."

"Aggie's my daughter," Junie said proudly.

"Aren't you both lucky?" Sister Nora asked. "The gift
of family."

"We were going to stroll by the house," Lucy said.

Nora checked her watch, which I was happy to see. She
might get direct orders from above, but the small things, like
telling time, were still up to her.

"Come see what we've done," she said. "I have a few
minutes before I make sure everything's set, and I need to
get something anyway."

We made all the polite protests, but by the time we'd finished, we were at the house. Everyone else was meander-
ing in the direction of the tent, and a line of three elephants
passed us, along with a pair of camels and four men carrying a bamboo pallet on which a woman in a black wig was
reclining. She was dressed in leopard skin and looked too
much like Pharaoh's daughter for my taste.

The house looked much better than the last time I'd seen
it. All those strong men and women had apparently turned
their hands to improvements. The roof no longer sagged; in
fact the roof was brand-new, a soft red shingle that was just
shades lighter than the freshly painted porch. The house was
now a soft yellow, and new forest green shutters matched the
door. Petunias and marigolds bloomed from big terra-cotta
pots flanking it.

"The front's our office. Yank and I live in the addition
in the back. Come see what we've done." She led us up to
the porch and through the house. The front looked official,
file cabinets and desks, computers and fancy calculators.
But once she unlocked the door on the other side of the

room, we were in an airy, open space with a small kitchen set off by an island from the rest of a pleasant room with windows looking out over the acreage. Vintage Nelson–Zimboni posters adorned three walls, sporting ringmasters, women pirouetting on tightropes and hanging from trapezes, and one with a buxom young blonde on a gorgeous white stallion. Unfortunately the fourth wall wasn't nearly as friendly.

"Some collection," I said, nodding to the rack of lethal-looking knives clinging to magnetic strips beside several powerful shotguns. The rack was as far from the kitchen as it could be and still hang in the room. Clearly these knives weren't meant for mincing onions.

"Yank's our knife thrower," Nora said, as if she were explaining that Yank was a lawyer, Yank was a tree surgeon. "You won't see him perform tonight, though. He has a cold, and his hands aren't steady enough."

I was glad to hear this, since a knife thrower with shaky hands sounded like plague number eleven to me and not one I wanted to witness.

"I hope Yank doesn't practice at home," I said.

"No chance. We just keep all the weapons here in the addition, pistols for the animal keepers and the rifles for tranquilizer darts. All valuables, too, important papers. We have good locks on these doors and a top-notch security system. Everything's perfectly safe that way and we can keep track. We don't want trouble."

She and Lucy chatted a moment about everything that had been done on the house. Then Nora disappeared, returning with a small whip.

"Just for show," she said. "I never whip my horses. But it makes a lovely cracking sound. Why don't you follow and I'll have you seated up front. We have a row reserved for the local clergy, but so far it's been empty. I'm sure they'll come, though. They'll want to help." She smiled a little. "Although I wish they would hurry. There's so much to do and so little time."

I didn't like the sound of that. "Until you build your biosphere?" I asked.

"There has to be a place where some people survive, and of course our animal friends, as well. It's not their fault we've disobeyed God's commandments. Man has greatly reduced his own chance of survival, and the odds will get worse and worse unless drastic changes are made. I've been given the task to save what we can. Now. Before it's too late."

She said all this so calmly, so assuredly, that we might have been having a conversation about books we'd read and loved. But I followed the others to the big top with an uneasy feeling. If Sister Nora had her way, someday, right here, just miles from the parsonage, a biosphere would house a few selected human beings and a circus load of animals. I was sure there must have been a few revelations along the way about oxygen, about food and water enough to survive, oh, conservatively, a millennium? Before the atmosphere cleansed itself, the glaciers began to reform, and life on the surface of the earth was comfortably habitable again. If such a thing could occur—and I was no scientist, so how would I know?

Of course this was screwy. Of course Nora was hearing voices in her head propelled by a very legitimate fear that our earth was not going to survive the abuse we leveled at it. There is a name for people who hear voices in their heads, and it isn't a pretty diagnosis. Yet here she was, warm and welcoming, the leader of a thriving circus, a performer of some renown, a manager with good sense and the ability to rally people—at least some people—to her cause. She'd even convinced a man with millions to join her and help support her vision.

I tried to put all this together and failed. The line between prophecy and psychosis? I had no idea. I was glad it wasn't my job to make that call.

5

"So first the band plays, and while they do, two guys in the front start a fight. They're pushing and shoving, and just when you think you'd better jump in and save somebody, one does a flip in midair, then a cartwheel, and pretty soon they've got a whole acrobatic act going, until they're both so exhausted they help each other out of the ring. This voice comes over the loudspeaker and says, 'Thou shalt love thy neighbor as thyself.' And that's the warm-up."

May Frankel, friend and member of Ed's congregation, shook her head. "An interesting way to teach the Bible."

"Right. You think, gosh, this is going to be some night. Then the band cranks up and the parade begins. Very old-timey circus, but traditional, no booming voices. Performing poodles, cantering horses, elephants dancing. But before that can bore you, the troupe begins the story of Moses leading his people from Egypt."

I paused for a breath. Besides, it wasn't possible to adequately explain my Saturday night adventure, not in so many words. If May wanted the full effect, she was going to have to go and see SNITS for herself.

"How did they do that?" May sounded sincerely interested, but then, she makes her living as a psychologist, and sounding interested pretty much comes with that territory.

"Well, for scenery they had teams stacked into human pyramids. I don't know how they just stood there for so long. Then they had people scurrying along tightropes, others swinging frantically from platform to platform on trapezes. They were trying to evade the Egyptians, who were approaching on elephants and camels. Then Sister Nora came riding in on her gorgeous white stallion, and all the Hebrews followed her. They did something amazing with lights and sheets of shimmering plastic that looked like waves, and when the sea parted, the good guys had gotten away and the bad guys had drowned."

"Ambitious. And creative. I don't remember a white stallion in the book of Exodus."

"Artistic license. They did the traditional stuff, too, sort of an abbreviated version of what you'd get at a regular circus. Then Nora did a speech about global warming. They dimmed all the lights, then brought up one huge spot, like the sun. And they'd created this tableau of a garden with performers dressed as trees and flowers, and as she spoke, they shriveled. Then the animals laid down, one by one, as if they were dying. An elephant, a horse, a bear, all the poodles. Even one of the big cats put his head in his trainer's lap—which was the scariest moment of the night. Finally Nora explains that she's here in our county because God told her to build a biosphere that will house as many species as she can find room for, and that this is how humanity and life as we know it will be saved from annihilation if things don't improve. It's the job of people in Emerald Springs to help make this happen."

"Uh oh." May has a cherubic face, which was now screwed into a grimace. "Let me guess. That part didn't go over well."

"Not so you'd notice. She cleared the place in record time."

Tara Norton, one of the Price Girls, appeared at the head of our stairs and posed for a moment like a runway model. She was dressed in leopard-print pants and a gold T-shirt with her dark hair teased and curled into a wild tangle around her head.

"Scary Price," I guessed, having boned up on my Spice Girls lore.

"I'm loud and boisterous, and I get into trouble."

Nothing could actually be further from the truth. Tara's a sweetheart. For a couple of years now, all the girls presently calling themselves the Price Girls have been part of a larger group named—unfortunately—the Green Meanies. I've never been fond of them banding together to promote envy among their peers, but the Meanies, despite their name, are for the most part nice kids who just like to spend time together. Some of them, like Carlene, otherwise known as Ginger Price, concentrate on being popular at school; some, like Tara and Maddie, May's daughter, are brainiacs.

Maddie joined us now, in a sweet little babydoll dress, which because of her mother's intervention, was longer than the girls wanted it to be. "Baby Price." She did a cute little curtsy.

Like May, Maddie is petite, blonde, and delicate. She looked appropriately cherubic with her hair in long pigtails. Deena came down right behind her in sweats, a spandex tank, and a headband, looking as if she were planning to run a marathon. I could tell from the expression on her face that she wanted to be anywhere else at the moment. Since "Sporty" has dark hair and I had refused to let her dye hers, she'd borrowed a dark wig from a friend which was fastened into a ponytail. I wondered if she was hoping nobody would recognize her. I hoped it didn't fall off mid-song.

Deena is at an age when confiding in me feels traitorous, but she had gone so far as to admit—as Lucy said—that she'd been railroaded into this performance. Now the big moment had almost arrived, and she and her friends were going up in front of Grady Barber and the other judges. I hadn't warned her that he might be less than charming. She'd found Internet accounts of other events like this one that he had judged. Humiliation seems to be the key to selling tickets.

Ed was next down the steps, followed closely by Teddy. Along with May the two of them were going to take the girls to the Emerald College auditorium, where they would wait their turn for this first round of the finals. I'd been there a good part of the day and had only just run home to shower and change before the evening began.

I definitely needed both. I'd spent a chunk of the afternoon crawling on the floor moving electric cords and wires right along with the stagehands every time Grady reconsidered where the judges' table should sit. Next to checking each plate of food destined for his stomach, next to helping Fred rearrange the upcoming schedule so Grady would have time for an hour of yoga each afternoon, next to finding a store in Columbus with medium-density down pillows that could be delivered to the hotel by evening, getting my jeans dirty and blisters on my hands and knees was nothing. A mere inconvenience. Besides, when they threw me in jail for murder, I would have plenty of time to clean up and heal.

"You girls are all set?" Ed asked. The other Price Girls, Carlene and Shannon, were going to meet them at the auditorium.

"Yeah, whatever," Deena said glumly.

"You have to be peppy. You have to have confidence," Maddie told my daughter.

"I need a lobotomy, then."

I wasn't sure where Deena had learned about lobotomies, but I rested my hand on her shoulder. "Just do your best, girls, and let the rest sort itself out."

Once they were all gone, I finished getting ready and left for the college myself. The campus is a nice asset for our small town, a center for culture as well as a place of higher learning. It's also a parklike oasis where townspeople can go for a stroll or sit by the creek that meanders between Rice Hall and Marlborough Center. Most of the buildings are antique brick or stone, with the requisite tendrils of ivy climbing toward slate roofs. Trees shade the expansive open areas, and beds of flowers break up long stretches of lawn.

Unfortunately a month ago the creek dried up, and the flower beds looked like a who's who of local weeds. I walked along the ditch where the creek had been toward

Marlborough Center and took the route to a side door. The Marlborough Auditorium has fifteen hundred seats, and most had been sold for the final Idyll round. Buses chartered in nearby counties were set to bring in patients from nursing homes and retirement villages. Church groups, civic associations, choirs, bands, and drama clubs had bought large blocks of tickets. At twenty dollars a head, we would make back Grady's fee in just one night.

I wasn't sure if we'd ever earn back his expenses.

Tonight for the opening round we were only about two-thirds full, and the ticket prices were cheaper. But even so, backstage there was an air of excitement once I was vetted and allowed in. As far as I knew, I had completed every assigned task that afternoon, and if all went well, I would need to fetch and carry only if the need arose. We had half an hour to curtain time, and I was hoping to find my Price Girl daughter for a quick hug before she and her friends faced the judges.

Instead I found the two female judges in a small dressing room, an overly bright, antiseptic place that needed Grady's bathroom bulb to warm it. Melanie Drew was a local woman who'd danced and sung in the choruses of two Broadway shows before she chucked Manhattan and came home to raise a family. Sandy Pierce had taught voice lessons in Minnesota and didn't yet have a job or students in town. Their credentials might seem thin, but nobody was coming to hear what they had to say anyway. This event was all about Grady.

Melanie and Sandy were quintessential Midwesterners, polite to a fault, anxious not to cause me any difficulty. When I asked if they needed anything, they assured me they were fine and wondered if they could do anything for *me*. Unfortunately there was nothing two accommodating middle-aged women or anybody else could do that would relieve me of the burden of one Grady Barber.

Of course Grady had taken one look at the male equivalent of the women judges' dressing room and insisted that we remake the most comfortable green room at the farthest end of the hall just for him, so that he would not be hounded by fans. With much grinding of teeth, I had. I headed in that direction now to make sure his wicker basket of organic fruit, mineral water, and trans fat–free whole wheat crackers had been delivered.

All hope of a quick check and a good night vanished while I was still fifteen yards away. I could hear an argument behind the closed door. Grady's voice was the loudest, and for a man who could sing so sweetly, he could also bellow like a hog caller.

"I'm fed up with your incompetence, Fred. I make allowances. I'm not that hard to please—"

"Are you kidding me? You're impossible. Nothing anybody does for you is good enough. And you're worse this week than I've ever seen you. What is it about being in Ohio that's got your head up your—"

"Who do you think you are? A miserable, overpaid, underworked loser—"

"Yeah? Well, I don't see you firing me. And I know why! Nobody else would work for you, and you can't make it without an assistant. I don't know why I stay. There are half a dozen people back in L.A. who want to hire me and—"

"Really? Then why don't you quit? Just walk out of here. You threaten to enough! I'll tell you why. Because you know the moment you do, I'll put the word out about what a loser you really are." He followed this with a tirade of profanity that was both creative and withering.

Fred's voice sounded closer now, as if he was moving toward the door. "Yeah? Well, let me tell you, you're walking the razor's edge, Grady. And if you slip, I won't be responsible for the consequences. You know what? If worse came to worst, there wouldn't be anybody out there that cared enough about you to bother picking up the pieces, anyway. You're a sadist, and you get your kicks out of making everybody around you miserable. You'd better watch out, or it's going to come right back at you! And I'll be standing here laughing my head off!"

I was rooted to the spot, of course. My so-called job description didn't include getting into any line of fire, but I was delighted to hear Fred fighting back. Until this moment I wasn't sure he had it in him.

The green room door flew open, and Fred came roaring out. Color flushed his cheeks, and he nearly ran me over before he even realized I was there.

"You heard that?" he demanded, as he stalked past me.

"Just the tail end." I spun around and raced to keep up with him. "Fred, hang on there. What's going on?"

"He's behaving like an ass—" He cleared his throat and glanced at me. "You get it."

"Where are you going? Please, don't tell me you're leaving me to deal with him by myself."

Fred slowed down a little. "It might be better."

"For who?!"

He stopped. His sigh was nearly as loud as their argument. "Nothing can please him. I could do every job a dozen different ways, and he'd want it done the one way I didn't bother with. He's lost his freaking mind. Is there something in the air here?"

"Maybe we need to pipe in a little smog."

"I was in pretty good shape when I took this job. Now my heart races, my gums bleed, my toenails are turning yellow—"

I was desperate to avoid the listing of hemorrhoids, impotence, or worse. "Take a deep breath, okay? Our air's good for you, and free."

"I thought dealing with his ex-wives was bad enough. But at least he left me alone to handle them. Since we got here, he's on top of me about everything. I'm two words away from quitting."

"Please, please don't say them until you're on your way out of town. I'll do everything I can to help you get through the coming week. Please, Fred." I grabbed his arm and pulled it, as if I were ringing a bell. "Please!"

"Yeah. Well." He took a deep breath, the way I'd suggested. "I gave up smoking about ten years ago. I'm going to find a cigarette."

He turned and stomped off. I knew better than to continue pleading. Fred hardly knew me, and his loyalty was already strained. I didn't want to push him over the edge.

I debated what to do next. I decided whether the basket had made it to the green room was a small problem. Staying away from Grady was a more worthy one, and I needed to focus all my attention on it.

Half an hour later Veronica, who had probably been here since dawn, found me trying to bribe one of the college student stagehands to fetch Grady from his green room. Grady was supposed to be in the wings waiting to be introduced before he took his seat at the judges' table, stage right, and Fred was nowhere in sight. So far the stagehand had refused my offers of a home-cooked meal, movie tickets with a popcorn coupon, or a road trip in my minivan.

"Where's Grady?" Veronica demanded.

"In the green room." I'm sure my eyes lit up. "Will you go and get him?"

"Why haven't you?"

She was dressed in a silver top and flowing pants, and she looked terrific. I, of course, looked like the gofer I was. In a burst of brilliance I made an issue of it.

"I think Grady responds better to power and prestige. Tonight I can only offer exhaustion and the desire to crawl into my bed and pull the covers over my head."

Her eyes softened. "You're doing a great job, Aggie. Everybody's talking about the miracles you've worked so far. Don't give up on me. We're almost there. Think about the children."

"Will you get him and make sure he's in place? Please?"

She lifted my hand and patted it. "You go on out and

take a seat. The second row's reserved for our volunteers. I'll take it from here."

I told myself the rush of love I felt was just Stockholm syndrome. My tormentor, my friend. But I smiled anyway and bolted for the steps down into the auditorium.

I make a point of avoiding reality shows. I figure, life's real enough, why do I need an ersatz version to entertain me? The Bachelor has been forced to choose his potential wife without my help. The Biggest Loser could pass me in the street and I wouldn't know to offer him a celery stick and a jog around the Oval. Survivors could swing from vines in my backyard, light bonfires, and vote one another out of Emerald Springs, and I would be none the wiser. But I will confess that once, just once, I watched *American Idol* on television. I was sick, and the remote was at the other end of the couch.

So while not an expert, I did have some idea how our night would go. The finalists would perform, receive helpful comments from the judges guaranteed to send them into therapy for a year. The judges would argue among themselves, and finally a young man or woman who could belt out a love song with loads of energy and even more volume would win. I would sink lower into my chair with every act, until eventually, I was so low I could drop to the floor and crawl out of the auditorium without anybody noticing.

I looked for Ed and Teddy, but I couldn't spot them. Since the lights were blinking for the last time, I settled for a seat on the volunteer row next to Camille Beauregard.

"Are you still okay with your daughter trying out?" she whispered.

"I try not to think about it."

"Have you warned her about Grady?"

"She was an inch from quitting. I didn't want to close the gap. The other girls would never speak to her again."

"I have Yorkies. They're easier."

"They might be more entertaining onstage, too."

"Don't take this the wrong way, but the girls won't make it past this round. So if you can get through tonight, you'll be okay."

I felt oddly comforted. Deena wasn't expecting to win. Maybe she and her friends would be so proud they made it to the finals, their self-esteem would get a boost powerful enough to take them all the way through high school. If not, at least everything would all be over with by the time we left for home.

The house lights dimmed once and for all; the spotlight came on, and the curtain opened. Veronica walked over to bask in it, and the applause began. I applauded, too. Nobody had worked harder than she had.

I was so tired I was able to zone out as she launched into a spiel about the Idyll, about the fun it had been—ha!—and the way it had turned a terribly hot summer into a memorable one. She moved right into the need for a new pediatric unit with a special ICU, the huge contribution Grady Barber had made by clearing his schedule and appearing as our celebrity judge. It was so much nicely done yada yada, and I had to fight to keep my eyes open.

Melanie and Sandy were introduced to polite applause, and they took their seats at the table. Lisa Lee, looking simultaneously arty and disheveled, just as she had at the party, came out and took her seat at the piano with a flourish. There was a drummer and a string bass with her for tonight's performances. Later there would be a larger ensemble.

Finally Grady was introduced, and the audience went wild. He favored the assembly with "Sailing toward a Rainbow," and got the same acclaim he'd received at the welcome party. Then he took his seat. A drumroll sounded, and the Idyll was officially on its way.

The first act was a brother and sister who sang "Seasons of Love" from *Rent*. The song was entertaining and upbeat, although neither of them had great voices. Still, they had every movement choreographed to perfection.

Camille leaned over to speak into my ear. "They've been

in pageants since they were babes in their mother's arms. She was Little Miss Midwestern Shopping Mall, and he was First Gallant Knight of Fire Prevention. Can you imagine what goes on in that house while other kids are doing homework?"

The song ended with remarkable energy. I was ready to pass them on to the next level, and so were Melanie and Sandy, who were warm and comforting and congratulatory. Not so Grady.

"I've been to Broadway. I've been *on* Broadway. I can tell you, kids, that what you just did? That's not Broadway."

The audience tittered. He stood and joined the two onstage. Both were thin and dark haired. She was younger, he was maybe eighteen at the oldest. They carried themselves with confidence, almost too much, as if that was their major asset, and they needed to make the most of it. Neither backed down as Grady approached, which gave them a boost on my virtual scorecard.

Grady got between them, signaled to Lisa Lee, and told her where to start playing. Then, as simply as that, he began the same lyrics, punching different words, pausing just enough and in the right places to give the words a whole new meaning. Then he asked the young man to try it. Courageously, he did. The girl followed suit when she was asked, and I could see the improvement. I imagined these two had been working with coaches all their lives and knew the drill.

Sadly, Grady didn't agree. He worked with them a little longer, shook his head a time or two, looked progressively more discouraged, and at last his attitude began to rub off. Their confidence visibly dwindled. They exchanged glances that said they weren't used to this kind of criticism.

Finally Grady patted them both on the shoulders before he took his seat, then he and the judges conferred. I squirmed as the siblings stood there looking more and more like whipped puppies and Grady dissected everything they had done into the microphone, from the way they moved to the clothes they wore. Melanie and Sandy were nodding faster and faster . . .

"Oh, neither of the women are going to stand up to him," Camille whispered. "Are you surprised?"

I'd just heard somebody stand up to Grady, and it hadn't been pretty. I wondered if Fred was still in the building somewhere. I really couldn't blame Sandy and Melanie for cowardice. They looked just the tiniest bit starstruck to me.

"I'm sorry, but we're going to pass on you," Sandy said after they had conferred again in lower voices. "Be proud you made it to the stage tonight, and good luck with everything you do in the future."

The audience applauded, there was a buzz through the assembled crowd, and I suspected some people, at least, were more excited now that the part where contestants got kicked in the butt had begun.

"I hate this," I said, as the boy looked bewildered, and the girl looked like she was going to cry.

"Toughen up," Camille said. "I'm no pro, but I bet that was Grady at his kindest."

"St. Grady of the Brothers of Malevolence."

The next act was good bordering on excellent. A young man in his early twenties came out with remarkable poise and something even I could recognize as stage presence. He sang "What Goes Around . . . / . . . Comes Around," which I recognized as a Justin Timberlake hit. I do have a young teenager in my house.

I liked the way he moved, and the voice was good, although the song didn't show it off very well. I was surprised when Grady agreed with me, and stood to demonstrate some vocal technique that the young man copied effortlessly. This time when Grady patted him on the shoulder, it didn't look like a rejection, and it wasn't. After tearing apart everything he'd done but not with much vehemence, the young man, Bart Jackson, was told to come back tomorrow night with another song.

"I guess he has to pass some of the contestants, or the

Idyll would end pretty fast," I told Camille. "This way the pain just keeps coming."

"You'll be surprised, but there really are some good acts to look forward to."

Those good acts weren't among the next three. Tap dancers from our local studio were summarily shown the door. The first time a baton was dropped, twin twirlers in red spangles and white boots were hustled offstage. Afterwards Grady made it clear to everybody in the audience that he wasn't there to judge anything that corny.

"What's next, hula hoop marathons?" he screeched. He seemed to be getting more and more worked up, more and more disdainful, and unfortunately, the audience seemed to like it.

My hands were sweating. I wondered if the Price Girls were still backstage, or if by now, they had run for cover.

After a man in his forties who fancied himself the next Clint Black was rudely dismissed, Madison Sargent came onstage.

"This is too much to ask of me." I squeezed my eyes closed. "This is one too many teenage girls to pull back from the brink of suicide tonight."

"Listen and enjoy. Just between us, it won't get better than this."

Resigned, I opened my eyes to note that Madison, always a pretty girl, was transformed into someone more spectacular under stage lighting. She wore a filmy red dress that bared way too much chest for a girl her age, but with a teenaged daughter myself, I've suddenly become very opinionated on that subject. Her gold sandals had heels that made Lucy's look demure. Her hair, normally straight, fell in magnificent highlighted ripples down her back.

"Wow," I whispered.

"She does look good."

Grady seemed to think so, too. Before she even began to sing, he told the audience that looking good onstage was half the job of entertaining, and Madison had nailed that

part already. Madison smiled a smile I hope Deena doesn't
learn until she's happily married.

I understood right away why Madison's not in our
church choir. Her voice is bluesy, throaty, a mature voice
suited to R & B, not anthems, and she knew it. She said she
had chosen Mariah Carey's "We Belong Together" for her
performance, and although she got something of a shaky
start, she took off about a quarter of the way through and
seemed to forget anything but the music. I sat there, hands
gripping the arms of my chair, and gawked as she played
with the notes, leaping octaves like they were inconsequen-
tial hurdles.

When she finished, the audience was silent. Then the
applause began and built. It built more when Grady got to
his feet, joined by his fellow judges, and applauded her.

"Well, well done," he said. "You're quite a talented girl."

Once the applause died down Madison, flushed and tri-
umphant, thanked him.

"It'll be fun to work with you," Grady said, remembering
to look at his fellow judges for confirmation that they were
as pleased as he was. "Come back tomorrow night with
something else for us, Madison."

Beaming, she left the stage. The glow I felt wore off
quickly when the Price Girls were ushered in. I tried to tell
myself the timing was good, that Grady would be so happy
to learn he had caught at least one substantial talent in the
Emerald Springs net, that he would be kind to the girls
when he threw them back. They were only thirteen. They
were cute as the dickens up there in their silly costumes.
He would let them down easily.

I risked zeroing in on my daughter's face. Clearly Deena
wanted to be anywhere else, but I had to give her credit for
standing there anyway and going through with this.

Grady smiled in a fatherly fashion. "So we have the
Price Girls tonight? And what are you going to perform for
us, girls?"

" 'Wannabe'," Carlene said, stepping forward. Her dress

was not quite as short as I'd feared, and tonight no thong was in evidence. She gave Grady a practiced, measured smile before she joined the other girls. Watch out boys of Emerald Springs, Carlene O'Grady was simmering nicely and just about to be served up at the banquet. I winced.

Lisa began the piano intro, the drums beat, and the girls began to bounce. And bounce. Then their arms began to swing, for the most part together, and they began to sing. Or at least I think that's what it was. The sound was part rap and part melody, and one sounded as unsteady as the other. They took turns with lines, just the way the Spice Girls did on the "Wannabe" video, which they had watched ten thousand times. Some were better than others. Deena, at least, could be heard, but I wasn't sure that was a good thing. Finally the beginning was over. I believe it lasted approximately six hours. Now they stood in two lines with Maddie in the middle between them and began to dance and sing the chorus.

The chorus was surprisingly good. Together, with one another's voices to rely on, they gained courage and began to project. Then, all too soon, they went bouncing their separate ways around the stage again. Deena, who hadn't done gymnastics since she was nine, did a credible flip over Tara, who had dropped to all fours. Amazingly they kept singing, and her wig didn't fall off. Finally they finished and ran behind the curtain.

"Is my heart still beating?" I thrust my wrist toward Camille.

"They are adorable. He'll be kind."

He wasn't, of course. He called the girls back out, and they returned to a healthy round of applause.

"Well, girls," he said. "You have considerable energy, and you know how cute you are, don't you?"

I knew from his tone that this was not a compliment. Judging from their faces, some of the girls had figured that out, too, but Carlene stuck her hand on one hip like a Paris streetwalker luring a john—or would that be a jacques?

"We just can't help it, we're cute without trying," she simpered.

The audience laughed. They, at least, were enjoying themselves.

"Well, being cute's just not going to cut it in the Idyll," Grady said with a cold smile. "I don't know who told you that you ought to go for the gusto here, but they ought to be shot. Cute as you are, this is not a junior high talent show. So scat. Go back to school, learn to sing and dance, add a few pounds in the right places. Then come back in a couple of years." He paused for effect. "Just please, don't come back if I'm the judge, okay? Never step on the same stage with me again."

The audience was laughing. Grady sounded as if he was teasing, a fatherly sort of teasing, but I was close enough to see the impatience in his expression and hear the edge in his voice. The girls were, too. Even Carlene lost her bravado and stepped closer to the others.

"Go. Scat. Good girls. Leave. Be gone. Out of here." He made shooing motions with his hands, and the girls turned tail and left the way they'd come. Quickly.

"Ouch," Camille said.

"Double ouch." I considered leaving to go backstage and be with Deena, but I was fairly sure May was already there, and maybe Carlene's mother, Crystal, as well. Nothing would be worse than to make too much out of this. Tonight I would remind Deena that she and the others had enjoyed some good times rehearsing the act, and that their friends probably thought they were cool to have made it this far.

I did think, though, that wearing a dark wig onstage had been an inspiration.

And now that I'd figured out what I would say to my daughter, I wondered what I would say to Grady Barber the next time we were face-to-face.

That moment came sooner than I'd expected. I left my seat at intermission. Backstage I found that the girls had already gone. May and Crystal had taken them out for pizza to celebrate their grit and determination, pizza being the adolescent equivalent of Spider-Man Band-Aids.

I hoped I could catch up with them since I'd also missed Ed and Teddy, who had gone home after the Price Girls were sent offstage in disgrace. If Grady needed anything for the second half of the night, he could get it himself. When nobody was watching, I left by the side door. I nearly tripped over Grady and Madison, who were talking in the shadows.

Grady moved away from her the moment I appeared. But the fact that he had to back away seemed more suspicious than the tête-à-tête itself.

"We'll work out a time," he said when I drew closer. He smiled at Madison, and sent me a cooler version. To my credit, I didn't stick out a foot to trip him as he walked past me and back inside.

"You were spectacular," I told her. "I had no idea you sang like that."

"Thanks, Mrs. Wilcox." She looked flushed, and just the tiniest bit unhinged.

"Are you heading home?"

"I need to get some sleep and figure out what to do tomorrow. Maybe not in that order."

"I'll walk you to your car. Unless you're waiting for your mom?"

"We drove separately. She's going to stay and watch my competition."

I couldn't help myself. Curiosity is as much a part of me as cellulite and hangnails. I wanted to know what they'd been talking about, and darn it, I wanted to know why Grady had been standing too close to her.

"I bet Grady was complimenting you on your performance," I said, having learned never to ask an adolescent a direct question.

"He says I have a lot of talent."

"He's right about that. I'll bet you want to pursue a showbiz career."

"My mom thinks I have what it takes." She paused. "I always thought I'd be a teacher. I'm good with kids."

"You help out in the nursery at church, don't you? I've heard you're terrific with the babies."

"I like to sing, though. Grady—Mr. Barber—says I have some things I need to learn."

"He would know," I said, keeping my voice light.

"He's going to coach me a little. Give me a few tips, if I want them."

I wondered if any of the other contestants were being granted this special favor. Madison seemed to realize how this had sounded.

"He says he always does this for the top candidates, but only if we want him to. I guess he'll be helping some of the others."

This had been related to me in confidence. I wondered if I had a right to bring up the issue of favoritism with Veronica. But wouldn't Veronica defend Grady no matter what I said? Maybe this was part of their agreement. Still, I felt uneasy.

"That would certainly give you an edge," I said, again making certain I didn't weight my words.

"Oh, he says it won't guarantee I'll win, or even get into the finals. He says coaching is just something extra he does, because people reached out to him along the way and helped him realize his dreams. He feels he owes the same to others."

St. Grady, again. I believed this explanation as much as I believed that at the end of the Idyll, Grady would donate his fee to the new pediatric unit. I wondered if he took his cut down the line when the contestants with the most potential actually made it to Hollywood, Nashville, or the local recording studio. Then he could point out that they'd gotten there because of him, and ask for favors.

Or maybe the favors began a lot earlier in the process.

I didn't know how to warn Madison that Grady might not be as benevolent as he sounded. We'd reached the parking lot, and I waited until she opened the door of a vintage Mustang.

"I know you'll always enjoy using that voice of yours," I told her. "But teaching's great, too. The important thing is to do what your heart tells you. Show business can be pretty cutthroat. I know you have good sense and you'll be careful."

"It's all so exciting." She smiled, then she reached out and gave me a spontaneous hug. I waited until she drove away. And for once, I was glad my curiosity had gotten the better of me. I had a new reason for keeping an eye on Grady Barber. And I was exactly in the right position to do it, too.

6

I survived the first week of the Emerald Spring Idyll, largely because Fred calmed down and remained as Grady's assistant. By Sunday I was ready to sit quietly in church, only parting my lips to sing hymns and greet my neighbors. The Idyll was down to ten contestants, and the audience had grown for every round. Madison was still in, of course, as was Bart Jackson. The rest were an assortment, from a middle-aged folk singer to a group called Catahoula Hounds who sang Cajun music with a rollicking accordion. We all knew that at the end, this would be a showdown between Madison and Bart, but in the meantime we'd had a variety of entertainment styles. This didn't make up for the process, not in my opinion, but it did make things more interesting for those captives who, like me, had to attend most of the performances.

Deena had recovered nicely, so relieved her days as Sporty Price had come to an end that she smiled more than she had for weeks.

I settled into the service, enjoying our pleasantly cool sanctuary, Esther's organ prelude, the opening readings and prayer. Halfway through Ed's sermon, however, I was pretty sure Deena's good mood was going to change quickly—in fact the moment Deena got wind of the story her father had chosen to introduce his topic.

I waited until the crowd had passed through the door stopping to chat and shake Ed's hand before I pounced on him. "I can't believe you used Deena in your sermon!"

Ed looked bemused. If I'd critiqued his sources, or his

use of one theologian versus another, he would have understood right away. But I could see he couldn't connect my tone to anything I'd said.

"She's going to be mortified." I lowered my voice. "Then she's going to be furious."

"No." He shook his head. I knew this expression well. He wasn't defensive, just convinced he was right. This, of course, is the problem with being married to somebody who stands in the pulpit every Sunday.

"Yes . . ." I hissed. "You drew attention to her failure at the Idyll, Ed. She was just getting over it."

"I used it as an example of courage, Aggie."

And indeed he had. Ed had talked about people who struggle against all odds. Famous people who suffer from attention deficit disorder or learning disabilities and go on to extraordinary careers. Cesar Chavez, who began life as the child of immigrant laborers, then founded the United Farm Workers. Christy Brown, the poet and novelist, who suffered from such severe cerebral palsy that no one except his mother believed him capable of learning. There had been others in this litany of failures and triumphs. Unfortunately Deena and her friends had been the comic relief.

"The sermon was about the indomitable human spirit," he said. "Every parent here could identify."

I poked a finger against his chest. "I'm not covering for you, buddy. You're on your own on this one."

"You're blowing this way out of proportion. She'll be glad I said good things about her."

I left him to go back to the pulpit for his sermon and reading glasses. I didn't really want to be in his vicinity when Deena caught up with him.

Since the church is visible from our backyard, the girls usually find their own way home. I debated spending the next week camping in the woods outside of town, since it would solve the dual problems of dealing with Deena and Grady. In the end I went to social hour in the parish hall to delay the inevitable confrontation. I knew there would be a confrontation, and I wondered how my insightful, compassionate husband could be so clueless about teenage girls.

Another mother of that species found me after I had gracefully extricated myself from a conversation about painting the sanctuary lemon yellow. I make a habit of not giving opinions on matters like that one. There's always the possibility Ed might get a raise someday, and the head of the committee, maybe a royal blue man, would hold this against us. Call me calculating, but in the not-so-distant future we'll need to think about college tuition.

"Aggie . . ."

I beckoned Tammy Sargent to my side, afraid if I met her halfway, the lemon yellow brigade would tackle me again, this time with color chips.

"How's Madison holding up?" I asked. "I wasn't able to talk to her the last few nights. She was always busy." I regretted this since my radar was still quivering. I knew I was probing where I didn't belong, but I had to add the next sentence. "She did say Grady might be coaching her a little."

"She's doing so great!" Tammy looked radiant, as if she was absorbing even more of her daughter's enthusiasm and youth. "Grady has been working with her, and the difference is incredible. Her voice, her presentation. I'm sure something wonderful is going to come out of this."

One of the newly announced prizes for the ESI winner was an audition with Fourteen Carat Records, a small but prestigious label with an eclectic list of artists. This alone would have eliminated the baton twirlers, of course, and the four-legged acts. I'm not sure how Veronica secured the new addition, but it upped the ante and sold that many more tickets for our final week.

"I'm sure all the contestants appreciate this extra effort of his," I said, hoping for more information.

She lowered her voice. "I'm not sure he's working with *everybody*. He concentrates where he thinks it will be most effective."

Now my instincts were vibrating hard enough to launch

me into the stratosphere. I had to try harder to keep an eye on those tryouts.

Tammy went on. "Anyway, Madison feels badly that so many kids from the high school tried out and didn't make it as far as she did. So we're throwing a party on Wednesday night for everybody who made the effort. She wants Deena and her friends to come, too. We'll throw some burgers and steaks on the grill, put *Wayfarers of the Ark* on television, have music. You know, maybe something a little classier than the usual, because Grady might drop by. But Madison wants to make sure nobody holds success against her."

There was something sweet about this. Madison in her moment of triumph was worried about her friends and their feelings. Okay, so she was also worried about what this would do to her social life. But that was beside the point. The gesture was thoughtful. And asking Deena and the other Price Girls to come, despite their ages, was kind.

It was also, most likely, unacceptable.

"This is such a nice idea, but I'll have to talk to Ed," I told her. "They're so much younger than the others."

"Deena's just three years younger than Madison."

"At that age three years is everything."

"Madison's always been so mature, I guess I didn't worry very much."

Madison *was* mature. Unfortunately more so than her mom sometimes. I knew Tammy didn't always think about possibilities and consequences, and it was a good thing Madison was innately sensible.

"I'll make sure Deena lets you know," I said, "but including her is very thoughtful, even if she doesn't go."

I dodged the sanctuary painters, the Women's Society committee determined to sign me up for the bake sale, Teddy's Sunday School teacher, who routinely wants to know if Teddy *always* asks so many questions. This left me no alternative except a scorching trip through the parking lot to the parsonage.

I was the first one there, which meant I might have a few

moments to prepare for Deena's arrival. Unfortunately that was not to be. The telephone was ringing when I walked inside. The manager of the Emerald Springs Hotel—who had become curiously unavailable to me as the days of Grady's residence dragged on—was on the other end. Ed, it turned out, really would have to deal with Deena by himself. I was off and running. At least the hotel was air-conditioned.

+ + +

The Emerald Springs Hotel and Spa is the finest establishment in three counties. Although it was built just after the Victorian era, the hotel manager has the face of a Dickens' undertaker, long and narrow, unsurpassingly dour. The black suit doesn't help, either, but I wasn't there to critique his wardrobe.

He greeted me in the lobby, as if he had been waiting to pounce. "They'd been shouting at each other for fifteen minutes before I called you, and nobody will answer the door. Our security guard's on a lunch break."

We headed immediately for Grady's suite, through green halls that always smell faintly of age, even in better weather than this. Now there was nothing nostalgic about the scent, and the citrus air freshener wafting through the cooling vents only made it worse.

"And you didn't use your key?" I asked.

"Would you?" he said tersely. "If we'd heard screams, it might have been different. As it is, I called you before I called the police. We've done you a favor."

If so, why didn't I feel overjoyed? Here's the truth. The manager didn't want to call the police because Grady Barber was the most important celebrity to stay here in years. The manager didn't want the publicity, and who could blame him? Grady being led away in handcuffs with the hotel in the background? Uh uh.

"I'll knock. Heck, I'll bang with both fists. But if somebody doesn't open the door, you have to go in. Better than the cops, right?"

He winced, a movement so at home on his gloomy face that it was hardly perceptible.

I could hear the shouting as we approached, although maybe it had begun to taper off, because it wasn't as loud as I'd expected.

"Calming down a little," he acknowledged.

We reached the door, which was at the end of the hallway, and I knocked. "Fred, Grady, it's Aggie. We need to speak to you."

The voices were still raised, but since they were shouting at the same time, I could hear only the occasional word. This was not a bad thing since what I did hear wasn't fit for anybody's ears.

I banged on the door with both fists. "Okay, you two. Cut it out and open up or the manager will have to use his key! Fred! Grady!"

There was a dip in the sound waves. I was pretty sure they'd heard me. I banged again. "Open up right now. You don't want the authorities called, do you?"

Silence reigned for seconds. Then, blessedly, the door opened a smidgen and two eyes peered out at me. It closed again; I heard the chain being lifted, and this time the door opened all the way.

I heard a door slam on the other side of the suite. Fred stood in the doorway, his hair disheveled, what looked like a bruise on one cheek.

"They could hear you in Timbuktu," I told him. "Are you hurt?"

He put his hand to his cheek, fingertips smack-dab on the bruise, but he shook his head. "I'm okay."

"Do you want me to call the cops?"

"No!" He swallowed, but his eyes still sparkled with rage. "Absolutely not. It doesn't matter anyway, because I'm out of here for good."

"Is Grady in his bedroom?"

He nodded. "Don't bother him. You don't know what that man is capable of. I'm just going to get my stuff and check out." He glanced at the manager. "There won't be any more disturbances. I'm sorry."

The manager *humph*ed, then he turned and strode down the hall the way we had come, leaving me to finish dealing with the mess.

"What happened?" I demanded. "If he hadn't gotten me on the phone, he would have called the police."

"*Grady* happened, that's what. I should have quit a week ago when I wanted to."

"Hey, don't blame that on me. You're paid to deal with him."

"Not anymore. I'm out of here."

This time I knew better than to protest. As angry as Fred was, he really shouldn't stay. I wondered if Grady was sporting bruises, too.

As if to prove the magnitude of his feelings, Fred slammed his palm against the doorframe. "He's made a lot of enemies along the way, and part of my job was running interference. Do you know what that's like? Trying to deal with his bad will, his ill temper, his lack of morals?"

"I have some idea. I've been doing it, remember?"

"Grady goes around the country judging events like this one, and everywhere he goes he treats contestants badly, raising their hopes, then smashing them, just for kicks and laughs. He's made enemies all over the country."

"Nobody told us any of this." Or if they had, I hadn't been privy to the information. Maybe Veronica had kept this a secret.

"Well, I know for a fact he's been involved with a couple of contestants who were too young to know better. Don't even get me started about the way Grady uses women to advance his career."

"Lawsuits?"

"If so, he's settled out of court. I haven't seen any paperwork."

I wondered if Fred was making this up or exaggerating

because he was so furious. Unfortunately it had the ring of truth.

"I'm just sick of it all," he said. "Between the enemies, the ex-wives, and worst of all *him*, the stress is just too much. Maybe he will blackball me with potential employers. But you know, enough people have seen him in action, they might write letters of recommendation explaining the problem. Besides, he's not nearly as important as he makes out."

That surprised me. "He looks that way to us."

"Between those two big hit songs of his? His career mostly consisted of B movies and quiz shows, and look what he's doing now, judging talent shows! If he doesn't manage another hit right away, he's going to be opening second-rate acts in third-rate hotels in Vegas."

I liked the sound of that. I have no desire to go to Vegas.

That positive thought was followed by the most negative one of a bad day. "Can he finish up here without you? Can he get along without an assistant?"

"Maybe it'll be good for him. Maybe then he'll appreciate what the next assistant does and leave him alone."

I had a feeling that this lesson in deportment and humility might come at a high price to the Emerald Springs Idyll. Grady had been unpleasant enough with Fred running interference. What would he be like in his final days with us?

"Do you have stuff that you need to take with you?" I asked. "I'll wait and make sure you get out alive."

Fred left and returned in less than a minute. I thought he already looked better, as if now that the decision had been made, even though he was still angry, a burden had been lifted.

He closed the door behind him, and we walked down the hallway together. We parted in front of his room. I wished him luck and he wished me the same. Of the two of us, I might need it the most. My next stop had to be Veronica's house, and I was not going to enjoy breaking this news to her.

Although the drive was short, getting in my minivan, which had been parked in the sunshine, was agonizing, and the air-conditioner did little to cool it. By the time I arrived, I had wilted into a pathetic pool of humanity. And by the time Veronica answered her own door, I was barely conscious.

"Aggie?" She looked surprised. "Did I know you were coming?"

"No, and neither did I. But we have a problem."

"Farley and I were just sitting down to lunch."

Was it still lunchtime? I could hardly remember. "I'm sorry. I hope this won't take long."

"I'll tell him to go ahead and eat. He has a two o'clock tee time. Why don't you wait in the sitting room." She gestured me into a small room off the foyer decorated with fabrics from Provence and photos of sunflowers and fields of lavender. Sitting there was cool and calming, which was a good thing since I heard the phone ring, and it took Veronica a long time to come back. By the time she did, I felt almost alive again.

Without introduction I launched into the story. "Fred's just quit his job after a huge fight. Luckily I was home to get the call or management would have called the police. Fred's gathering his things and heading out of town. There's no way he'll stay and that's probably wise. We don't want a murder."

Veronica lowered herself to the sofa beside me. "I know. That was Grady on the phone. You're sure Fred won't stay? We can't bribe him?"

I shook my head. Vehemently. "Grady treats him badly."

"Grady was always such a sweet, patient boy."

"Grady is no longer a boy." I thought about telling her what Fred had said. But what was the point? Veronica looked at Grady Barber and saw the high school student she had known and admired. I didn't think I could change that.

"Did you talk to Grady, too?" she asked.

"No. He shut himself in the bedroom, and my first priority was to get Fred out of there alive."

"He's very upset. He says Fred screwed up one too many times, and he fired him. Fred was abusive, and he admits he snapped."

"Maybe it doesn't matter what happened between them. We just have to get through the next week."

Veronica was biting her lip, something I'd never seen her do. "Aggie, Grady says he can't go on without an assistant. There are just too many details he can't handle alone. There's no time for him to hire a real replacement. Not with his schedule here. He wants us to assign him a volunteer."

"Good luck finding one."

Veronica was silent, but her eyes never left my face.

I held up my hands, as if warding off an attacker. "Oh, no, don't even think about it."

"Look, who else could do it? From the moment they arrived you're the one who's been helping Fred. You have the lists. You know all the arrangements. You understand the situation better than anybody else. You're good at working with people. You handle everything with tact, and you know how to keep from antagonizing him—"

"I'm not sure there's any way not to."

"Don't you see? You're the only person who can do this."

"It took two of us, Veronica. Fred *and* me. Two to keep him calm and somewhat in line. And even that was tough. Now you want me to handle everything by myself?"

She leaned forward earnestly. "No! I'll get somebody to help. I promise. Camille will do it. She likes you."

I wondered if this meant Camille was the only committee member besides Sally who did. "Camille's great, but she's already busy."

"Not that busy. She did the first round of tryouts, remember? They're over now. I know she'll help. She thinks you're great." Now she realized how that sounded. "Of course we *all* think you're great, but Camille will go that extra mile to help. The two of you can do it together. You can do whatever Fred was doing, and Camille can be your go-between with everybody else."

"Don't you dare say, 'Think of the children.'"

She sat back. "I can see I don't have to. So I'll say this instead. He's really upset. Maybe upset enough to walk out on us if we don't fill Fred's shoes with somebody else. Please, Aggie. Tell me you'll do this. There's just one more week to go, and we're making so much money for the hospital. Please!"

On the way home I asked myself why I'd caved in and said yes. It wasn't as if these women were going to be my enduring friends. We would nod when we saw one another on the street, maybe stop to reminisce a moment or two. But our paths would seldom cross. I didn't have to impress anybody, and in truth that's not what this was about. Despite all the hassles, I was feeling good about what I'd done for the hospital, if not with the process, and I didn't want one Grady Barber to ruin that. Veronica was right. We had one week. I could survive one week. We all could.

I pulled into the driveway with trepidation. There had been enough time since I'd left for the thunderclouds to gather and the storm to begin. The tiniest possibility existed that Deena hadn't heard any reports about Ed's sermon. An even tinier possibility was that, as Ed believed, she had been proud to have her failures trotted out in front of the congregation as a humorous example of courage and fortitude.

Right . . .

I gathered my purse and my own courage and went inside to see.

"Do you know what Daddy did?"

Deena was standing by the door and didn't even wait for me to close it. She jumped out at me the way a mugger might, but I'd been expecting it and didn't use any of her grandfather's blocks or kicks.

I was hoping with all my might that this was about peanut butter sandwiches for lunch when Deena had asked for grilled cheese. "Why don't you tell me?"

"He talked about me in his sermon! He told everybody about the Price Girls and how we got thrown off the Idyll."

"He absolutely did not put it that way."

"Are you defending him?"

I believe in united fronts. Parents standing together arm in arm to combat the ravages of colic, teething, and adolescence. I also believe in honesty. I did my best to straddle that considerable distance.

"I think your dad is really proud of you for trying out, and proud of the way you handled not making it to the next level. We both are. I know he didn't realize mentioning that in his sermon would upset you. He would never do anything to hurt you, Deena. But sometimes it's hard to put yourself in somebody else's shoes."

Her eyes were narrowed; her hands were on her hips. "Why didn't you stop him! You knew I'd be mad, didn't you? You figured that out, and you've been practicing what you were going to say to me!"

"Only a little. And I mean every word of it."

"Why didn't you stop him?"

"I don't read his sermons, and he didn't tell me. I would have suggested he ask you how you felt first. But you'd better believe he'll always ask you in the future. I know he understands that now."

"I have never been so humiliated. Not in my whole life! Do you know how many people came up to me afterwards and patted me on the back and told me it was okay that we didn't win?" Tears glistened in her eyes.

"Sweetheart, I'm so sorry you're upset. Really, I am. And I know you're feeling—"

"You don't know! Did your father ever stand up in front of hundreds of people and tell them all about your most embarrassing moment?"

Actually, once when I was fourteen and visiting Ray for the summer, he'd climbed up to the top of the water tower for a small town in Minnesota and spray painted "Cheat the IRS" in bold red letters. I'd been so embarrassed that when the local police hauled him off to jail, I'd called Junie and insisted she send me a bus ticket back to wherever she was living at the moment. She'd done one better and gotten me a seat on the next plane out and a cab for the two-hour ride to the airport.

But no, that was not quite the same thing.

"There weren't hundreds of people sitting there," I said. "It's not Christmas or Easter, and half the church is on vacation. Nobody's going to remember this by next week."

"I will. I'll remember it until the day I die!"

She thundered into the hallway and up the stairs.

When her bedroom door slammed, Ed came in from his study. Sunday afternoons are never his best time. I'm usually here to pump food and liquids back into him and protect him from all domestic dramas until he's breathing normally again. Clearly today my absence had been missed. He looked ten pounds lighter and fading fast.

"I guess you heard," he said.

"Uh huh."

"For the record, I more or less got down on my knees and begged for forgiveness."

"You don't believe in astrology, do you? It's not part of your personal theology? Because whether we believe it or not, I can pretty much guarantee our stars aren't aligned today. Something's in retrograde or ascending and descending simultaneously. I'm thinking a meteor shower or a black hole in the vicinity. We might need to get in bed and pull the covers over our heads."

"I think we have to put this mess down to good old-fashioned human failing."

I went to him and put my arms around him. "I think we'll be doing that a lot until the girls leave home for good."

7

Despite wanting to resume his place in Deena's affections, Ed agreed that she couldn't go to Madison's party. The other Price Girl mothers agreed, too, although, of course, Crystal O'Grady had to be talked into compliance. Until we intervened, Carlene had planned to attend without her friends, which was like throwing harmless Fourth of July sparklers into a keg of dynamite. Now Deena wasn't the only Price Girl who was angry at her parents. I figured it was just as well Deena was already upset with Ed. We were getting a two-for-one bargain, and now she wasn't speaking to either of us.

I also told Ed my suspicions that Grady's reasons for coaching Madison had nothing to do with altruism and everything to do with her nubile sixteen-year-old body. Like me, he was concerned, and like me, he wasn't sure that telling Tammy with such scant evidence would do more good than harm. Tammy has always been sensitive to anything that implies her parenting skills might be lacking. Ed and Tammy have sidestepped a couple of blowouts about the church youth group, but only just. He was afraid that she might go out of her way to prove I was wrong by reinterpreting every sign I was right. We decided to watch closely and play this by ear.

Astonishingly, in the two days after Fred resigned and left town, Grady Barber was, for the most part, on his best behavior. He gave me a long list of things to do, but he stayed out of my way. We met each morning, went over phone calls I needed to make and lists of errands to run. He introduced me to his manager and publicist by way of conference call, and gave me access to his calendar. He clearly had an aversion to paperwork, preferring that I do as much of it as I could, even if a few mistakes were made. So I wrote letters and gave them to the hotel staff to key in and fax. I checked incoming contracts from other organizations that wanted him for their own versions of the Idyll, and I noted questions in the margins, going over them point by point when we were together, since he never seemed to have time to read.

"He even gave me an amethyst bracelet," I told Junie on Wednesday morning, after an hour in Grady's suite in which he had not shouted or used more than a whiff of sarcasm. I held out my wrist. I thought the bracelet was nice, small, emerald-cut amethysts interlaced with silver charms in the shapes of rainbows, jungle animals, doves, and arks. In a few years it would suit Teddy well.

She looked it over with a practiced eye. "Nicely done," she pronounced. "Not cheap, but not so expensive he'll necessarily expect a favor in return."

Junie believes in positive thinking, but not stupidity. She understands the world of men and women, and so do I. I suspected Grady had a cache of *Wayfarer* bracelets that he gave out on all sorts of occasions, some of which I didn't want to dwell on. But I had been surprised he'd wanted to impress and even thank me. Possibly the man still had a good instinct or two deep inside him. More likely he just wanted to endear himself, so I'd work harder and faster.

I lowered my wrist. "I may survive Grady, but I'm not sure I'll survive Deena."

A customer came up to us, and Junie gave advice about one brand of thread versus another while I waited. When we were more or less alone again, she pulled me close for a hug. "Just enjoy the silence, precious. It will end."

Deena knew she would never be allowed to get away with not answering when we spoke directly to her. That would be an unforgivable offense. Still, she hadn't initiated a conversation with either of us since Sunday.

"It's not a blackout, exactly, more of a brownout," I explained.

"Is Teddy making up for it?"

"She's beside herself. She's a fixer. She keeps trying to bring everybody together. Deena's stopped speaking to her, too, because Teddy keeps telling her that when somebody says they're sorry, they're supposed to be forgiven. And since they've been studying the Ten Commandments in Sunday School, honor thy father's been coming up a lot."

"Oh, my."

I finished with a flourish, ending my daily news broadcast. "Last but not least, your buddy Nora's been to see Ed, as well as every other minister in town. Ed said some of them are meeting regularly to discuss how to get rid of the tent show."

"Ed, too?"

"You jest. He's a 'freedom of religion' man. But he's concerned things might get nasty, and some of the people most upset about Nora and her animals could take matters into their own hands."

"It's an odd world, isn't it? She's asking people to take care of the planet and respect it, and they're afraid she's the problem."

I didn't think things were quite that simple, but Junie definitely had a point.

Another customer appeared at Junie's side—a sale was in progress—and I said good-bye. I didn't leave, though, because just then Tammy Sargent walked in and headed straight for the notions room.

Since she hadn't seen me I followed to say hello, although I wasn't really fooling myself. Despite Ed's well-founded concerns, I was still hoping that somehow I could ease into the subject of Madison and Grady. I had decided to alert Camille to my suspicions, and neither of us had come upon any alarming episodes. But we couldn't be with

Grady twenty-four hours a day. If Tammy admitted to even the weakest of doubts, I might be able to bring my concerns into the open.

Luckily no one else was in with the notions, since fabric was on sale, not seam rippers or flying geese rulers.

"Hi, Tammy. I saw you come in," I said, when she didn't look away from a revolving rack.

"Aggie." She looked pleased to see me, and I hoped that lasted. "I can't believe you have a whole minute off."

I laughed obligingly, but I was glad we'd gotten to the subject of Grady so quickly. "Looking for something special?"

She lowered her voice. "I found a great sequined tube top at Here We Go Again, and I think it'll be perfect with capris for one night of the finals. Trying to keep up with all these costume changes is expensive. But the top is missing some sequins." She put her hand just above her breast to demonstrate. "So I'm looking for something to cover the spot."

Here We Go Again is our local consignment shop, and I was glad to find Tammy wasn't spending Madison's college fund—if there was a college fund—on clothes for the Idyll. "If you don't find what you want in here, Junie has boxes of trims and beaded appliqués upstairs. She's going to put together a little bridal gown corner in the spring. You can tell her what you need and she'll help."

Tammy's eyes lit with pleasure. "We're so happy she moved in and opened this shop."

"Our family's happiest of all."

"Speaking of which, I'm sorry Deena's not coming to Madison's party tonight."

I was glad she knew and I wouldn't have to give Tammy the news myself. I didn't know what excuse Deena had used, but I wasn't going to spoil it now with my own explanation.

"I'm sorry, too. I know everybody's going to have a great time," I said.

"We're going to do this one up right. A couple of friends

from the church are going to help me set up. I really hope Grady will come. That would make it perfect."

My luck was holding. "That would really be a special favor, wouldn't it?"

"He's been so good to Madison, it wouldn't surprise me."

"He works her pretty hard onstage."

"That's nothing compared to their private sessions. She comes home so tired she doesn't even want to talk to me."

My heart sank. "That doesn't sound like Madison. I've never met anybody easier to talk to."

"This has been tough on her. It means so much, the Fourteen Carat audition, all the attention, the possibility of a real career. The stress is difficult, I know, but she can do it. She's such a trooper."

"She is." I paused and asked myself if I should go on, but in the end, I knew that even if I alienated Tammy, I had to try.

"Tammy, is it possible there's something more going on than just the Idyll auditions?"

She frowned, and I could see she was completely clueless. Tammy was blinded by the glamour of having her daughter do so well in front of our entire town. I wasn't sure how much winning the Idyll meant to Madison, but it definitely meant a lot to her mother.

"I don't know how to say this . . ." I chewed my bottom lip hard enough that I winced. "It's just that . . . I've heard rumors about Grady and other contestants in other places, and they worry me. Nothing concrete. But if Madison seems more stressed out—"

"Of course she's stressed out! She's been onstage for every round. She's learning new songs, new ways of presenting herself. She's working with her voice teacher, Lisa Lee, the stage crew. I'm surprised at you."

Maybe I should have stopped there, but I just couldn't. "I saw Grady talking to her that first night, in the shadows of the auditorium. He was standing so close it gave me pause. I was worried then, and I'm more worried now that I know they're spending time alone together. And those rumors I heard? I'm afraid they're from somebody who knows him well."

Tammy lifted her chin. "Madison can take care of herself. Grady's been nothing but kind to her."

That worried me most of all. Because despite his good behavior for the past two days, despite the bracelet, I was afraid Grady Barber didn't have a kind bone in his body.

"I'm sorry I upset you," I said. "I really am. I've debated talking to you because I don't have any strong evidence things are out of whack between them. But Tammy, please watch out, okay? If you see anything that fits with my suspicions, if you see any sign Madison's not just stressed but scared—"

"I can deal with my daughter, thanks." She turned back to the rack, dismissing me.

I hoped she *could* deal with her daughter, but I was afraid she wasn't going to. In many ways Tammy was a good mother, but her ambitions for Madison were like blinders. Now I hoped that she wouldn't set out to prove me wrong and ignore every signal that things were not as perfect as she desperately wanted them to be.

+ + +

As Grady's new volunteer assistant, I was expected to be on call for emergencies. As if he understood my frustration threshold was a lot lower than Fred's, there hadn't been many, and I'd been able to handle them all quickly. Tonight I was even marginally optimistic I could have an entire evening with Ed. In preparation for the three-night final round, which was to begin on Friday, there were no Idyll performances. Grady was having dinner with the Hayworths and some of our town leaders at the country club, so I didn't have to worry about Madison. I even knew what he would be eating since I'd gone over the menu with the country club chef.

Our children had cooperated without being asked. Deena

was spending the night with Posh Price, aka Shannon Forester, and Teddy was spending the night with Junie. Ed and I needed some time alone, and I'd bought an assortment of mushrooms from my favorite grocery store to make a luscious new lasagna recipe. We hadn't had a really good home-cooked meal since Grady came to town. We hadn't done anything even more fun for a while, either, and we were both looking forward to that, as well.

We were just sitting down to eat when the telephone rang.

"Don't answer it," Ed said. "Don't even listen to it ring."

"It could be one of the girls."

"It sure won't be Deena."

That was probably true. It was temporarily beyond Deena to even mutter "hello" if she didn't have to.

The phone rang for the third time. I tapped my fingers on the table. "It could be Teddy."

"Your mother knows where we live if there's an emergency."

But the moment he'd said the "e" word, we both knew the game was over. If you live in a parsonage, answering the telephone comes with the territory. I got up and caught it on the fifth ring.

I closed my eyes when I recognized the voice on the other end. I listened carefully, asked a few questions, which were answered with snarls, asked a few more anyway, then I hung up.

I made another call before I turned to tell Ed what was happening, although I was sure he'd guessed most of the details by now.

"Grady decided to drive himself out to Lake Parsons before his dinner at the club. One of the committee members loaned him her BMW. On his way back somebody plowed into him at a stop sign."

"Is he okay?"

I couldn't tell from the way Ed asked the question what answer he was hoping for. I gave him the benefit of the doubt. "He's fine, the car is not. I just called our towing service. Now somebody has to go out and get him. He's not a 'ride along in the passenger seat of the tow truck' kind of guy."

"Surely not you."

"He called Veronica first. She's already at the club, and for some reason her cell phone is off. I kind of get the feeling he's not used to punching in numbers on his own, so he didn't know how to dial directory assistance. Maybe that was Fred's job."

"Can't you call somebody else to pick him up? Call the club yourself?"

"He's about fifteen minutes away. If I go right now, I can drop him off at the club and be home in half an hour. If I start calling people, it'll take at least that long to find somebody else who's willing to go." I didn't add that I was hoping to get to the scene lickety-split, since the police were on their way, and I really didn't want Grady talking to them the way he had just talked to me. Okay, I'm human. Grady in jail is worth a grin, but Grady not judging the Idyll when we're counting on that revenue? Not funny at all.

"We were about to eat. Remember?"

I smiled, but my eyes were less friendly. "How many meals have I warmed up because you've been called to the hospital, Ed?"

I waited for him to tell me that this was different. This was Grady Barber, spoiled and apparently incapable of taking care of himself. Ed's emergencies were important. Mine had to do with some deep-seated emotional need to prove I was an intelligent, capable addition to our community.

Wait . . . Ed didn't have to say that. I'd done a pretty good job thinking it all by myself.

"Go," he said, instead. "I'll just be glad when he's not in our lives anymore."

"Hey, nobody will be gladder than me." I kissed the top of his head as I walked past to grab the minivan keys out of our key basket.

I knew exactly where the accident had occurred. Grady

was waiting at the four-way stop sign on a back road into town. A four-way stop means that everybody traveling that way has to be polite and take turns. Most of the time our locals are able to contain the urge to be first, and they patiently wait in line. I was afraid our star had simply assumed everybody knew he was the most important person ever to drive through the intersection, so he hadn't even slowed to a crawl.

I tried not to imagine how the authorities would view that attitude.

I didn't exactly speed, but I did get to the scene in record time. On the way I kept my foot on the gas pedal by fantasizing the best scenario. The cops would have arrived and taken all the information. Grady would be apologetic if he needed to be, or understanding if somebody else had been in the wrong. He would be chastened as I drove him to the country club and sorry that he had snapped at me. He would write a big check to Diana Feldspar, whose car he had borrowed, and promise to pay anything that his own auto insurance—if he had insurance—wouldn't cover. Then we would all join hands and sing "Sailing toward a Rainbow" together.

Things didn't go exactly that way.

First, the troopers had arrived just before I did. There was a cluster of people on one side of the road where a pickup loaded with bales of straw and a Toyota of some model no longer produced had pulled onto the shoulder. Diana's BMW was on the other side, and the right front looked like a larger version of a Catahoula Hound's accordion. Grady was shouting and gesturing toward the people on the other side, and two older women were holding a young man— I was guessing the pickup driver from his straw-covered jeans and feedstore cap—who was trying to get to Grady. When I parked and got out I could see that the front end of the pickup had been totaled.

"Move along, miss," one of the state troopers said, as I tried to get to Grady. Dressed in gray, with the traditional campaign-style hat, which sat just inches above a thunderous scowl, he didn't look like anyone to fool around with.

"The man in the BMW called me," I told him. "I'm supposed to give him a ride back into town."

"Grady Barber?"

I was sorry the trooper had recognized him. "Yep. That would be the one. I guess he told you who he is."

The trooper sneered. He'd obviously had a lot of practice. "No, ma'am. I went to school with Mr. Barber."

The two men were about the same age, so this seemed plausible. The trooper looked like he'd lived a harder life, but it sat well on him.

"Do you know whose fault it was?" I asked softly. "I'm on the committee that brought him here for the Emerald Springs Idyll. We'd sure like to avoid any trouble."

"You might ought to have gotten somebody else as your judge, then. Considering the way Barber was raised, it's no surprise his people skills are so lousy."

There was no time to follow up on that. Grady's voice was rising exponentially.

"Any chance you can calm him down?" the trooper asked. "Because my fellow officer isn't too big on patience. And I have even less."

"I can try."

"Be my guest."

He let me pass. I stayed on Grady's side of the road, and the trooper went over to calm the young man on the other side, who clearly wanted to wrap his hands around Grady's throat.

I really didn't know what to say. But desperate measures were called for. I did the only thing I could think of. I shouted. "Grady!"

That got his attention. He turned and pointed a finger at me. "What took you so long?"

"I've yet to perfect teleporting." I pointed my finger right back at him. "I am here now, and I want you to be quiet. Right now. No arguments."

His eyes widened, and his chin dropped, but only to let out another shout, aimed this time at me. I glanced at the trooper and smiled. "May I speak to him alone a moment?"

"Miss, I'm not sure he's safe."

"My self-defense skills are beyond reproach."

I blocked out the outraged bellows coming from Grady's lips until the trooper had moved away a little. Then I grabbed his wrist, snapped it back, and shook it. "Shut up right now! You're about to get thrown into jail. And if that happens, I swear I'll call every major newspaper I can find a number for and report what happened here. And I'll make sure you look like a total jerk."

I didn't really expect that to work. But it was as close to a plan as I could come up with in the seconds given me. I should have worked on it on the trip, instead of imagining the best scenario. Call me an optimist.

I'm not sure what got to him. The way I was holding his wrist? Jail? Bad PR? Whatever it was, he abruptly fell silent.

I dropped the wrist, but I stepped closer and lowered my voice. "So here's what we're going to do. You're going to co-operate with the troopers and give them your statement. If they don't throw you in jail, you can get in my van and I'll take you to the country club. A tow truck's on the way for Diana's car. And while we're together in my van, you will remember I am a volunteer. I have no real reason not to dump you by the side of the road if you get abusive. And buddy, let me tell you, I can do it, too. If you want a demonstration, I'll give you one right here and now."

He looked like he was considering my offer. Or maybe he was just considering whether he could afford a hit man.

I spread my hands, palms up. "I can leave. You never have to see my face again. You can find another way back. I really don't care."

He took me up on my first offer, although silently. When the trooper saw we were finished, he moved back and took Grady's statement, which went something like: The pickup had come out of nowhere. He had come to a complete stop, no matter what the loser in the feedstore cap was saying. This was not Grady's fault. The trooper glanced at me with a raised brow. I was careful not to shake my head, although my neck tried every which way to thwart me.

Sunset had come and gone by the time I was allowed to whisk Grady back to town. Although my cell phone and I don't always see eye to eye, I'd been able to reach the club and leave a message for Veronica, who had called back in a panic while we were waiting for the go-ahead. She promised that she and the others would wait as long as it took to get Grady out of this mess. She stopped short of saying she would always be there for him. She did say she would be eternally grateful to *me*.

I wasn't sure how grateful she would be tomorrow when I told her I was going to resign.

It was almost nine when I dropped Grady off in the circle outside the country club. He hadn't spoken to me since my tirade, and I hadn't trusted myself to speak to him. There was no apology and no acknowledgment of my help. He opened his door and got out. He didn't even close it. He just walked into the country club without a backwards glance. Luckily somebody else saw the door and gave it a shove so I didn't have to get out and do it myself.

I had managed to call Ed once, to tell him to eat without me. That had been an hour ago, and when I finally parked outside the parsonage and went inside, I had no appetite, and, I was afraid, no pulse.

Ed was putting on his shoes when I walked into the living room. I wondered if he was leaving me.

"Deena . . ."

My hand flew to my chest. "Is she okay?"

"Not so much. Tammy Sargent just called. We have to pick her up."

This didn't make sense. "What does Tammy have to do with it? Deena's at Shannon's house for the night."

He beckoned for me to follow; then he waited until we

were both in the van and he was backing out before he explained. He drove as quickly as I'd driven to get Grady. Luckily the Sargents' house was a lot closer.

"The message was garbled. Tammy was in a hurry. We'll find out how this happened when we get there. But apparently the girls showed up and Tammy had put out quite a spread. She didn't know Grady was busy getting arrested . . ." He glanced at me. "Was he?"

"Missed it by the skin of his teeth. Go on!"

"Tammy wanted everything to be perfect, so she borrowed serving pieces from church, including the punch bowl. I think she probably got Norma to go along with that."

Norma's the church secretary and sometimes too willing to please. But now I knew things must be dire. Ed wouldn't have mentioned my nemesis the Women's Society punch bowl otherwise. Punch bowl and I have a history, none of it good.

"Somebody broke it? Again?" But that hardly seemed the important question. Why were we picking up our daughter? I knew Tammy, and she wouldn't have reported Deena to us. Since Deena had declined the invitation herself, I doubted Tammy even knew that Deena had been forbidden to attend.

"No, somebody spiked the punch," he said.

We were on Tammy's street now, and Ed stopped talking as he looked for a place to park. For a quiet, residential street, this one was surprisingly crowded. Cars were parked everywhere, a few side by side, and Ed had to concentrate hard to miss them. Luckily for us, somebody pulled out just as we drove up behind them, and Ed was able to edge the van in and turn off the ignition almost in front of Tammy's house, an aluminum-sided shoe box with one medium-sized tree in the yard and withering shrubs.

We didn't have a chance to finish the conversation. I saw kids being hauled outside by parents, then I realized, for the first time, that one of the city's rescue squad vehicles was parked in Tammy's driveway.

I got out and started at a trot up the sidewalk. Ed joined me.

"Tammy says Deena's okay," he said. "We just have to get her home."

I sprinted now and reached the open front door, not pausing to knock. Inside we were greeted by chaos. I saw two men from the rescue squad bent over one teenager who was sprawled on Tammy's couch. They appeared to be taking vital signs. I saw kids hanging out of chairs giggling. One lying on the floor. I caught a glimpse of Tammy kneeling between two others who were sitting with their heads between their knees.

Before I could find out anything else, I saw my daughter and her friend Shannon in the dining area between the living room and the kitchen. The church punch bowl was still on the table. I could have sworn it winked at me, as if it had finally paid me back for whatever sins punch bowls believe are committed against them.

Both girls were resting their heads on crossed arms amid a jumble of plates and platters. The house smelled unpleasantly of vomit, and I could see that not all of it had been cleaned up.

Ed caught up to me. "Apparently the medics told Tammy that somebody probably got hold of pure grain alcohol and added as much as a whole bottle. It's tasteless, odorless, and packs a triple whammy. None of the kids would have known it was there, and if they drank a lot . . . I guess it was supposed to be a joke."

I wondered if the kid in question hadn't made it past the first round of tryouts and wanted to punish those who had. I was beyond appalled and hoped that whoever had done this got a good scare from the local authorities.

I put my hand on Deena's shoulder. She didn't seem to know I was there. "Deena. We're taking you home." I looked up at Ed. "Do you know if the medics checked her out?"

"Tammy said she and Shannon got here late and didn't have much to drink."

"Deena." I shook her. Deena finally lifted her head and narrowed her eyes, as if she were seeing several sets of parents in front of her. "You're . . . not supposed . . . to know I'm here."

"But we do."

The Foresters arrived just then. Tammy may not have been watching the punch bowl well enough, but she had managed to call parents when the party deteriorated into moaning and vomiting. I had to give her credit for that.

Grace Forester is absolutely sure that all teenagers are on a one-way street to perdition, and she guards Shannon like a junkyard dog. I found it astonishing that the girls had made it to the party on Grace's watch.

"My son was in charge while we were out," she said shortly. "See if that ever happens again."

Shannon's brother was a student at Ohio State and home for the summer. Shannon worships him, and that kind of adulation can make even sensible young men think of themselves as heroes.

"The girls should know better," I said. "Deena's responsible for her own behavior."

"I'm really sorry, Aggie." Grace thumped her daughter on the back. "He says Shannon and Deena decided they'd go to Madison's party, and he thought it was no big deal, that nobody—like us—would be the wiser. They'd just stop by for a little while, see what was going on, then head back to our house."

Explanation finished, she thumped her daughter again. "You are going home, young lady. And you're going to stay there a long, long time."

Shannon sat up. Her eyes were as unfocused as my daughter's. "Is . . . s . . . s your fault . . ." She couldn't seem to remember why. Her head dropped back on the table.

Ed got Deena under one arm, and I took the other. Between us we lifted her to her feet. Surprisingly her legs remembered how to move. We walked her slowly toward the door. That's when I saw a punch-drunk Madison sprawling on a piano bench, her back and arms resting on the keys. Tammy was standing over her, and even though I was busy with my own daughter, I could see she was trying to quiet hers.

"I tell you . . . he's not acting . . . like a father. Maybe I don' . . . have a father . . . but father's don'—"

Tammy rested a finger on her daughter's lips. "Be quiet, Madison. You don't know what you're saying. Just be quiet."

I hadn't heard enough to know what they were talking about, much less whether Madison was sober enough to make any sense. More important, my own hands were full with Deena. But as we walked our disoriented daughter out to the van, Madison's words haunted me.

8

I didn't resign from the committee. Not just because Grady sent a huge bouquet of flowers with a florist's card apology. Not just because Veronica called after I got home from the Sargents' house with my chastened and sick-to-her-toenails daughter and begged me to stay. Not just because Thursday morning Camille came to my front door with a basket of baked goods from the committee and a promise she would quit, if I did, because I was the only reason the whole Idyll farce was bearable. Not even because I was convinced I had to keep an eye on Grady and Madison, because now I knew that Madison's mother wasn't going to.

The biggest reason I didn't resign was because I really did not want to stay home. Deena was grounded, possibly for all of eternity. She now had in her possession a long list of chores she had to perform before we discussed the resumption of a normal life. Additionally all her privileges had been revoked, including attending the final round of the Idyll and sitting with the other contestants in a special block of balcony seats.

I wasn't all that keen on staying close by and watching this family drama unfold. I had no doubt whatsoever that Deena would comply with our edicts, and we wouldn't see another fit of rebellion like this one for quite some time. But between Ed's confusion about where we had gone wrong, Teddy's frantic attempts to make everybody behave reasonably, and Deena's contemplative silence, home was no haven. Ed could supervise the fallout as he researched sermons and made phone calls. I preferred mopping up after Grady.

Although he didn't apologize again once we were face-to-face Thursday afternoon, Grady *was* on his best behavior with me. I went over papers, made a half dozen phone calls, and ran interference with the hotel's morticianlike manager when Grady complained that somebody had searched his room while he'd been at breakfast. By this point, even if Grady had found somebody lurking in the closet and strung him from the shower rod with bedsheets, the hotel wouldn't have believed him. Grady's multiple complaints and infractions had destroyed his credibility. My job was just to keep the manager from hurling him out the window.

Friday dawned with the promise that the Idyll would soon be over. If we'd had any rain in the past months, I would have expected a rainbow as confirmation.

Tonight was the beginning of the final round. There were only three contestants left, Madison, Bart, and Julia, the folk singer. By Saturday night there would be two, and on Sunday the winner would be declared. A huge gala was planned after the Sunday night show—with a steep price for invitations, of course—and Veronica had wisely chosen the hotel as the venue. She wanted to make up for Grady's stay there.

I spent most of the day finalizing party plans with Veronica and Camille, dealing with Grady's insurance agent about Diana's car, and performing, almost by rote, the dozen or so other chores that cropped up. By now I could vet menus with one hand and organize Grady's to-do list with the other.

By the time I got home, I was beat. But I knew better than to pay attention to that. I had to eat, shower, and change in time to be at the auditorium for the sound check.

Teddy greeted me at the door. "Deena says I can't go tonight if *she* can't. Why is that fair?"

For most kids the first sentence would have been the most important. For Teddy, who thrived on moral dilemmas, the second was the interesting one.

"It wouldn't be fair," I agreed. "If you'd like to come tonight, you can. I'll find somebody you can sit with if I'm busy."

She looked disappointed. My solution was too easy.

"I'll stay home." She put her arms around my waist and rested her head against my breasts. Since Teddy's not normally a cuddler, I took her up on this display of affection and wrapped my arms around her, too.

"Deena didn't know there was anything bad in the punch," she said after a while.

At least Deena was still talking to her sister. "Deena was told not to go to the party. She shouldn't have been there drinking punch or doing anything."

"People don't always get caught, do they? When they make mistakes? Timmy Snyder always pulled my ponytail . . . when I had a ponytail . . . and nobody ever stopped him."

"I'm afraid that's the way things are. Life's not always fair."

"Do we know how many people get caught and how many don't?"

I ruffled her hair. "Why, are you calculating your odds? It's just better to do the right thing and not worry whether the wrong thing will get you in trouble."

"If I help Deena with her chores, will that be wrong?"

"This time it would be. But you can keep her company."

"I don't think she'd like that."

"Could be she just needs time alone to think."

"Daddy's sad." Teddy looked up at me. "Can't you *do* something?"

I was touched that she still thought I had magical powers, but I had to kiss her forehead and tell her no, I couldn't.

I thought about that conversation once I was on my way to the auditorium, dressed in a skirt and blouse of the lightest fabric in my wardrobe. Our family has really entered a new phase. By the time Deena is no longer pushing hard against us, Teddy will be. And knowing Teddy, the form will be more existential. If Sister Nora is still around, Teddy will probably run away and dig her way into the biosphere.

Things were already buzzing by the time I dragged my perspiring body into the auditorium. The stage crew was running from one side of the room to the other, talking in headsets and switching lights on and off. Sound checks were in progress and microphones were screeching. Melanie and Sandy, Grady's sidekicks, were down in front talking to a group of admiring senior citizens. I waved to Veronica, who was heading for the balcony with Diana. Probably to rope off seats for the first rounds of contestants.

Camille intercepted me as I was heading for the stage and beyond.

"Some guy was looking for Grady. I sent him back-stage, but he didn't look familiar. He must have showed somebody identification to get in here, right?"

Theoretically that was true, but in reality, security was a little loose. Early in the evening the guys at the door had a habit of just waving in people who looked familiar. Once the ushers arrived, the rules were less likely to be bent, but right now it wouldn't be that hard to get inside the auditorium with a group of people who looked like they belonged.

"I'll go back and check," I said. "I have to find him anyway and see if he needs anything before the curtain goes up."

"Want me to come?"

"It's plenty busy back there. Nothing can go wrong."

I knew Veronica had a list of people who needed to be thanked from the stage tonight, and she'd asked me to check it and make sure everyone had been included. I glanced at my watch, then made my way backstage as fast as I could.

I was halfway to Grady's green room when a youngish, dark-haired man nearly ran me over. I jumped back. "Hey!"

He didn't stop, and he didn't look around. He wasn't running, but his stride was long and determined. Before I could do anything, I saw Grady coming toward me, too.

"You come back here, and I'll have my lawyers all over you!" Grady shouted.

The man stopped, and for the first time I got a good look at his face. It was just a touch familiar, but that was as close as I came to recognition.

"Yeah? You try it, Barber. I'd love to have this out in court. We still may, but at my instigation. And not every town will have a stake in protecting you!"

Grady started after him, but the stranger swatted a hand in his direction in dismissal, turned, and stalked out the stage door.

"Grady . . ." I jumped into Grady's path to keep him from going out the door after the man. "Are you okay?"

This time the swatting hand—his—flew vaguely in my direction. He opened his mouth to say something, then seemed to think better of it. Maybe memories of Wednesday night intruded. Maybe his wrist still ached. He snapped his lips together and stood there, as rigid as a fence post.

"Do you want me to call security?" I asked.

He shook his head. Then, as if he knew that opening his mouth was going to lead to more trouble, he turned on one heel and disappeared down the hall. I guess he made it to the green room, because I heard a door close with a resounding thud.

Mistress of timing I'm not, but even I knew this wasn't the best moment to ask Grady if he needed anything before the show. In truth I was afraid he needed to take a swing at somebody, and I wasn't being paid enough for that. Oh, wait. I wasn't being paid at all. If he wanted me, Grady would have to come and find me himself.

The next half hour flew by. Melanie and Sandy had baked cookies and brownies for the stage crew, and I helped pass them out. I found assistants to help the band carry in equipment and set up in the orchestra pit below the stage. We had ten instruments now, and all the contestants had been working with them for this final round. I tried to visit each of the contestants to see if they had everything they needed, but only Julia had arrived before I had to go out front again.

There was a problem with the curtain, another with the lights. I had no expertise, but I was good at telling people where more knowledgeable people had gone and what they were doing. They kept me busy.

Twenty minutes before the curtain was to go up, a reporter for the *Flow*, the Emerald Springs daily, begged me to take him backstage to ask Grady for a quote, but Grady ignored us when I knocked.

I apologized to the reporter, who was young enough that shaving was probably a biweekly event.

"Maybe afterwards," he said cheerfully.

I hoped Grady would be in a better mood by then. Voting people offstage seemed to jack up his serotonin levels.

Ten minutes before the band started their prelude a harried Veronica found me in the ladies' room backstage. She was beautifully dressed all in black, and not a hair was out of place, but worry creased her forehead.

"Aggie!"

I flushed the toilet, straightened my skirt, and opened the stall door. "This may be an all-time low. Whatever it is couldn't wait thirty seconds?"

She followed me to the sink. With Veronica right beside me I couldn't hum "Happy Birthday" to make sure I washed my hands long enough, but I did my best.

"Madison's not here," she announced.

I cut short the hand-washing ritual and grabbed for a paper towel. "Nobody's heard from her?"

"No, and she's supposed to be up first. I tried her home number, but nobody answered."

I'd gotten a phone call from Madison that afternoon. She had apologized for the events at her house, and I'd assured her that I knew it wasn't her fault. She'd told me that the young man who'd doctored the punch had confessed to the police. Tammy had agreed not to press charges if he spent the rest of the summer's weekends working at our local food bank. Hopefully the parents of the kids at the party would go along with this.

But she hadn't said a word about not coming tonight.

I faced Veronica. "Did you ask Grady? He's been coaching her. Maybe something happened in one of their sessions."

If she understood what I was hinting at, she gave no sign. "I haven't seen him, either."

I followed her outside. "I guess I'd better go and get him."

Tonight she didn't volunteer to do it for me. "Ask him about Madison, then. And be thinking where else she might be. We have to have three contestants or this whole thing will fall apart. I'll change the order, but that's the best I can do until I know."

Now I had no choice but to wind my way back to the green room and pound on the door again. "Grady? Ten minutes until we start. And we have a problem with Madison. She hasn't arrived yet. We need to talk to you."

I waited, but there was no reply.

"Grady, I'm going to have to come in there and make sure you're all right unless you at least answer me." I figured that would work, since Grady regarded the green room as his own space, not to be defiled by underlings.

Still no answer. Now I had to make good on my threat. Dealing with Grady was like dealing with my girls. They got one warning, then I had to follow through or they'd never believe me again.

Sighing, I turned the knob and pushed the door open. I was surprised to find the room was lit only by an emergency flashlight plugged into a wall socket in the corner. The light was actually a nice touch. Every room backstage had one, in case the power went off. Even when the power was working they functioned like night-lights. I flipped on the overhead and did a quick inventory, wondering if maybe Grady and Madison had eloped together. I had no idea where he'd gone, but this was beginning to get spooky. Madison's disappearance was bad enough, but if I didn't find Grady and fast, the show couldn't go on at all.

I turned to leave, then something made me stop. I hadn't been in the room very often, but on the few occasions when I'd been allowed to step foot over the threshold, the room had been orderly, in keeping with Grady's rampant perfectionism. Furniture had been neatly arranged along walls. Now the table at the far end was pulled out at an angle. Nothing remarkable, but definitely different.

Suddenly I didn't want to know why the table had been moved. I had one of those hairs-lifting-at-the-nape, goose-bumps-rising-on-the-arms moments when I knew something was amiss. I thought about getting somebody else to investigate with me, but what would I say? Come in here a second and take two steps across the room with me? I have the strangest premonition?

Swallowing whatever was rising in my throat, I gingerly slid one foot, then the other to cross the room. Even at that pace, it took only seconds to see that my intuition had been correct. The table was askew for a reason. There was a body lying half under it. First I saw a shoe, then the cuff of a pair of beautifully tailored pants. The rest came into focus a piece at a time. Belt, shirttail, pale hand lying with fingers spread on the utilitarian speckled carpet.

My eyelids closed, but only for a moment. They flew open and I moved closer and knelt beside Grady, trying to make myself feel for a pulse in his neck. But there was no pulse to be found, because the gash in Grady's neck was so wide and so wet, that there was no place where I could put my finger. And the knife that had made the gash, a bloody knife that looked as if it had been made for just this purpose, was lying not far away.

Grady's eyes were open and staring blankly at nothing. I thought he looked surprised, then I realized I was wrong. Because Grady hadn't died instantly, only stunned for seconds by his imminent demise. After the attack, he had lived long enough to manage, somehow, to crawl under this table and scrawl three letters on the wall behind it in blood.

Three lowercase letters. *n . . . o . . . r.*

I thought the *r* had probably been his dying declaration. There were no letters after it.

The Idyll would not take place tonight or any night in the future. Much, much worse, Grady Barber would be the ghost that forever haunted this room, this auditorium, and the imagination of every citizen of Emerald Springs.

9

Finding a murder victim doesn't make for a good night's sleep. I knew that from past experiences, so when I finally made it home, I took a long shower, then swallowed Junie's cure for everything—warm milk and whiskey with honey. Finally I pulled the pillow over my head, so the nightmare monsters wouldn't find me. Of course, nothing really helped. All through the long night, I relived discovering Grady's body and the moments afterwards.

After the shock of finding him, I had gotten to my feet, backed away carefully so as not to disturb more of the crime scene, gone outside, and closed the door behind me. Then, as I stood guard, I called the police. After I told the dispatcher what had happened, I called Veronica's cell.

People seem to react to this kind of tragedy in two ways. There are those who weep and wail, and those who put their emotions in deep freeze to take out a sliver at a time once they're able. As I stood there, my own in cold storage, I saw both. The security guard, pale-faced and shaky, wanted to go inside, but I wouldn't even let him open the door. He was young enough to join the *Flow* reporter for a night of hitting on college students, and I was fairly certain that his training, if he had any, had not extended to preserving evidence.

Although she was openly weeping, Veronica supported my blockade. The other committee members and the two female judges arrived, and the embracing and tears were quickly followed by debates on what to tell the audience. We needed to send them home without argument, but also without fear they might be the next victims, an assurance we couldn't honestly give. Veronica was too upset to make an announcement, but Melanie's show business experience propelled her to the stage, where she explained there would be a delay and an explanation very soon. Even from my post at the doorway, I could hear the rising tide of speculation from the auditorium.

Uniformed cops arrived first and relieved me of duty. I gave them my account of what had happened, and they told me a detective was on his way, so I should remain for questioning.

Emerald Springs has more than one detective, of course, but I knew who would show up for such a high-profile victim. Our best and brightest, Detective Kirkor Roussos. Roussos and I go back a few murders. He's a dark-haired, dark-eyed Greek American hunk who would be my heart-throb of choice were I not happily married to Ed—which I am. So Roussos and I hold a different place in each other's hearts. I make his life miserable by sticking my nose where it doesn't belong, and he does everything he can to stop me.

I wasn't wrong. Roussos arrived, went into the room with the medical examiner and another man, then returned about fifteen minutes later, when he noticed me. He took one look and lifted a brow. "Tell me you're not involved in this," he said.

"I was Grady's assistant while he was here. Oh, and I found the body."

"You've got to stop doing that. We had a nice break. I was hopeful."

"Me, too."

His gaze softened, or maybe it was just the light. "He's a friend?"

"No, and I don't think he had many." I kept my voice low, because there were still people close by, and I didn't want to be overheard. "If he had an endearing side, I never saw it." I told him quickly about the accident on Wednesday, about the fight with Fred and Fred's resignation, even about the incident at the welcoming party with the server. "That's the way Grady treated almost everybody," I finished.

"You, too?"

I chose my words carefully. I sure didn't want to sound like a suspect. "We had our moments, but I stood up to him, and he backed down enough that we could keep working together. I can't say I liked him, although I'm still sorry he's dead." I paused. "It's awful." And it was.

"So who do you think killed him?"

For a moment I thought Roussos had asked me for my opinion. I almost laughed, until I realized he actually had. "There was a stranger backstage tonight, and the two of them were arguing. I stepped right into the middle of it."

"You're good at that."

"Tell me about it." I explained what I had witnessed. "I had the idea I'd seen this guy before, but I can't remember where or when. While I was waiting for you to arrive, I racked my brain. No luck."

"Give it some thought tonight and let me know if you figure it out. You can give a description?"

"Tall, dark haired, in his forties somewhere. Thin, I think. Dressed casually, jeans, a polo shirt of some dark color like navy or forest green. Camille Beauregard spoke to him and sent him backstage. You might want to check with her."

"Will do."

"I knocked on Grady's door about ten minutes before I finally went in. If I'd just gone in earlier . . ."

"Don't beat yourself up. It wouldn't have done any good. He was a dead man from the moment he was stabbed and his throat . . ." He stopped.

"He found time to scrawl letters on the wall."

"Somebody scrawled them. But judging from where we found him, it does look as if he crawled to the wall to do just that."

Roussos went back into the green room, and eventually I was sent home. In the meantime the police chief arrived and announced Grady's death to the audience, although not the circumstances. He told people to leave quietly, and warned them there would be extra police in and around the parking lots and local streets to make certain everybody behaved. Of course, I knew that wasn't the real reason for the extra police presence.

Melanie followed the chief onstage and told people to keep their ticket stubs. Anybody who wanted a refund would get one, but it might take a day or two to work out logistics. She didn't go so far as to say the Emerald Springs Idyll was now history, but the message was clear.

After everything, all the work, all the imagination, all the hope, all the kowtowing to Grady's demands, the pediatric unit was now nearly as far out of reach as it had been when we began.

When I woke up on Saturday morning, sun was blasting straight through the shades and curtains on our bedroom windows. There was no pillow thick enough to block it, and definitely none thick enough to block my memories.

I rose and went downstairs to find Ed cooking breakfast in our substantial country kitchen. He told me Deena had taken a stale muffin and gone back to her room. Teddy was sitting at the table buttering toast. A reporter had called from a Columbus paper, but Ed had told him I wouldn't be making any statements. I figured they wouldn't be the last.

"Lucy called, too." He held out a plate half covered by one of his signature add-whatever's-in-the-fridge omelets. I didn't have the heart to tell him I might have permanently lost my appetite. I took it with thanks and set it down long enough to pour myself a mug of coffee.

"What did Luce want?" I added a piece of Teddy's toast to my plate and wondered where I could dispose of the contents without being caught.

"I know you're not hungry," Ed said, with his gaze still glued to the omelet pan, "but give that a try anyway. You'll feel better."

He was right. After forcing down two bites of toast and

one of omelet, my stomach settled a little. The coffee helped,
as well.

"Lucy wanted your version of what happened last night.
Of course," Ed added, as if the question wasn't worthy of
my high IQ.

I cut to the chase. I knew what had come next in their
conversation. "So when is she coming over?"

"In about thirty minutes."

My stomach was half full; I'd had another shower, and
I was dressed presentably by the time Lucy arrived. Ed
planned to be home all day with Deena and Teddy. I was
free to suggest a field trip in exchange for my information.

We were backing out of the driveway before I told her
where we were going. "Nora's," I said. "Drive slowly, and
I'll tell you everything."

We were more than halfway there before I finished the
basics. "I'm not sure about all the worst details. Roussos
said he was stabbed *and* his throat was cut. I saw the throat,
and that's all I needed to see."

Lucy was shaking her head in sympathy. "The *Flow*
said he'd been murdered, but they didn't give much in the
way of details."

I figured the details wouldn't stay secret for long. Too
many people knew the truth.

"Even somebody like Grady Barber deserves a better
death," she added.

I thought so, too. Call me foolish, but I'm always hopeful that, like Scrooge in *A Christmas Carol*, nasty folks like
Grady will have a sudden change of heart and live out the
rest of their lives doing good works. Now Grady would
never have a chance to put his talents to a better use. Someone had robbed him of that possibility.

"After all that, what's the connection to Nora?" Lucy
asked. "Unless this trip has nothing to do with Grady?"

"Do you remember the other night when we were inside
Nora's house?"

"Sure."

"Do you remember what was on the wall in their living quarters?"

"Circus posters."

"Knives. She said her boyfriend, Yank, was a knife thrower, remember?"

"She said they kept guns, too." Lucy didn't ask where this was going. She understood. "What makes you think one of Yank's knives did the deed? Did you get a good look at it?"

Honestly, I had tried not to look. The knife had been less important to me than the victim, and unnecessarily gruesome to contemplate. But during my middle-of-the-night review of the crime scene, I had begun to wonder if the knife that killed Grady Barber had been one of the set on Nora's wall.

"I don't think the murder weapon was anything ordinary," I explained. "Not a kitchen knife, that's for sure. Not a hunting knife."

"What would you know about hunting knives?"

"I've seen a lot in my dad's compound. Almost everybody there has one on his belt."

"Don't tell me why."

"Chores, for one thing. Cutting rope, hacking down vines, as well as skinning animals."

"I told you not to tell me."

"Their knives are hefty, with handles that make them easy to grip. The knife that killed Grady? I don't think it had a handle, not a separate handle, anyway. It looked like it was all one piece, and the point looked as sharp as an arrow."

The better to stick into a target after a multitude of flips through the air.

"Is that the only reason we're going?" she asked.

I hadn't told her about the letters scrawled in blood on the wall, because I didn't know what details the police planned to keep to themselves, which could be why, besides deadlines, our local paper had given only a few. Now

I decided to tell her anyway, because I knew Lucy could keep a secret if I asked her to.

"The knives are the biggest reason," I said. "I want to get a look inside the house if we can and see if the knives on that wall look familiar." Then I told her about the letters.

"Aggie, why would somebody from the circus kill Grady Barber?"

I noted she had already discounted Nora as a possibility. "I have no idea whatsoever. He has a lot of enemies, but to my knowledge not a one of them wears a curly wig or sticks his head in a lion's mouth."

"One thing's for sure, Nora wouldn't have had anything to do with it. I've never met anybody so dedicated to peace and good works."

I had to agree. Surely there were many explanations for *n . . . o . . . r.*

"I can't imagine a connection between them, can you?" I asked at last, having tried to think of one. "I can tell you global warming never came up in any of my conversations with Grady."

We discussed possibilities until we arrived. Lucy drove right into the gate and dispensed with trying to park on the road. There were a few protesters, but the unrelenting heat had sapped their energy and numbers. Maybe after a good rain they would reunite, to be joined by the press, who were still probably trying to find Emerald Springs on their maps.

"If the knives look too familiar, or we note some connection with Grady, I'll have to tell Roussos," I said.

Lucy pointed in the direction of the house. I leaned over to see beyond the tree to my right.

"I'm betting you won't have to tell him anything," Lucy said.

There were police cars parked in front of the house, and a small crowd had gathered just beyond them.

"We can turn around and go home," Lucy said, as she unbuckled her seat belt.

I followed suit. "What are the chances?"

"You've given up investigating murders, remember?"

I recognized the taunt for what it was and gave her my coolest stare. "I'm not investigating anything. We're supporting a friend."

"Tell yourself anything you need to."

We couldn't get as close as we wanted. The police had prepared for trouble, and there were enough of them to make sure they didn't get any. We were rows back, surrounded by tall men and muscular women, who were behaving admirably. Luckily Lucy recognized Henry Cinch, Nora's millionaire—or was it billionaire—benefactor, and we edged our way over to him.

Henry did, as Lucy had told me, have a little topknot of hair on an otherwise bald head. He was small, probably over seventy, and both gnarled and tough. Judging from the worn Stetson clutched in his hands and the string tie with a bucking bronco clasp, I was betting he'd wrestled his money from Texas oil fields.

"Henry," Lucy said. "What's going on?"

He tore his stare away from the unfolding drama inside the house, which was, of course, invisible to us. When he saw who was speaking, he nodded in welcome. "They're railroading Nora, that's what. Charging her for something she didn't do."

"What?" Lucy asked, although we both knew the answer.

"That murder last night. They think she did it."

"Do you know why they think so?"

"One of Yank's knives was found at the scene."

I pointed out the obvious. "Then why aren't they arresting Yank?" Although, let's face it, Grady had not traced *yan* on the wall before he died.

"Yank was here all night. A dozen people vouched for him."

The crowd was buzzing, but Henry fell silent. A resounding silence, under the circumstances.

"And Nora wasn't?" I asked when he didn't volunteer more.

He didn't answer.

Just then Nora came out on the porch, hands cuffed, a uniformed officer at each arm. They put her in the backseat of the closest police car while the crowd began to grow noisier. For the first time I was sorry I had decided to embed myself in their midst. If there was a riot, this could be difficult to explain to Ed.

A tall, good-looking man came out of the house and held up both hands.

"Yank," Lucy told me.

"Nora wants everybody to go about their business," he said. "No trouble. Have faith things are happening this way for a reason."

Minister's wife I may be, but my faith isn't that strong. I couldn't imagine that arresting Nora, unless she was truly guilty, was good for anybody or anything.

The cops doing crowd control motioned for people to divide so the car carrying Nora into town could pass. There was still some rumbling, a little shoving, but eventually people moved. In just a few minutes she was gone. People began to disperse toward trailers and tents, including Henry Cinch, who blessed us with a snippet of wisdom before he departed.

"Nobody wants to hear her message about saving the world. They're trying to shut her up." He stomped off.

"Your buddy," Lucy said, nodding toward the house.

Detective Roussos had come out to the porch, and he was talking to two other men who were unfamiliar. Just as I was debating how best to approach him, he caught sight of me. I'm almost sure his eyes narrowed.

"My *buddy's* going to come down here in a moment, ask me what in the heck I'm doing here, and harangue me about getting involved. Won't that be fun?"

"You do know how to throw a party."

We waited while Roussos finished a brief conversation, then started toward us.

"You're here," he said. "Like you have an antenna for bad news."

"Then the news is bad? You've arrested the wrong person and you've already figured it out?"

"You know the right one? Come on, tell me. I'll arrest him without anything except your opinion."

"You remember Lucy, right?"

Roussos looked at her and nodded. "Hard to forget either of the Dynamic Duo."

"Can you tell me why you've arrested Nora?" I asked.

He considered, which is more than he usually does.

I ventured a guess. "Somebody told you the murder weapon was one of a set used in Nora's show."

"You didn't tell me that last night."

"Last night I was pretty upset. Am I right this morning?"

He gave a slight nod.

"Detective Roussos, the knives were kept in a rack on the wall. Anybody could have taken one."

"Uh-huh."

"There's more, right?"

He considered again, then he sighed. "It'll be common knowledge before long. She was seen backstage last night."

"No! I was there. I didn't see her."

"You were backstage the entire night? Guarding Barber's door?"

I remembered my trips out front. "Well, no . . ."

"Uh huh."

"Why would she be backstage?" When he lifted a brow I hurried on. "And don't tell me she was there to murder Grady. But let's say she was there. Would you know the reason?"

"That's going to be common knowledge, too. Maybe you should wait and hear it with everybody else."

"Please tell me. I found the body. I happen to like Nora. That gives me something of a connection, right?"

"History repeats itself. You always have connections."

"Please?"

"They were seen arguing, okay? A stagehand saw them together, and he said that Barber was furious with her."

"Grady was furious a lot. Nobody else thought of stabbing him." I watched his expression. "There's another connection, isn't there? Something you haven't said."

"There is a connection. Yes. Other than the knife coming from her house. Other than *nor* on the wall, scrawled in his blood as he was dying. Other than her being there last night and fighting with him in the half hour before he was found."

The evidence already sounded incredibly damning. But I wanted all of it. "And the rest? The part you aren't telling me?"

"You find it in the tabloids every day. Nora Nelson and Grady Barber had a special bond. A long time ago she was Mrs. Grady Barber. Nora Nelson of Sister Nora's Inspirational Tent Show was Grady Barber's very first wife."

10

When I left the parsonage on Monday morning, Henry Cinch was leaning against the side of a dark SUV parked in front of the house, with his arms folded around his Stetson. He wore black-rimmed sunglasses with temples wide enough to suit a chain gang boss, and sported a toothpick protruding from the side of his mouth to complete the image. At the rate he was chewing on it, I didn't think it would remain there long.

I was glad Henry was waiting and not one of the reporters who had nosed around since they'd finally located our little burg.

"Mr. Cinch?" I shooed Teddy into the minivan with her backpack of notebooks and pens. We were on our way to the Frankels, where she and Hillary were planning to shoot a screenplay they'd written using the Frankels' video camera. At Teddy's age I spent my summers on all fours pretending I was Scooby Doo. I'm glad Junie didn't have a video camera to record it.

Teddy went willingly. She'd told me she wasn't satisfied with the screenplay climax, in which the bad guys—two stagestruck neighbor boys—are caught stealing bicycles. She felt there needed to be a scene where they admitted how badly they felt about what they'd done. I was glad she wasn't going to make the film too realistic.

She settled herself on the van floor by the sliding door, swinging her legs and happily scrawling notes in the margins of her script. I went out to see what Henry wanted.

"How's Sister Nora?" I asked. "Have you been able to see her?"

"Yank's talked to her by phone. They're just holding her in town until they can arraign and transfer her to the regional jail. We can visit tomorrow night if she's still there."

I had tried not to think about Nora since the arrest. Clearly I'd already exceeded my involvement quota. A fair portion of this had simply landed in my lap, but I didn't want that to send me off and running to find a murderer. The police had their woman. The evidence was convincing. So what if it felt completely wrong? Like my mother, I wasn't one bit psychic.

"I'm kind of surprised to see you *here*," I said.

"After Nora was arrested, I saw you and Lucy talking to that detective, Roussos."

"We've met," I said, in classic understatement.

"More than that, I'm told. You've helped him find a couple of killers."

"I don't think he'd put it quite that way."

"How would he put it?"

"That I've stuck my nose where it doesn't belong more than once and almost died in the process."

"You didn't die."

"Yes, well, I seem to be like a cat, only there's no proverb promising how many lives I've been assigned."

"Nora didn't kill Grady Barber. She doesn't have murder in her. Back down East Texas way, I knew men, and a few women, who did. Once in some oil patch or the other a man got stomped into the ground and left for dead just for eating somebody else's share of corn bread. That takes a right lot of meanness, and there was plenty to go around back then. So I know murder, and I know mean, and I know when a woman's got neither inside her. Nora Nelson's the finest human being I know, and I plan to make sure she doesn't go down for something she didn't do."

I glanced back at the van. Teddy was still swinging her legs. "I'm glad you're on her side."

He pocketed the toothpick, and took off the glasses. "So you think she did it?"

"There's some pretty strong evidence."

"That's not what I asked you."

I thought I could see how this man had made so much money. "It's hard to believe," I admitted. "I don't really know Nora, but why on earth would she kill Grady Barber? They've been divorced, what, twenty years?"

"More like twenty-four, and she hadn't seen him since the decree."

I knew Henry believed this. And so far the newspaper accounts of their marriage and divorce hadn't reported any recent connections. But Grady had died on Friday, and this was only Monday. Evidence takes time to assemble.

"What was she doing backstage?" I asked. "If she hadn't seen him since the divorce, why on earth was she visiting him on Friday night?"

"I'm not sure. She told Yank she was going into town to deliver a message. We weren't performing that night, on account of not wanting to draw crowds from what you folks were doing, since the cause was good and all."

"Was good, yes. Now there's no chance we'll reach our goal anytime soon."

"Not because of Sister Nora. She's caught up in this mess, sure, just like you are, but it's not of her making. Somebody wanted her to take the fall, planned and executed it that way. Why use one of Yank's knives if not for that? You think Nora would have taken a knife so easy to trace, kill her ex-husband, then leave it lying there?"

I'd gone over that in my head a dozen times, and it made no sense to me, either. "Maybe she was scared off. Maybe she meant to remove it after she killed him, and the whole Grady dying in front of her thing was so awful she got spooked and left."

"She doesn't spook. She'd stand up to the devil himself, if she thought she was supposed to."

Prophets are pretty good at that, I suppose. Who else would be willing?

I reminded him of another puzzle piece. "Grady traced *nor* on the wall before he died." That was now common knowledge, and all over the papers.

"*Somebody* wrote it. Maybe the same person who stole Yank's knife."

From what Roussos had said, I knew this was unlikely. "What message was she delivering, Henry? I hate to say it, but maybe it was the one Grady got. The last one he'll ever get."

"No." He shook his head.

"What do you want me to do?"

"You've got a relationship with the detective. You can ask him to keep looking, not to stop just because it's easier. And whether he does or not, you can help us figure out who really did it. I can get lawyers. I can get the best, and will. But that's legal mumbo jumbo, and I want answers." He smacked his fist into his palm. "I want the real killer caught and punished."

"You could hire your own detective."

"I offered. Nora says no. But I know that you were with Grady Barber a whole lot while he was here. You've got a head start. You're the one who could dig up those answers the fastest anyway."

"I'll be glad to talk to anybody you hire if she changes her mind, but my investigating days are over."

He regarded me with ancient eyes. "Nah," he said at last, shaking his head. "You're fooling yourself." Then he smiled. "That husband of yours think Nora did it?"

I hate it when I get pinned down. "He wonders."

"Good." He nodded. "Clergy get special visiting privileges at the jail. You can talk to Nora."

"Ed's the clergy, not me."

"Something tells me nobody there'll be splitting hairs." He pushed away from the SUV and dug something out of his pocket and handed it to me. It was a business card with numbers where he could be reached. Then he held out his hand. "Where I come from, we shake when a deal's done."

"Where I come from, we shake just to be polite." We shook.

"I've talked to that mother of yours, you know. She tells me you're not from anywhere, and you spent as much time in Texas growing up as you did anyplace else." He put the sunglasses and Stetson back on, fished the splintered toothpick out of his pocket, and stuck it in his mouth. Then he nodded, went around to the driver's side, and drove off.

Henry Cinch was slick as a gusher, and twice as forceful. My sense of reality was distorted. I wondered if I'd just bought a piece of oil-depleted East Texas, or worse, sealed a deal to let Henry drill in the backyard of the parsonage. More realistically I was afraid he had sensed weakness and read my character, like the tycoon he is. Henry knew he'd planted a seed that was going to grow like a magic beanstalk.

Once I dropped Teddy off at Hillary's house, I decided to go and see Roussos for a ray of daily sunshine. Maybe I wanted him to convince me they had the right person for Grady's murder. Or maybe Henry had gotten to me. I didn't examine it too closely.

As I drove I thought about what I knew for sure. I'd been busy all weekend trying to help with details relating to the end of the Idyll. By Saturday evening Grady's manager had sent his own assistant to pack Grady's things and take care of details, and I had given up my notes and everything else relating to Grady's stay here. She'd thanked and dismissed me, promising she would call if she needed anything else. She did tell me that once the body was released, Grady would be flown back to Los Angeles for burial. On an even less personal note she'd said that her boss was going over Grady's contract with our committee to see what was owed his estate, since Grady had not completed his commitment. The whole transfer of responsibility had been surprisingly cold-blooded, and I suspected that Grady had never endeared himself to the people who represented him. I found that sad.

I pulled into the parking area of the new Emerald Springs Service Center, which finally housed our police station and jail as well as the garage where all county vehicles and equipment are parked and serviced. There's also a salt dome, a playground and exercise trail, and, since the start of the summer, a community swimming pool. The timing for that last expenditure had been just right. Without it we might have had a summer of riots. For once the county hadn't waited until crisis struck before they spent our tax dollars.

I walked over to the station, trying not to think of an evening I'd spent here almost two years ago being chased by a murderer. That was the night I'd learned for the first time that meddling was not for the fainthearted. At least nowadays, the police would be on the premises if history ever repeated itself.

I was used to the old station downtown, held together by duct tape and testosterone. Once inside, this shinier, antiseptic version made me nostalgic. I felt like a stranger. I told myself that was a *good* thing.

I asked for Roussos and got the evil eye from the woman in uniform behind a Plexiglas partition. For a moment I thought she was going to come out and frisk me. I took a seat in a plastic chair—the discomfort, at least, was familiar—and leafed through pamphlets about home security and the evils of pets running free. I thought that last pamphlet ought to be mailed to the new residents at the old Weilly farm.

I fully expected to be summoned back to the window for another dose of evil eye and a recommendation I never show my face again, but a jeans-clad Roussos came out to welcome me. Okay, *welcome*'s not quite the right word. At least he didn't chase me off the premises.

"Let me guess. Either another person close to you has gone belly-up, or you're here about the last one."

"Door number two."

"You can tell me outside."

Roussos isn't fond of allowing me into his private space. Whenever we've had the opportunity to chat, it's always elsewhere. I tell myself he looks on me as an informant, and he doesn't want anyone else to guess my identity.

More likely he's embarrassed someone will discover that he tolerates my interference.

The sun was busily destroying epidermal layers when we stepped into it. Roussos nodded toward the exercise trail winding through a grove of young trees that were yet to cast much shade. This was the best we could do.

"I've been thinking a lot about Sister Nora," I said, when we were no longer in earshot of anybody else. "I know you have good evidence that points to her, but Roussos, anybody could have planted the knife and traced those letters on the wall. I guess I just need to tell you one more time that there were a lot of people who disliked Grady. I just spent a few hours with somebody from the agency that represented him, and you know what she told me?"

"Is this where I'm supposed to pretend I care?"

Having expected this, I continued. "She said that everybody was shocked he'd been murdered, but nobody was surprised. When I asked what she meant, she said Grady was good at pissing off people. Her exact words, by the way, in my quest for accuracy."

"Thanks. Four-letter words make all the difference. Case closed."

Again, I ignored him. "So I've been making a mental list of people I know he upset. There was the guy I told you about who showed up backstage that night. Did you find him, by the way?"

"I remember how you slip in those little questions."

"Well, did you?"

"We didn't. Mrs. Beauregard was unable to furnish a better description, and nobody else remembered him."

At least Roussos had followed up. I was encouraged. "Then there's Fred, Grady's former assistant. Grady was awful to him. I was called in to break up a fight in Grady's suite, and when Fred came to the door, his cheek was bruised. Supposedly he left town after he quit his job, but what if he didn't?"

"You're wasting your time."

I plowed on. "He was hateful to the contestants he kicked out of the finals. One of them might have killed him. He upset everybody at the hotel. I wouldn't be surprised if somebody there snapped. The car accident I told you about? The young man in the pickup that Grady plowed into looked ready for murder."

I didn't mention Madison or her mother, who I was afraid might have had their own good reason to want Grady Barber dead. Madison had been missing that night, but maybe she had actually come . . . and gone.

"When I said you were wasting your time, I wasn't just moving my lips to keep them lubricated," Roussos said. "We have our suspect."

I waited, because I had the darndest feeling there was something he wasn't saying.

He turned around, and we started back toward the station. We were halfway there before he spoke again. "This is a high-profile murder. We're under pressure to solve it."

When silence fell again, I mulled this over. "Are you saying that in the rush to show what a fine department we have, justice might get edged aside?"

"Not me."

"Roussos, are you saying that you're not really sure Nora's the murderer?"

"The prosecutor thinks he has a good case. Your Sister Nora's a kook. She's also the victim's ex-wife. But I don't need to tell you any of this. You know it all."

"She's not a kook."

"Then she's converted you?"

"I was converted to a need to stop global warming a long time ago."

"She's got the whole town up in arms."

"So she's fodder for the local lynch mob."

"I don't make these decisions."

That was as clear a statement as I would get, but again, I was encouraged. Roussos wasn't exactly on my side, but he had doubts about the side he was on. I decided this was the right moment to ask my last question.

"I'd like to see her. I know you have visiting hours and all kinds of rules. But can you bend them for clergy?"

"You're not wearing a collar or carrying a Bible."

"All those board barbecues and bake sales I've cooked for, all the nights rearranging pews or chairs in the parish hall. All the rummage sales! You have no idea how many rummage sales and bazaars I've staffed. That has to count for at least three years of seminary."

He actually smiled. Fleeting, but unmistakable. "Why do you want to talk to her?"

"Isn't that privileged?"

"Don't push your luck."

"I want to see if she needs anything. I want to see if she'll tell me why she was backstage."

"You're investigating again, aren't you? You didn't learn anything last time?"

"I'm not!"

"You don't think I can tell?"

"I swore off investigating. I've taken up committee work."

He stopped and turned to look at me. "You hate it, don't you?"

I closed my eyes for just a moment. How had he known? "With every fiber of my being. But I'm good at solving problems."

"If I put in a good word and we get you in to see her, promise you won't solve this problem? Leave the investigations to us."

I parted my lips to do just that, but they closed of their own volition. The second time, the intended message was a little different, but more acceptable. "I'm not planning to solve anything. I'm not going in with that in mind."

"I ought to lock you up, too."

"Think of the trouble I'd cause."

Back inside the station he pointed at the chair I'd vacated, and I took it without another word. Half an hour later a cop in uniform came out and led me back through a maze of hallways to what was now the Emerald Springs jail. This was what Ohio called a five-day jail, a short-term facility meant for overnights and for holding prisoners before transfer. Luckily Nora was still here.

He sat me at a counter with a window separating me from a room on the other side and told me how to use the telephone intercom once Nora was brought in. Then he left me alone.

I made a mental list of questions, starting with "How are they treating you?" but I abandoned that when she was brought in. She was chatting with the uniformed woman, and Nora laughed at something the woman said. When she spotted me, her smile widened. She looked relaxed and confident as she took the seat across from me.

I picked up the receiver and she picked up hers.

"Aggie," she said, and under the circumstances I was touched she'd remembered my name. "It's a pleasure to see you."

"Well, I wish the circumstances were better."

"I'm not worried, and you shouldn't be, either. Things will work out the way God intends. We're in His hands."

My personal theology was more along the line of "God helps those who help themselves," but I wasn't there to question.

"Henry came by this morning and asked me to see you. Everyone's worried."

She shook her head fondly. She looked rested, clean, thin—but that wasn't new. "Henry's faith is tried at times like this."

I hoped this was simply an expression, and there hadn't really been "times like this" in her past. Previous murders would certainly be a black mark against her.

"Nora, I was backstage most of the night Grady was killed. Were you really there? Because I didn't see you."

"I wasn't there for long. That morning I had a strong premonition Grady was in danger. I prayed about it, and I was led to go and see him. Grady had strayed terribly through the years. Evil is like a magnet, it attracts more evil. Grady was sinking under the weight."

"Is that what you told him?"

"Yes, and I told him it wasn't too late to change his ways, but if he didn't, I saw a terrible end for him. I asked him to join us, to use his money for good and help us build our biosphere. He wasn't happy to see me. He didn't recognize me at first, then he was angry I'd sought him out. He knew I was in town, of course, but I think he believed I would stay away because of old hurts."

"It's none of my business, I know, but Henry asked me to find out what I could from you . . ."

She smiled. "You want to know about those old hurts, don't you? I can understand that, although I imagine they'll be public soon. I met Grady on a movie set. We were both impossibly young. He'd made a splash in *Wayfarers* and the studio tried to follow up his success with something in the same vein, fantasy, legend, or history with a sentimental score to go along with it. He made two movies in quick succession, both with limited appeal. Next they decided to do something colorful and completely different. They had a script that had been floating around for years about a young man who joins a circus to hide from a murderer. It was called *Circus Train to Nowhere*."

"I'm sorry. I've never heard of it."

She smiled, as if that was understandable. "I was traveling with our family circus, and a talent scout tapped me to try out for the female lead. I was blonde and photographed well. They thought my act would look great on film, and they were sure I could be trained to act. They were wrong about that part. The movie was dreadful, and I was dreadful in it. Grady wasn't much better. It flopped, but by then neither of us cared. We were madly in love, the way only people that age ever can be. We married right before the premiere, and right afterwards we both knew it was a terrible mistake."

The woman who'd brought Nora into the room looked at her watch.

I spoke faster. "You weren't married long?"

"His contract with that studio wasn't renewed. He had nowhere to go and nothing to do, so he traveled with us, Nelson–Zimboni that is, for about six months. Several months into it he convinced Caprice Zimboni to have an affair with him. Caprice was a few years younger than I was, and although I wasn't wise, she was even less so. She was the Zimboni star, a lovely young woman who had all the family athletic ability. She was a high-wire genius, and my best friend."

"I'm sorry."

"Oh, it was a long time ago. It lost its power to hurt me. Now I know Caprice was simply seduced by a master. She was young and not very sophisticated. Her parents were old school, and they watched over her like she was a chest of precious jewels. Unfortunately Grady was my husband, so not to be feared. I'm sure he told her that he and I had fallen out of love, that I wasn't treating him well. All the usual. I learned of the affair the same day I learned she was pregnant with his baby. Our families had been together for generations, and suddenly we were torn asunder. I divorced Grady. The circus divided assets, and we went our separate ways. Then Grady left Caprice at the altar. He didn't want her or their child any more than he'd wanted me. He had been bored and between movies. We all paid the price."

"And you hadn't seen him since?"

"No. Not even on the silver screen. Not until the night he died."

Nora's jailer tapped her wrist, signaling that we needed to wrap this up.

"What happened to Caprice?" I asked quickly. "And the baby?"

"Caprice took the child, a girl, I've heard, and moved to Italy where the Zimboni family originated. I wish I knew where she was so I could tell her I forgave her a long time ago. Everyone was damaged. For years, I'm told, the Zimbonis talked about a vendetta against Grady. But I'm sure that was only talk. They weren't violent people."

I was sure the police knew this history. And what a motive for murder, both for Nora and Caprice. But twenty-four years after the fact? That seemed a tad long to wait for just the right moment to kill him.

The jailer held up her arm, watch turned toward me. I nodded and held up one finger in plea.

"Nora, could somebody have gotten into your house and taken Yank's knife? Do you know how that could have happened?"

"I'm sure it did happen, since I didn't carry it there myself. Yank and I are so careful. It's not that we don't trust those who travel with us, but it's our job to protect them from themselves. In a moment of anger, tragedy can be averted by keeping weapons away from those who might want to settle a score. And there are children traveling with us who must be protected, too. So no, I don't know how or when it might have happened. I just know that it must have."

Our time was up. I told Nora good-bye and wished her luck. I also told her I would do whatever I could to help. Then I watched her being led away, poised, serene, and sure that all was still well.

What had I meant by those parting words? What could I do? Nothing had changed. I was still powerless. I was still an outsider in the investigation.

But something *had* changed. I had come here not knowing whether Nora Nelson had killed Grady Barber. I hadn't been sure of anything. Now I was sure that she *hadn't*. She had said she was a terrible actress. But even if she hadn't said so, I was positive she hadn't been acting today. Someone else had killed Grady, and nobody with authority was going to investigate any further.

Where exactly did that leave *me*? And wasn't that a moral dilemma worthy of even Teddy's consideration?

11

After lunch Ed left for a meeting of the local clergy. Deena, who had been as visible as a ghost since the night of Madison's party, took a sandwich to her room and mumbled that she was going through her clothes to see what no longer fit. Since that was one of the chores she had to complete before we talked about restoring privileges, I felt somewhat encouraged that our standoff would eventually end. Deena hadn't had much to say for herself after her hangover subsided, and that had continued. So far we hadn't received an apology. I suspected she was slowly processing what she had done and why, and eventually we would be able to talk about it. For now, though, silence reigned.

As good as alone, I contemplated my choices. The Idyll was over, and the remainder of the summer beckoned. Lucy had a couple of houses in mind for us to buy and flip, but the owners had inflated ideas of their worth. By late summer, if they hadn't sold to someone else, we could start negotiations. In the meantime I could run errands and carpools, clean the house from top to bottom, put lots of casseroles in the freezer while fresh vegetables were readily available. And . . . or . . . I could do just the tiniest bit of sleuthing.

Sister Nora wished that she knew what had happened to Caprice Zimboni. Me, too. That seemed harmless enough. If I stumbled on the fact that Caprice was living here in Emerald Springs under an assumed name, then that would be an *investigation*, and of course, I'd turn that piece of information right over to Roussos and back away fast. More likely I'd discover Caprice was living in Venice, cheerfully walking a tightrope over the Grand Canal, and this would simply bring peace of mind to a fine woman who was unfortunately facing murder charges.

So Caprice went on my list, but she was hardly more than an asterisk. Buy paper towels at the grocery store and caulking at the hardware store. Oh, and find Caprice. Not enough.

Roussos hadn't chosen to investigate Fred as a suspect, or at least he hadn't admitted to this. How hard would it be to simply dial Fred's cell phone myself? I had the number, of course. I even had it on speed dial thanks to Deena, my techie expert. When Fred was in town we had talked often. Was this investigating? Or simply one friend checking on another after a traumatic event?

"Checking works for me," I said, cautious Aggie talking to free-spirited Aggie, and unfortunately, doing it out loud.

I knew I was making excuses, but they were good ones, and I was proud of them. I decided to start with Fred since I didn't want to brave the Internet without somebody riding shotgun beside me. With my luck the moment I typed Italy into a search engine, I'd end up with a prepaid trip to Rome, Florence, and Sicily. One way, at that.

I got my cell phone and proudly pressed the correct key and waited. Fred didn't answer, but his voice mail did. I took no chances on skipping the message by pressing another key. I know my limits. I listened, then waited until it was my turn to speak.

"Fred, this is Aggie Sloan-Wilcox. I'm sure you've heard about Grady. I just wanted to touch base with you. Will you give me a call? I wondered what you might know about his relationship with Nora Nelson, his first wife. Any info would be appreciated." I left my number in case it had been deleted from his address book.

I actually did want to know what Fred could tell me about Nora, but even more so, I wanted to know what Fred could tell me about Fred. Of course I wasn't going to leave that part on his voice mail. I hung up and wondered if he would ever return my call. If not, I would keep trying at odd hours and hope he picked up by accident.

"Well, that took a full minute." I plopped down on our sofa and stared glumly at the fireplace. Even having a fireplace seems an abomination in this heat.

I wondered if there was anything else I could check on while I had time. After all I . . . I was running out of excuses. The desire to ease Nora's mind. Comforting Fred. Truth was, I wanted to know more. I just did. Unanswered questions bother me. Not the big, existential ones that seem to worry Ed and Teddy. But the more manageable ones I can really sink my teeth into.

Like, who killed Grady Barber and tried to pin it on Sister Nora?

My mind drifted to the evening of Grady's accident. The trooper at the scene had said something about the way Grady had grown up here. What exactly? Something about Grady's people skills being so bad because of the way he had been raised. The version I'd heard of Grady's years in Emerald Springs hadn't hinted at this. He was the product of a poor but hardworking single mother who taught her son the importance of following his dreams.

In what way would that upstanding background teach the guy poor people skills? Somehow I trusted the trooper's version more than I trusted Grady's publicist. Maybe it wasn't important which version was true, but without jetting off to Los Angeles or the scenes of the other shows had judged, this was something I could check out in my spare time. And what better place to start than with Veronica, his childhood friend?

I had receipts and bills I needed to be reimbursed for, and some lists that would help Veronica as she worked her way through the remaining Idyll paperwork. As soon as Ed came home to make sure Deena didn't get a tattoo or run

off and join a motorcycle gang, I had the perfect excuse to
visit Emerald Estates.

✦ ✦ ✦

At four o'clock I knocked on the Hayworths' door. I hadn't
spoken to Veronica since the night of Grady's death, although I had heard she was planning a memorial service at
her own church in a week or two. I was beyond relieved
that Ed wouldn't have to do *that* eulogy.

Just before my knees gave way, Winona answered the
door. She looked tired, but not as grim as usual. She almost
seemed glad to see me.

"I was afraid you were a reporter," she said.

All the local Ohio newspapers and television stations had
sent crews to dig up whatever they could, but luckily their
enthusiasm had fallen short of a media blitz. A couple of
news programs had offered me a moment of fame on camera
if I would tell them about finding Grady's body. I had refused, as had everyone with real information. Instead, only
people who knew absolutely nothing had been recorded
for posterity. Passersby with strong opinions, people who
knew people who had once crossed our city limits. I hoped
the hubbub would die quickly. Grady just hadn't been
enough of a star to keep the news in play until a trial.

"The media's been after me, too." I held up the folder of
papers I'd brought. "Is Veronica in? These are leftovers
from the Idyll."

"I can give them to her."

I held on tight. "She's not home?"

"She's not seeing anybody." Maybe Winona read the dis-
appointment in my expression, or maybe her own defenses
were lower, because she explained. "She's upset. Still. She
says she's not fit company."

"Their friendship went back a long way."

Winona didn't say anything, which I'd come to expect.
But just as I was about to give in and hand over the papers,
she spoke.

"You know, I went to school with him, too. The three of us were there together."

This surprised me. "Part of my reason for showing up today was to see what I could find out about his years here."

"Why?"

This didn't seem like the best time for that truth, whole truth thingie. Instead I gave her a sliver. "I guess I'm trying to make sense of it, you know? It's like putting a jigsaw puzzle together, and until I feel like I have a picture in my head to work on, it's just a bunch of pieces."

"You did a lot of work up close with him, didn't you?"

I gave a short nod.

"Did he ever mention me?"

"Honestly? He never mentioned anybody in this whole town. Not to me. I don't think he even said anything about Veronica. But the other night somebody else mentioned his years here. A man who went to school with you, a state trooper?"

She smiled a little. "That would be Hal Jorgensen. Big guy?"

"Savvy, too."

"What did he say?"

"Let's just say Grady wasn't at his best when he and Hal were, *ummm* . . . reintroduced. Hal told me that considering the way Grady had been raised, his lack of people skills made sense."

This time she laughed. I was surprised at the way laughter changed her face. Different clothes, lose the headband, and Winona would be a pretty woman.

"That's Hal all right," she said. "Straight to the point."

"Would you know what he meant?"

She propped a shoulder against the doorframe now, more relaxed than I'd ever seen her. "Grady and I grew up in Weezeltown. Not far from the button factory. You know Weezeltown?"

"Enough." There were plenty of poor but honest folks in Weezeltown, the least attractive section of our fair city.

There were also plenty of people who didn't fit into either of those categories. Weezeltown was not the community of choice for raising children.

Winona looked over my shoulder as if she were seeing a different time and place. "Veronica grew up on the other side of town in a house with five bedrooms and a live-in housekeeper. On her sixteenth birthday her father gave her a red convertible. Her mother and her mother's bridge club used to bring discarded clothing and toys to be distributed to the needy in my neighborhood. I probably wore some of Veronica's old skirts and blouses to school, and felt lucky to have them."

"And Grady?"

"I doubt Grady's mother bothered picking through hand-me-downs. He wore his clothes until they fell apart. His mother worked as a cocktail waitress at a seedy bar downtown and probably drank up a lot of her tips, so she was gone all night and slept all day. Not alone most of the time, either. Grady was left to raise himself. I remember winter afternoons when he had noplace to go, and he'd come to our house just to get warm. His mother would lock him out, her idea of not corrupting his morals, I guess, if she had a boyfriend staying over."

I felt a flash of pity. "So his life was tougher than we were led to believe."

"Not nearly as picturesque, that's for sure. He got through it by dreaming about leaving Emerald Springs. Of course none of us thought he'd ever make it. Maybe if he'd spent his time studying, so his grades improved, but Grady was too busy dreaming. I used to help him study, and it was like everything we'd learned from homework hadn't penetrated. He wasn't stupid. Not by a long shot. If we studied together, he could pick up enough of what he needed to pass. But grades didn't mean a thing to him."

"So you were that close? He came to you for help?"

"We were friends. He used to talk about his plans for the future, about being a star, about having a fancy house and a

Corvette. He always said the day he was able to buy a Corvette was the day he would know life was worth living."

"I never heard any of this."

"Oh, you wouldn't. In his own way he was very private. I'm not sure that many people knew how bad things were at home. I think most of them probably thought he was lazy and just didn't care. I read his autobiography, and none of what I'm telling you was there, either. I wouldn't be surprised if he blocked it out and started to believe his publicist's lies."

"Autobiography?"

"Yes, it came out a few years ago. But it was hard to find. Not much call for it. I'm surprised it wasn't reissued after 'Think of Me in April' became such a hit."

I wasn't sure which was more surprising. Winona's sudden chattiness, or the fact that there was an autobiography of Grady where I could get all the information I needed.

"It must have been strange to have him back here," I said. "I hope you had some time to catch up with him before . . ." I didn't know how to finish.

"No, Grady was much too important to bother with me."

From her tone I knew that she meant Grady had *thought* himself too important. I was sorry his general hostility had extended to old friends.

"I did ask him if he ever got the Corvette," she said, just the shadow of a smile playing on her narrow lips. "He said if I knew anything, I'd know Corvettes were so yesterday. I told him that under the circumstances, then, a Corvette seemed like an absolutely perfect choice for him."

✦ ✦ ✦

We had homemade pizza heaped with mushrooms, fresh tomatoes, and mozzarella from a local farm. Teddy and Ed made a salad, and Deena silently sliced lemons and poured iced tea. Very soon I thought we might digress to taking bets on when she would finally begin to communicate with us again.

After we say grace we always talk about our days over dinner. No matter where my own family was, or what was going on, or who happened to be traveling with us, Junie had always made sure we sat down as a family and had dinner together. I've carried on that tradition, although nobody's required to talk.

Teddy told us about her bicycle theft movie, which had been harder to shoot than she'd thought. The boys had acted stupid and hadn't followed the script. Had Ed not been there, I would have explained how much more mature girls are at her age than boys, but that seemed impolite.

Ed suggested that maybe the boys didn't like being told what to do and ought to have some say in the script. Mars and Venus in eternal battle.

Ed had already told me about his clergy meeting. Now he regaled us with research for his next sermon about Jewish mysticism. He saves his most esoteric subjects for summer when church attendance is lower. I had to drop my silverware a few times to keep the girls awake.

"I hope I'm not in that one," Deena muttered.

"Not unless you've take up study of the Kabbalah," Ed said without flinching. "Then I might ask your advice."

His calm and his answer won points from me. Most fathers would have overreacted, but Ed had already apologized for his mistake and knew the rest was up to Deena. He wasn't going to wrangle with her indefinitely.

Nevertheless I jumped in, just in case things deteriorated. "I didn't do much. I did some errands, checked out a few things . . ." Why had I said that?

"Relating to Grady Barber," Ed said, reaching for the pizza platter and offering it to us before he took another slice. "I wondered how long it would take you to get started."

I chewed slowly, considering my next words. "I can imagine that starting at all doesn't please you."

"You please me." He looked up and our eyes met. "The way you are, not the way I sometimes wish you were."

"Less curious?"

He shrugged. "Less likely to put yourself in harm's way. But I appreciate that sitting by and watching an innocent woman languish in jail is completely against your nature."

I felt a weight drop off my shoulders. I'd been resisting the inevitable, as much for my family as for myself. "I'm just looking into a few things. I'll be careful."

"We'd all appreciate that."

The girls did the dishes. I heard lowered voices in the kitchen. Deena was speaking to Teddy, but I hoped that didn't mean poor Teddy would continue to feel she was in the middle. Family dynamics give me a headache.

Teddy finished her portion and went up to her room to work on the screenplay. I had a feeling that despite Ed's suggestion, the boys might find themselves playing bit parts in the newer version. When Deena started to follow a minute later, I stopped her.

"I need some help on the Internet. Do you have a little time?"

"Other people's mothers can turn on a computer and move the mouse by themselves."

"I like to think of myself as the reincarnation of some pure but possibly primitive being too spiritually advanced to use technology."

"You are too weird."

"That won't be the only time you'll say that."

She looked torn. Deena was staging her own version of a sit-down strike. Helping me didn't fit into her plans.

"Do I have to?" she asked.

"Nope. It would be kind if you did, though. A favor to the woman who labored for fourteen hours to bring you into the world."

"That's gross."

"After the first thirteen hours I thought so, too. But really, most of the time, I think it was worth it."

She rolled her eyes, and she's getting quite adept at it. Just a few years ago she was a beautiful child, all peaches and cream complexion, strawberry blonde hair, big blue eyes. Now she was turning into a woman, face and body changing composition, complexion not always as perfect. Inside she was changing, too, her heart and brain sometimes at war, her hormones flourishing. I knew she had to find her way without us leading her by the hand. I only hoped she could still reach out when she needed us.

"I could try on my own, I guess," I said. "I just hope I don't reinvest your college fund in junk bonds."

"Let's go."

Once we were seated and the computer was safely on, I told her what I was looking for. "The woman's name is Caprice Zimboni. She used to be in a circus. She walked a tightrope. The last I know she and an infant daughter were living in Italy, but that was over twenty years ago. I'd like to see where she is now and what she's doing."

Normally Deena would ask why. Now she simply went to her favorite search engine and asked me how to spell Caprice's name.

"When was the last time you checked your e-mail?" she said, as she waited for the computer to spit out results.

"Last November. Your aunt Sid sent me an article about flipping houses." Okay, I'm not a good candidate for an e-mail account. I worry about every piece of mail. I mean, what if I did win a lottery in the Netherlands, or what if some man in Zimbabwe really is my long-lost uncle and left me a million dollars, and I've sent my only chance at lasting wealth into our spam folder?

Deena did the math. "That was eight months ago."

"Your aunt gave up on me. Now she goes to the post office or calls and reads me stuff over the phone."

"That's pathetic."

How could I fault her for telling the truth? "Let's check these sites."

Deena reads quickly. She scanned the first few, then ignored them. "These are bogus. And this third one will find her if you pay them for information. Only you won't know if what they have is any help until you've sent them the money."

"How do you know all this stuff?"

"Everybody knows it."

She clicked on the fourth result on the list as I contemplated being the only person in the entire world who *hadn't* known.

When the website came up, we both read through it. It was an informal history of aerialists, and the Zimboni family was mentioned, along with names of family members who had been renowned for their prowess. Caprice appeared with nothing else about her. The website mentioned the Nelson–Zimboni circus and stated that when the split occurred, most of the Zimboni acts had just been absorbed into other circuses.

Five more results and I was getting discouraged, even though there were pages and pages left to go. "Don't the most likely sites come up high on the list?"

"Not always. Advertisers pay for that, too. But we're at the real sites now. I can add a few more words to filter stuff, but sometimes you miss the good things that way."

"Why don't we add 'daughter' and see if that helps."

"You don't know her name?"

"No idea."

She added "daughter" and for good measure "Italy." Then we waited a moment for the new results.

"Italy wasn't a great idea," she said. "A lot of these are in Italian."

"Believe it or not, I can make out what they say."

"You speak Italian?"

"No, but I can read it pretty well." Too many years in graduate school and nothing much else to show for it.

"That's cool."

I basked in the unexpected approval. "Click on this one," I told her, pointing to the fifth result. She did and the website came up. Unfortunately "O Sole Mio" was playing in the background.

"I hate it when sites have music," Deena said. "Try sneaking on the Internet when you're not supposed to. Then suddenly there's loud music."

"I haven't personally had that experience."

"It happened to me once at school."

What kind of sites had Deena been checking? Were they playing stripper music in the background? I got cold chills.

"Oh, don't worry," she said, reading my mind. "I was trying to play a word game, that's all. I was supposed to be researching a term paper on a school computer. I don't go to *those* kind of sites." She glanced at me. "Just because I did something I wasn't supposed to one time, and you caught me, doesn't mean that now I'm going to wallow in online porn."

"Well, that's good to hear."

"It's demeaning to women."

"Indeed."

"I still have principles."

"I'm glad to hear it."

"You probably made a mistake or two along the way yourself."

"Some corkers."

She waited for me to explain, but she would have to wait a very long time for that. I believe in sharing my feelings with my children, but not necessarily sharing every stupid thing I ever did. I don't want to give them ideas.

"If you made mistakes, then why are you being so hard on me?" she demanded.

"Because you haven't learned anything from your father's good example."

"And what was that? That I should stand up in front of an audience and embarrass somebody I love?"

I struggled to be calm, despite the taunt. "No, that if you make a mistake, you apologize before you move on. You're stuck at the apology, Deena. And it's an important thing to learn."

"You and Daddy always talk like you're giving sermons."

I sat back. "That would be a good sermon," I said carefully. "Forgive us our trespasses as we forgive those who trespass against us. But I think somebody else beat your daddy to that one."

"I wish Daddy sold cars."

"If he did, he'd give you a great deal when you turn sixteen. Because you know, he absolutely adores you."

I hit home with that one. She looked away.

I focused on the computer screen and began to read to myself. "Listen to this," I said at last, translating for her. "This is a website for the town of Siena in Tuscany. Somebody had a good-bye party in the Campo—that's a big square in the center of the historic district—for Caprice Zimboni and her daughter, Felice, because they were moving to Michigan." I looked up at the top for a date. "Two years ago."

"Let's take out Italy and put in Michigan," she said, going back to the search engine and making the alterations.

The very first result was exactly what I needed. Deena clicked on it, and a newspaper article from a Michigan weekly came on the screen. The article was dated May thirteenth of this year. For the second summer, Caprice Zimboni would be working with troubled teens in a program called Performing for Life based in a suburb outside Detroit. With the help of several charitable foundations, she and six other instructors had assembled a small circus and would teach performance as well as the nuts and bolts of putting on a show, skills designed to build self-esteem and give the kids business experience. There were testimonials, a glowing report of the first show of the season, and a blurry photo of a young woman walking a tightrope. Beneath it was the caption "Felice Zimboni, of the famous Zimboni circus family, teaches the art of the highwire."

Grady's *daughter*, Felice.

"Bingo," I said. "One day's drive."

"What do you mean?"

"Can you print this for me?"

The eyes rolled again. "You mean turn on the printer and press Print?"

"I'd appreciate it."

She turned on the printer and let it warm up. "Are you taking Teddy to visit this circus or something?"

"Just the opposite. I need to figure out if this particular circus ever visited Emerald Springs." I stood and kissed the top of her head. "Thanks for your help."

"Maybe someday you'll learn to do this yourself."

"Don't count on it." I was glad I hadn't tried today. I thought I would remain computer challenged just as long as I needed an excuse to spend time with my daughters.

12

On Wednesday morning Teddy and Ed happily went off to a father–daughter softball game organized by our parks department. Deena went out to the old detached garage at the back of the parsonage property to sweep and organize the contents, although unfortunately I can't say *she* went happily. I stayed inside to try Fred again—no luck—and chop farmer's market vegetables for a chunky marinara sauce to simmer in the slow cooker. Vegetarians are happiest when tomatoes are in season, but this year because of the drought, everything cost a fortune.

I was just finishing the last of the Japanese eggplant when our doorbell rang. I rinsed my hands, then dried them as I went to answer it. I suspected this might be another bushel basket of zucchini. Despite the drought and heat, this had been a bumper year. If Nora's right and global warming persists, life as we know it might end, but the planet will never lack for zucchini or cockroaches.

I opened the door to find Veronica. She had dressed down for this occasion, assuming, I suspect, that wearing designer duds to my doorstep might be a tad assertive. The black jeans and zebra-striped T-shirt probably hadn't set her back the equivalent of a month of Ed's salary. I silently applauded her tact.

"I brought you a check." She held it out until I took it. "I didn't want to make you wait."

Since local mail delivery takes only a day, I knew there had to be more to this visit. I opened the door wider.

"I just finished my morning project. Why don't we have a cup of coffee? I've got home-baked bread to go with it."

She stepped right in, as if she'd hoped I'd ask. "I just had breakfast, so I'll skip the bread. You bake your own?"

"Sometimes. When I have time." And when I need something to punch.

"Then you weren't baking it a few weeks ago."

"My girls were happily gorging on Wonder Bread."

She followed me back. I waved her to the table, which bisects the impossibly large room. I can only assume the first residents of this house had twelve children.

"I'll make a fresh pot," I said. "I'm ready for another cup myself."

Veronica looked around, and I imagined she saw the stark contrast between her designer mansion and the parsonage, which is simply decorated with imagination, furniture we've purchased through the years, and the hand-me-downs Ed fondly calls Early Unitarian. Still, I'm perfectly happy with the way things look. Junie made every apartment, house, or trailer I lived in as a child feel like home, and she taught me well.

"This is really cute," Veronica said. "I feel wrapped in warmth."

"We don't have air-conditioning."

"Well, that, too, but that's not what I mean. It feels homey, like a place where people want to spend time. No matter how many times I redecorate our house, I never get that feeling."

"I like your house. You've done some beautiful things with it."

"It is what it is. When I'm bored, I redecorate. I watched my mother do the same thing. She put up new window treatments, bought new furniture, played bridge, lunched at the country club, drank martinis, and at the end of the day she went to bed as bored as she'd been when she woke up. Nobody could understand why she was so calm when she learned she was terminally ill a few years ago, but I did."

"Wow."

"I'm sorry. I seem to be saying a lot of things these days before they get a chance to pass through my good-sense filter."

She had come to talk. Now I understood, even though I was surprised she'd chosen me. Maybe because I wasn't part of her regular circle, and she could be frank.

"You don't need to apologize," I said. "It's just kind of a bleak portrait. Did your mother ever consider going to school or getting a job?"

"Job?" She sounded incredulous. "Sanderson women specialize in fluffy little lives. It's what we know best, and Mother did it with determination and goodwill. Unfortunately I want to be more than that. I want to use my position in the community to *help* the community. It's important to make a contribution."

I set about making the coffee while Veronica put her purse on one chair and picked out another for herself. "There was nothing fluffy about the Idyll," I said, when I'd finished. "At least not the reason for having it. Women have been in charge of raising money and funding important projects for centuries. I hope you're proud of what you tried to do."

"Tried to do. Yes."

I rested my back against the counter and folded my arms as I waited for the pot to fill. "Veronica, it wasn't your fault. Nobody can possibly hold you responsible for what happened."

"Do you know how much money we have to return to ticket holders? And I just found out we have to pay Grady's estate about 65 percent of his fee. If he'd left on his own, we would have been free and clear. But nobody can argue that he wanted to be murdered."

"I guess not."

"When the books are balanced, we'll have very little for

the new pediatric unit. We'll have to start all over with a brand-new idea." She shook her head. "And I'm not feeling all that creative. How about you?"

What I was feeling was exhaustion. I couldn't imagine starting all this again. The pediatric unit was every bit as important as it had been, but I hoped the hospital found a different way to fund it. Robbing a bank sounded preferable to another Idyll.

"How are you doing otherwise?" I asked. "You knew Grady for a long time. He was an old friend. That wasn't true for most of us."

"I guess I'm in shock."

Veronica didn't say anything else until I'd poured coffee and brought it to the table along with a pitcher of half-and-half.

She accepted her cup with a wan smile. "I keep asking myself if I hadn't pushed the committee to bring him here, would he still be alive."

"You can't blame yourself. He was murdered. Whoever did it might have tracked him down anywhere."

"Whoever? You don't think it was Nora Nelson?"

I might be coming to terms with being an amateur detective again, but I wasn't sure I wanted to acquaint the world with my decision. I answered as carefully as I could. "There seem to be a lot of questions that haven't been answered."

"But the knife that killed him was from a collection in her house."

"True. But that collection hangs on the wall in plain sight. I've seen it. If the door was unlocked for even a minute or two, anybody could have taken the murder weapon. I bet if the police had looked harder, they would have found flaws in Nora's security system."

She lifted a brow, as if she thought I was reaching when there was no need. I suppose I'll be getting a lot of that if I talk openly about my doubts.

"It sounds like you're friends with this woman."

"We've met. I can't imagine her killing anybody."

"I don't know . . . She was seen backstage. Those horrible letters on the wall . . ."

"Yes, well there's a lot going against her, that's for sure."

She managed a smile. "Am I right in assuming you're not going to let this rest?"

"What makes you think that?"

"Nonie says you were asking about Grady."

"Nonie?"

"My housekeeper. She goes by Winona now, Winona Unger. But she was Nonie Wysocki when we were in school together."

I filed away Winona's last name, just in case. I was glad the subject was moving away from me and my doubts about the murderer. "I was just trying to reconcile what the state trooper said about Grady's family life on the night of the accident."

"I'm sure Nonie told you that the truth wasn't anything he would have enjoyed recounting to the media."

"It sounds like he had a lot to overcome."

"Kids can be cruel, and from kindergarten on Grady was something of a misfit. I didn't know him until high school. Then we were in choir and later drama club together. I hate to say this, but back then I was part of what they called the in crowd. And Grady, of course, wasn't. My friends either ridiculed or pitied him. But they were blind to his talents. I saw what he had to offer."

Over the rim of her coffee cup, I saw her eyes mist with tears. "I hated that he was teased so much, so I tried to befriend him. The music department put on *Oklahoma* in our sophomore year, and I made him try out for the part of Curly, even though sophomores never won the leads. He got it, though. He had the best voice in school, and he could act, too. And I got the part of Laurie, even though my voice was nothing special."

"Are you saying you were a couple?"

She laughed a little and wiped her eyes with a fingertip. "Goodness, no. I wasn't *that* much of a do-gooder. I had a reputation to maintain. I was just a friend. I cheered him on. Besides, he already had a girlfriend. Nonie."

"Nonie said they were *friends*." I tried to remember if she'd said "just" friends.

"Oh, they were more than that. They were always together. But when he won the role of Idan in *Wayfarers*, he never looked back. He left Emerald Springs, and that was that. He dropped poor Nonie, and she was crushed. Up until then she'd been a top student, on her way to a full scholarship somewhere. After Grady disappeared she just stopped caring, and her grades plummeted. She didn't even apply for college. When she graduated, she stayed in Emerald Springs and took one menial job after another. After I got married I hired her as my housekeeper because I felt sorry for her. I guess I was on my way to being a professional dogooder even then."

"Part of your charity work?"

She looked chagrined. "No, I'm sorry it sounded that way. Nonie was a great choice, but the personal stuff gets sticky after a while. After shoring up Grady, then Nonie, I moved on to wider interests. Eventually I ended up on the national board of A Hospital for Every Child. We work with communities all over the country to develop better pediatric facilities. I'll be leaving for our semiannual meeting before Grady's memorial service, which is why it's been scheduled so late. Maybe Santa Barbara will be cooler than Emerald Springs."

"No wonder the hospital here was such a priority for you."

"Farley and I weren't able to have children of our own. I want other people's children to have the best treatment available."

This was a more human side of Veronica, and I liked her better. "Not such a fluffy little life. It sounds like you're doing a lot to make a difference."

"You know what they say. Bloom where you're planted. And I seem to be planted here for good."

"Maybe that's not so bad. Grady got out of town, but I don't think he was a happy man."

"His life certainly didn't turn out as well as I'd hoped." She finished her coffee and looked at her watch. "Neither did he, for that matter. I know how much trouble he caused you. I'm sorry that's the person he turned into, quarrelsome, demanding, difficult. But I'm sorry he died, too."

"Especially here and now?"

She nodded ruefully. "Especially here. If this had happened somewhere else, he would have been a footnote to Emerald Springs history. Remembered for his roots, his remarkable success. Now he'll be remembered for being our very own murder victim."

"I'm sorry, too. That he died at all. That he did it on our watch. That we're expected to pay 65 percent of his fee . . ."

"That the circumstances are suspicious?"

"Call me eternally curious."

She got to her feet and picked up her purse. I walked her to the door.

She paused at my threshold. "Just be careful, okay? If Nora Nelson's not the murderer, that means the real one's still on the loose." She paused. "But quite honestly, I think you're perfectly safe."

"Because the murderer's already in jail."

"Too many coincidences otherwise."

"You're certainly in the majority."

She held out her hand. "You'll be at Grady's service?"

I knew better than to say no. "I'll see you there."

"We need to put him to rest and move on."

But as I watched her walk to her car, I wondered how possible that was going to be. Growing up here, Grady Barber might have been a loner and a misfit, but now he would cast one of the longest shadows ever seen in our fair city.

+ + +

The moment Nonie had told me about Grady's autobiography, I'd called Book Gems, the local bookstore where I had once been employed, and asked them to find and order it. Today, after Teddy and Ed returned victorious, I decided to run into town and see if the book had arrived. Instead, just as I was gathering my keys, the store called to tell me the book was out of print and no longer available. I'd have to look for a used copy or try the library. I decided to start with the latter.

The Emerald Springs Library is small and cozy, with that old-book smell that seems to be missing in the most modern versions. I missed having a preschooler young enough for story hour, so I could sit and watch the children's librarian perform the magic trick of turning a child into a lover of books.

I missed having the time to thumb through the jokes in *Reader's Digest*.

Since our library has replaced the card catalog with a computer, I went to the desk and told the bespectacled woman behind it what I was looking for.

"You're kidding, right?" she asked. "*Sailing toward a Rainbow*?"

"There's a waiting list?"

"We had one copy. Somebody stole it. I'm sure it'll show up on eBay. The autobiography of Grady Barber from the library in the town where he died. That will jack up the price."

"Yuck."

She shrugged, as if to say that was the way of the world.

"Why just one copy?" I asked. "He was a local celebrity."

"We probably started with more, but when there's no demand for a book, it's donated to our book sale in the spring. Too bad we didn't know—" She paused. "It would be in demand," she finished.

Too bad we didn't know he was going to die.

I was disappointed. Thanks to Veronica and Nonie, I knew something about Grady's years in Emerald Springs. I wanted to know more about the later years, too, even if Grady's book was probably a gross exaggeration. Still, it would give me a place to start.

Somebody tapped me on the shoulder, and I turned, expecting to be told to move on, since it seemed like that kind of day. But the woman behind me had a friendly face.

"Esther." I gave our church organist a quick hug. "Hiding out in the air-conditioning?"

Esther, more energetic in her midseventies than most twentysomethings, pretended to fan herself with her hand. "I have a route. If the parsonage had air-conditioning, I would be visiting you regularly."

"That's a reason to ask the church board for window units."

The woman behind us cleared her throat, and I apologized and stepped aside. Esther went with me and gave up her place in line.

"I heard what you were asking for," Esther said.

I tried to think of a good excuse. I was stumped.

"You wouldn't be the first," Esther said when I didn't explain. "I think we're all a lot more curious about Grady Barber than we were before this happened."

"I spent so much time with him. I'm hoping the book will give me a more pleasant perspective."

"I heard he was a handful."

Esther was one of the helpful women who had gotten me into this mess in the first place. I couldn't hold it against her, though. Like Sally Berrigan, Esther had just wanted to keep me busy.

"You're smiling," Esther said.

I told her what I was thinking. "You got me into the Idyll, you and the others, to keep me out of trouble, didn't you?"

She smiled, too. "If that was our reason, it certainly didn't work. But that wasn't the reason. Why did you think so?"

"I have this wee history . . ."

"No, you just seemed at loose ends. We thought we'd put your talents for solving problems and finding answers to good use until something better—or worse—came along."

That was a much nicer slant. I told her so.

"I'll find you a copy of the book," Esther said.

"Really? You have one somewhere?"

"No, but I'll find one."

She would, too. Esther was a treasure hunter-and-gatherer. She had the gift of finding things of value in places no one else would look. Apparently this extended to Grady's autobiography.

"That would be great." I started to say good-bye, so she could get back in line, when I thought of something else. "By the way, did you know Grady personally? I know you taught piano before you retired, and I know he sang in the school choir. Did your paths ever cross?"

"As a matter of fact, they did. One of my students played the piano for him. There was some kind of concert, I think, and she accompanied him during a solo. I remember he came to her lesson, so I could give pointers. He had a voice like an angel. Very memorable."

"Who was your student?"

"I can't recall. Over the years I had half a dozen or more who played for the school choir. I can't remember which one it was, but maybe I will if I think about it."

I thanked her and gave her another hug before we parted.

I wasn't done with church folks, though. Since they tend to pop up out of nowhere, I always try to be on my best behavior in public, or else slink around in the shadows. Sometimes both are easier said than done. Luckily this particular church member was somebody I did want to see, so I carefully placed myself in her path.

"Tammy . . ."

Tammy Sargent looked up from the magazine shelves on the other side of the librarian's desk. She didn't smile, and she didn't look all that happy to see me, but she did nod. "Aggie. I was just looking for something new to make for dinner."

I'd already seen she was clutching *People* magazine and *Us*, which aren't magazines I consult for their recipes. She was looking for details about Grady's murder. I carefully didn't glance at the magazines as she set them down again.

I lowered my voice. "I wanted to say I'm so glad Madison was late on Friday night. I'm happy she wasn't there when everything happened."

"We were in a mess. She was getting a final fitting on her costume, and a seam ripped as we were going out the door. So poor Madison was standing there wrapped in a towel while our seamstress tried to fix it, and the clock ticked and ticked. She was frantic."

Tammy had been talking rapidly, but she came to a sudden halt. Her shoulders drooped. "I guess it was all meant to be. It spared my poor daughter that awful scene."

"You had a seamstress working on her costume? What a good idea. My mother knows everybody in town who can thread a needle. Maybe she knows her." I looked expectant.

Tammy hesitated. "Sue Grossman. Over on Eagle Street."

"I guess I'll never need her with Junie in town, anyway."

"I heard *you* found him."

I nodded. "I went to get Grady just before he was supposed to go out onstage. Somebody else had been there first."

"Somebody else? You mean Nora Nelson."

This was not a subject I wanted to debate for the second time that day. I lowered my voice still more. "Tammy, Ed can find the name of a good counselor to help Madison process everything that's happened. I'm sure the whole thing has been—"

"We don't need anybody else. She's got me. Don't you think I can handle this? Grady Barber's dead, and Madison just has to move on. Case closed."

I wondered why Tammy was so defensive again. What exactly was she afraid that Madison might say to somebody? And had she sounded just a shade too happy Grady was history, or was that my imagination?

I tried to pacify her. "We all need help sometimes. This parenting thing is harder than I ever thought it would be, and I've got Ed. I just thought you might like somebody to share that burden. You haven't really had that."

"And Madison's turned out just fine."

"That's not in question."

"You and Ed don't think I know what I'm doing. This isn't the first time this has come up, and it's worse now because of that party."

I apologized, although I wasn't quite sure for what. "I was trying to lend a hand at a tough time. In no way was I implying you're not a good mother."

"Great. For once, just stay out of whatever doesn't concern you."

Sometimes the best thing to say is nothing. I watched her stomp away, and I hoped that Madison really had been having her costume pieced together while Grady lay dying on the green room floor. Because if this scenario was an out-and-out lie, then I had to tell Roussos. And fingering a member of our congregation as a murder suspect was as good as asking the church board to fire my husband.

13

On Thursday, Feeling Quilty was feeling the heat. Except for those quilters without air-conditioning, shopping was low on agendas, and the store was almost empty. Those who did drag themselves in were less enthused than usual.

"After this heat wave nobody believes they'll ever have use for a quilt again," Junie said. "I'm offering a class on home-dec sewing. People still believe in place mats and pillow shams."

We were down in the basement, and I was helping Junie dust and straighten. Not because the classroom area really needed it, but because this was a cooler place to chat than the backyard or porch. By nine AM the thermometer had hit ninety, and by ten thirty the temperature had climbed two degrees. We were rumored to reach triple digits tomorrow.

"Surely we'll get some rain soon and cooler temperatures," I said.

"Tempers are short. Yesterday I separated two women who were about to come to blows over the last yard of fabric on a bolt. I had to promise I'd special order more and give it to them at a bargain."

Even in the basement I still felt too hot for beating around the bush. "It's always nice to see you, but I do have another reason to be here. Do you know a woman named Sue Grossman? She's a professional seamstress. She does alterations, tailoring, makes clothes to order." I had looked Sue Grossman up in the phone book, so I knew Tammy had been telling that much of the truth.

"Sue's in here every once in a while. She might teach a dressmaking class in the fall."

Encouraged, I told Junie what Tammy had said about being at Sue's house the night Grady died. "I need to find out if she really was," I finished. "I could ask her myself, but I doubt she'd tell a stranger something like that."

"Oh, you want me to help you get Nora out of jail." Junie looked thrilled.

I held up a hand. "I'm not sure I'd go that far. But I'm trying to figure out who else might have murdered Grady. The police aren't going to look any further. They're perfectly happy just to say a suspect's in custody."

"I can talk to Sue." Junie's eyes were glowing. "I wonder what I should wear?"

"Please, no Sherlock outfits, okay? Just talk about other things, then slip in the subject of Grady, and maybe mention Madison. Say you understand Madison had a costume problem the night Grady died, and Sue tried to fix it. Maybe what a good thing it was that Madison wasn't there when Grady's body was found."

"I'll work on my lines. This is exciting."

I had a twinge of doubt. My mother's terrific, but I wasn't sure I should have enlisted her help. Junie's lines might go something like: "Were the Sargents with you on Friday night when Grady Barber was murdered? Because, you know, if they weren't, they probably murdered him."

My cell phone rang before I could repeat that this was really a simple thing, and she should approach it simply.

I opened my phone and put it to my ear. This much I can manage.

"Aggie? I just heard about Grady." The line crackled, but the voice was unmistakable.

Fred! I pointed to the entrance to signal I was taking the call outside and headed there while I greeted him, hoping the reception would be better.

Outdoors the heat was smothering, and I rested against the side of the house where there was a couple of feet of shade. "Thanks for getting back to me. Where have you been that you just heard? It was all over the news."

"Not where I was. I've been at a retreat center in Big Sur. When they say retreat, they mean retreat. No phones. No newspapers or connections with the outside world. I needed to get my head together. I went straight there from Emerald Springs."

This would be easy enough to check, but I was inclined to believe him. Plenty of time had passed since my first phone message, and Fred could well have invented a better scenario if he'd needed one.

"Sounds like a place I need to go," I said. "What's the name of it?"

"The Enlightenment Center, just south of Carmel. I'd say you need a day there for every three you spent with Grady. What in the heck happened? His ex-wife murdered him? Nora Nelson was the only one in the bunch who wasn't after him. I should know."

"What do you mean?"

Fred sounded happy to be gossiping again. "He was married twice more after Nora and lived with another woman long enough that she got common-law status. Nora was the only one who wasn't constantly dunning him for more money. I don't think he ever paid her a cent. I never spoke to her or communicated with her in any way. She was well and truly out of Grady's life."

"I'm having trouble believing she did it."

He must have realized he was a suspect, but Fred didn't sound the least offended. "Well, it wasn't me. I can see why you might wonder, but my story'll check out. So who else is on your list?"

"There was a man backstage that night, fighting with Grady. I caught the end of it. He looked a little familiar, but I can't remember where I saw him the first time. Tall, dark haired, a little older than I am maybe. Thin. He was dressed casually. I know that's pretty vague."

"Could you have seen him at the welcome party?"

"I don't think—"

"As the police chief was evicting him?"

"Oh!" That was exactly where I'd seen the guy. I'd only glimpsed him on Veronica's porch, which was why I hadn't been able to place him. Still, the circumstances should have alerted me. I was chagrined.

"His name's Rob Taylor," Fred said. "Remember when Grady jumped all over me that evening because I wasn't at his beck and call the moment he arrived? I couldn't tell him in front of you, but I'd been out on the street trying to deal with Taylor. I followed the guy after the chief sent him away. He was fit to be tied."

"What's his story? And where can he be found?"

"His wife was a contestant in an event like your Idyll, only in Pittsburgh. He's from some little town north of there. Zelienople I think. She was talented. A country, soft rock voice and repertoire. Pretty, too. Grady was taken with her, too taken with her, if you catch my drift."

"The way he was too taken with Madison Sargent?"

"I'm sorry. I hoped that wasn't the case."

"I don't know for sure, but I'm afraid it was."

"Grady just never caught on. I did a lot of damage control. I don't know why I put up with him so long. The money was great, and every time I would threaten to leave, his manager and accountant came up with more. I got greedy. I just kept milking the cash cow and ignoring my beef with him."

"The Enlightenment Center probably serves a vegetarian diet, right? You're fixating."

"I'm starving. I'm on my way to get a steak. Anyway, Taylor's wife told him what was going on, and he came after Grady. He was ready to kill him. Grady denied it all, of course, and what proof did she have? Grady said she was blackmailing *him*, making up stories so he would be forced to declare her the winner. But Taylor was smarter than some of the others in the same situation. He started tracing Grady's steps, going back to towns where he'd been and interviewing contestants. He compiled a list of women Grady had come on to. A couple of those who had succumbed even said Grady had videotaped them together, and he was holding that over them."

"That's beneath contempt."

"Yeah, he was a scumbag. I never saw any tapes, although I do know he had a camera set up in the bedroom of his house out here. I came across it once when I was looking for something he'd sent me to fetch. He said it was just for fun, that he and his last wife had enjoyed taping themselves and playing back the tapes when they got bored. I guess that should have been enough of a clue, huh? Anyway, I never saw irrefutable proof Taylor wasn't making up at least some of his story to get even. I do know Grady had affairs with contestants, and broke a few hearts along the way. But I wasn't there. I didn't know who initiated what. So I just ignored what I could and went on until I couldn't go on anymore."

"What did the two of you fight about that last day? The day he fired you or you quit. Whichever."

"Rob Taylor had gone to Veronica Hayworth, but she tossed him out and said he was just trying to destroy a good man's reputation."

I tried to put myself in Veronica's position. Childhood friend. The reputation of our fund-raiser in jeopardy. No good way to verify Taylor's claims without hiring an investigator. Still, had she done anything to protect the Idyll contestants, just in case? I wondered if she had spoken to Grady and asked for his version. I bet she had, and I bet she'd been snowed by his response.

"And you fought *why*?" I asked.

"When I got to his room that last morning, I found a purse."

"Madison's?"

"No, Julia's."

Julia, the folk singer.

Fred went on. "I told him this had to stop, that I wasn't

going to do any more damage control with contestants, no matter how much he paid me. I reminded him Rob Taylor was after him, and all the guy needed was more proof. Eventually Veronica or somebody like her would listen to Taylor, and nobody would ever hire Grady to judge again. Grady said Julia was an adult, single at that, and that he hadn't made any promises. They were just hanging out, and one thing had led to another. I asked him if he'd made a tape of them together, and that's when he hit me."

"It sounds like you believed he was capable of blackmail."

"Yeah. It came to that when I stopped looking the other way. In fact maybe that's why I never had any contact with Nora Nelson. Maybe Grady had something on her, too. Maybe his career as a blackmailer went way, way back."

I supposed that was possible, although there again, Nora didn't seem like the kind of person who would put up with blackmail. She'd admit her sin, whatever it was, ask forgiveness, and move on.

"Do you think this Taylor guy was angry enough to kill Grady?" I asked.

"He was furious. And more furious because nobody was taking him seriously enough."

"What about Julia? Would she have been angry?"

"Doubtful. I'm sure she was going to be eliminated after the next round, he as much as told me so. He called her Joan Biased in private and said she was hopeless. So maybe after she got the axe, she would have been furious, but not before. Look, I need a T-bone. Or ribs. I love ribs."

"Just one more thing, Fred. Please?"

"Quick, quick. Onion rings are calling my name."

"You said once that Grady's career wasn't all it was cracked up to be. I've been trying to find out more. I want to read his autobiography, but so far I can't find it."

"They printed very few copies. Remember, it was published before he came back into the public eye with 'Remember Me in April.' I'd send you my copy, only I burned it a couple of months ago. Very therapeutic."

"Somebody's trying to find me one."

"Well, when you read it, look for all the things that aren't there. Friends who are real players on the Hollywood scene. Big contracts. Major films. 'April' was a surprise hit, but not another song on that CD went anywhere. When he sang other people's material, he was okay, but nothing special. And he didn't record another song of his own that was worth listening to. Out here you're hot only as long as you're making money for everybody. If his next album hadn't had another 'April' on it, he would have been toast."

I thanked him for everything. "Any jobs on the horizon?" I asked in closing.

"Three offers so far, all promising. Grady's death was good for me, even if it wasn't so good for him. Now I don't have to explain why I'm not working for him anymore."

I hung up so Fred could get his steak, although I did suggest a big salad and a baked potato to go along with it. He had given me a lot to think about. The least I could do was keep him from heading straight from meditation and spiritual cleansing to a heart attack.

+ + +

Since so much of the case against Nora revolved around the knife from Yank's collection, I decided I had to make another trip to the farm to see if he had any ideas how one could have ended up in the green room. Nora had extolled the security in her living quarters, but clearly something had gone wrong. How long had the knife been missing? Had Yank paid close enough attention to his inventory that he would have noticed? As I remembered it, the knives had been distributed across a magnetic strip. Could someone simply have spaced out the remaining knives, so no gap was evident?

Before I left the quilt shop I told Junie I planned to talk to Yank that afternoon. She offered to accompany me, and since people will tell Junie the oddest things, I was happy to have her ride along. We debated whether to bring Teddy, but since I wasn't sure how the tent show performers might feel about anyone from town, now that Nora was in jail, I decided to leave her at home with Ed, who was writing his sermon. He had promised there was no mention of family in this one, a situation that would continue, I was fairly sure, well into retirement.

Junie dressed down, which meant she wore khakis, a leopard-print camp shirt, and something too close to a pith helmet for comfort. The "helmet" was tied under her chin with a camouflage scarf. I decided to steer her away from the menagerie tent, just in case her ensemble brought up bad memories.

The picketers were out in force today. Nora's arrest had probably stirred them to additional action. Despite temperatures inching their way to a record high, there were eight adults and three elementary-school-age children carrying signs. I could tell the heat had sapped all creativity, or perhaps the subject didn't lend itself to any. "You're not wanted here" went straight to the point. I wondered what these people were most upset about. Wild animals, an influx of strangers with children to educate, the lights and noise of the tent show, Nora's claim that God had chosen a circus performer as his newest prophet, or just her message.

I suspected the message trumped everything else. Even people who believe every dire prediction linked to global warming aren't happy to hear they're required to make serious personal changes to combat it. It's easier to think of it as somebody else's problem. And easiest to think of it as some subsequent generation's hurdle. Nora claims disaster is imminent. Easier to get rid of Nora than fix the things that are wrong. All through history there's been a lot of that going around.

I hadn't met Yank, but I had seen him the day of Nora's

arrest. Now, after one of the residents pointed us in the right direction, Junie spotted him under the big top. From a distance Yank looked like any reasonably sincere male on the midway, working hard to win a stuffed bear or kewpie doll for his lady love. He was tossing something at what looked like a target, but as we drew closer, I saw the tossies were knives, maybe even from the set that had killed Grady Barber, and the target was a spinning disk with what looked like a human form attached.

Junie, who apparently saw nothing to be alarmed about, caught me up on his history as we headed in that direction.

"Yank grew up in a circus family. He's fourth-generation in the impalement arts."

"That's what he calls it? Impalement arts? Has he ever, uh . . . missed?"

"Your genes run true, precious. I asked him the same thing."

I tried to imagine in what other ways I might be like Junie. As much as I love her, I wasn't sure how good that piece of news might be. But then, would I be happier to more closely resemble my father? Would Ed be willing to join me in a commune or compound someplace where land was cheap and neighbors looked the other way as the walls grew higher and higher?

"What did he say?" I asked, stowing away thoughts of genetics for a rainy day—if we ever had one again.

"He said he's nicked his assistant a time or two, but never more than a simple flesh wound."

"Does this seem even slightly odd to you? This desire to throw deadly weapons at people?" I narrowed my eyes and saw, to my vast relief, that today there was only a spinning dummy for Yank to avoid. I wondered how this act fit in with Nora's message. Yank as the devil in Nora's interpretation of hell? I hoped I could avoid that particular night's entertainment.

"I think it's exciting. I'd let him throw knives at me. I even volunteered."

"You didn't."

"I think I'm too stately. He probably wasn't sure the wheel would spin fast enough. Of course he was too kind to say so."

Junie is short, chunky, and very blonde. None of her daughters fits that description. The reminder made me feel better about my genetic lottery. Mother Nature can be a wonderful comedian.

"Please don't volunteer for anything else here, okay? I'm sure they have plenty of skilled *umm . . .* artisans to do everything that needs to be done."

"I just feel so badly about Nora being thrown to the lions this way."

"Better watch the imagery, too. Wrong place, wrong time." As if to corroborate, a lion roared somewhere nearby.

We were close enough to Yank now that conversation ceased. We stood about twenty feet behind him and waited for the last knife to be thrown. He hit a switch with his foot, and the disk stopped spinning.

"Yank?"

Without knives at his fingertips, Yank looked much more approachable. He turned and smiled at Junie. "Ms. Bluebird. What are you doing here?"

"Have you met my daughter Aggie Sloan-Wilcox?"

Yank extended a hand. "So you're Aggie. Nora said you were helping her."

That seemed a huge overstatement, which I tried modestly to correct. "I'm not. Well, not really. I mean, I don't know if I can."

"Aggie will find the real killer and make sure Nora gets off," Junie said, clearly believing every word.

"Nora's convinced this was all preconceived and meant to be." Yank looked to be in his late forties, thin like a runner, dark curly hair slowly going gray, lightly tanned skin, and eyes as dark as olives. I wondered how long he and Nora had been together and how much he knew about her relationship with Grady.

Junie thoughtfully excused herself, leaving me there to question him without interference. She promised to meet me outside in a little while. I hoped that in the meantime nobody talked her into taking up sword swallowing.

"I did get in to see Nora on Monday," I said after Junie had gone. "I guess she's been moved to the regional jail by now?"

"At least they have regular visiting hours. We can see her on Saturday."

"I wonder if you'd mind answering a couple of questions? I honestly don't know if I can do a thing, but I do know there were a lot of people who didn't like Grady Barber. And in my mind, the evidence that points to Nora is just too clear and clean, almost as if somebody was planning to make it look that way."

"Almost?"

I liked this man, and I didn't know why. I mean, Yank hurls knives at people. He's shacking up with a woman who talks to God and believes everything she hears. That's just fine if it really is God putting words in Nora's head, but these days we're more likely to assume it's a lack of medication.

"I don't think Nora killed Grady." I turned up my hands. "But let's face it, I'm in a real minority."

"Ask away. Let's blast away any remaining doubts."

I had a vision of Yank shooting me from a cannon, but I thrust that one aside, as well.

"Okay, did Nora ever talk about Grady with you? At the very least, he was her first husband."

"Only husband. And not a good experience, as she probably told you."

"Then she did talk about it?"

"She felt Grady was a hurdle she had to overcome. In order to be worthy of the visions she was experiencing, she felt she had to really forgive every wrong ever done to her. Grady was the hardest, but she triumphed. At the end she only wanted to save him from himself."

"Was she hopeful she could?"

"Faith moves mountains. But Grady needed the faith, and hers couldn't suffice for him. He didn't listen. He died."

"Free will?"

"If all it took to turn a bad person into a good one was a little prayer here and there, the world would be a much nicer place to live."

I thought quite possibly Yank was the force that held Nora to the earth. I imagined he was a daily dose of common sense. I was really warming up to the guy.

"So, in your opinion, Nora only had the concern of one human being for another to bind them together? She wasn't looking for anything except his, *umm* . . . conversion to a better life?"

"That's all she wanted. She came home disheartened, but not unreasonably so. She hadn't expected a miracle, although she believes in them. She said Grady was still Grady, that he hadn't changed except that the youthful, sweet-faced innocence was only the thinnest of veneers now and would soon be gone entirely. She said in the future, people wouldn't be fooled so easily, and that, at least, was a good thing. But honestly, she didn't expect him to have much of a future. She saw a very dark cloud over him."

This was beginning to sound like a tarot reading. I pictured old Grady about to turn over the Death card in some cosmic spread, and Nora with her compassion and sensitivity had been attuned enough to recognize it and warn him. I wondered why that interpretation bothered me less than the one Nora believed, that God had intervened and requested her to make one more attempt to bring Grady to the light.

Since this whole situation required me to move beyond those notions to get even the slightest sliver of objectivity, I shook these thoughts off as, well, a philosophical Labrador retriever emerging from a theology-encrusted pond.

"Tell me about the security system at your house," I said. "Nora praised it the evening she gave us a tour."

"We kept everything in the house and put in an alarm, motion detectors, special locks on the doors and windows. Not keeping a weapon was a requirement of traveling with us. Anybody found to have one was asked to leave. We were so careful. I was taught to be careful from the time I was old enough to hold a knife in my hand." He raked fingers through his curls, clearly agitated. "I can't believe I might have been responsible for what happened."

"What do you mean, Yank? Were you careless one day? You forgot to turn on the alarms, or you left the door unlocked? You made it possible for somebody to get in and steal a knife?"

"Nothing like that. Only I've been racking my brain trying to remember something, anything, that might have made it possible for somebody to slip inside. And last night I remembered an incident. About two weeks ago I was in the house getting ready for a rehearsal here." He gestured to show he meant the big top. "There was a commotion outside, and somebody set off one of the alarms in the menagerie tent. I took off to see what was going on, and I can't remember now whether I locked up first or not. I don't think I did. When that alarm goes off, we go running."

"What was the problem?"

"A door to one of the cages hadn't been shut tight, and it hadn't been locked. Somebody went in and found our white tiger with her paw in the opening, more or less playing a game with herself. He sounded the alarm to make sure he had backup if she decided to spring when he closed and locked it. It was all taken care of by the time I got there. I wasn't gone more than a few minutes."

"Do you remember if you had to unlock first to get back in your house?"

"No, I was in a hurry, already late for the rehearsal. I can't remember anything but that. But if I didn't lock up, it never really registered with me. I never felt guilty or worried. It all happened so fast, I guess it just didn't seem like much of an event."

"How long would it take somebody to slip in and steal that knife?"

"Less than a minute. And it's doubtful they would have been noticed. Everyone was heading for the cages. People go in and out when we're in the house. Nothing would have seemed out of place."

"Have you told the police?"

"I spoke with the detective in charge this morning. He wasn't impressed."

Roussos, of course, and he wouldn't have been.

My head was filled with questions, but the most important one was obvious. "Let's say somebody did get into the house, steal a knife, take the time to spread the others on the magnetic strip so that you didn't notice the absence—"

"That's what I think happened. Because if there'd been an obvious space, I would have seen it right away."

"So who might have done it? Does anybody here have a reason to want to frame Nora? Better yet, does anyone have a reason to kill Grady Barber and frame Nora for the murder? Anybody with a connection to both of them?"

"I can't imagine who. If somebody does, they've kept it to themselves."

"Nobody who's mentioned knowing Grady? Nobody who was particularly interested in the Idyll?"

Yank shook his head. "Nobody like that, at least not that spoke to me. And Nora's never mentioned it."

"Ask her on Saturday, would you? But if that's a dead end"—I tried not to wince at my own words—"who might have killed Grady just to frame Nora? Did she have enemies in the tent show? Anyone who wanted to see her brought down in a big way? Someone who wanted control, or wanted to stop her from living her, *um* . . . message?"

"Nora's the heart and soul of the tent show. Nobody would listen to a detractor. Anybody who didn't like her and didn't want to follow her would simply pull up stakes and leave. There's nothing to be gained here, no resources to grab, no power that doesn't come directly through her."

"You can't think of a single person who might be angry and want to see her arrested?"

"I've thought about it a lot, and no one comes to mind. Of course I don't know every thought every person has. And we have some people who've only cast their lot with us in the past months. So in some ways, they're still strangers."

"Was there anybody you or Nora was worried about? Somebody who wasn't fitting in? Somebody who might have been here just waiting to do mischief?"

"But why would they be? What would they have against Nora?"

I wondered, as well. One religious fanatic determined to take out another? Calling Nora a fanatic felt odd, since her message was about peace and saving the world from itself. In my mind fanatics always preach hate and destruction. She had the destruction part down pat, but only because we were heading down that road and she was trying to stop us.

I wasn't coming up with anything, and I wanted to, badly. "Could somebody dislike her for her ideas? Is there a test of some kind to join you? A profession of faith in Nora's abilities, maybe? And somebody whose profession didn't quite ring true to you?"

He smiled, and gestured again as he did. "This, everything you see here, is not about Nora. She'd be the first to tell you so. It's about doing what's right. Not about dotting every *I* in every word she says. No one is required to make any kind of statement. This isn't the easiest life. Nora assumes that anybody with serious doubts won't put themselves on the line with us."

"Anybody who just doesn't quite fit in? Any of the new people?"

This time he laughed. "Look around you. We're circus people. We never fit in."

"I mean *here*, with each other. Not the world in general."

"I don't want to start looking at my brothers and sisters with suspicion."

"I understand, but somebody stole that knife. Either that, or Nora took it to the Idyll the night Grady was killed . . ."

I knew Yank didn't want to believe the worst about anybody, but there was a choice to be made here. Somebody had taken the knife. Somebody had betrayed a trust.

He looked uncomfortable. "I just don't know."

"Would you be willing to give me the names of anybody you don't know well enough to trust completely?"

Yank didn't shrug me off. I could see him struggling. He wanted to deny the possibility that somebody was trying to hurt Nora by killing Grady Barber, but there were only so many possibilities.

"There are a couple of young men who joined us back in the spring. I've never been sure they're here for the right reasons. I've even wondered . . ." He glanced around, but I thought it was more likely he was giving himself time to compose his thoughts than to see if anyone was listening.

"What did you wonder?" I didn't want him to compose too much.

"If they were running from something or someone. The law, most likely."

"Is this a good place to hide out?"

"It can be. Circus people take care of each other. We offer protection from outsiders. This may not be a circus anymore, but we're still a community. What doesn't hurt the community, you know, things that happened in the past, stay in the past. It's no concern of ours."

"So the men in question might have joined hoping you wouldn't look too closely or ask too many questions." I paused. "Could you give me names?"

"I could give you the names they go by here."

I saw his point. "There must be paperwork, Social Security numbers, that kind of thing."

"The bare minimum, easily faked. But I can give you

whatever we have. To help Nora." He paused. "But I wouldn't give it to the police."

"And I won't, either. Not without your permission."

"I'd appreciate that. And discretion if you investigate them?"

I reassured him. Satisfied, he walked to the target and began to remove his knives, carefully placing them in a carved wooden case. I watched, then asked the obvious question.

"Yank, why do you put them in the case here, then take the time to put them back up on your wall? Aren't they safer in the case?"

"Oh, these aren't the same knives. That set belonged to my father. They're for display. Sort of a sentimental thing, I guess, that got me in trouble. If one of these knives had been taken, I would have missed it immediately."

That made sense to me, but was little help. As we walked toward the exit I asked what I hoped was my last question.

"Just one more thing. You talk about loyalty here, the way circus people take care of each other. When it goes wrong, it can really go wrong, though, can't it? I know there was trouble in Nora's past with Grady, that the Nelson–Zimboni circus was dissolved after a scandal."

"It's odd you'd bring that up."

"Why?"

"Because Caprice Zimboni is here today. Did you know?"

"Here? In Emerald Springs?"

He looked relieved. "Here on the grounds. You didn't hear it from somebody else? It's a coincidence you're bringing it up now? Because none of us wanted her presence to become a news item."

My mind was whirling again. "It's hardly a coincidence her name would come up. Caprice is one of the links between Grady and Nora. I heard she was the reason they divorced."

"More that Grady turned her into a link. She was young,

innocent, tired of being sequestered by her family, and completely snowed by everything he said to her. That's what Nora's always said. And I imagine if you talk to Caprice, she'll tell you the same thing."

I couldn't believe he hadn't brought this up right at the beginning of the conversation. "When did she get here? How long has she been in town?"

"Just since this morning. Of course she heard what happened to Grady, and she heard Nora was arrested for it. She came to see what she could do to help. It's pretty clear she feels like she's at least partly to blame, even though Nora and Grady have been divorced for decades."

"*Umm* . . . Did she happen to mention if this is her first trip to Emerald Springs?"

"You mean, did she happen to stop by the night Barber was killed?"

"Something like that."

"She didn't kill him."

"And you'd know this how?"

"She's not a killer."

I crossed Yank off my helpful-witness list. He sounded much too sure of himself. I wondered if he, like Nora, thought he was getting special-delivery messages straight from above. Maybe the messages had brought them together. Kind of a divine dating service.

"Can you tell me where I can find her?" I asked when we'd reached a parting of the ways. I saw Junie in the distance talking to a couple of people, and thought I'd better find out what she was doing.

"No problem. She and her daughter are probably in the cookhouse—"

"Daughter?"

"Yes, Felice is here, too, and she's as unlikely a killer as her mother. You'll see what I mean. Caprice feels awful that she hasn't asked Nora for forgiveness face-to-face, and now she may not have the chance. She'll do whatever she can to help."

I thought my luck was extraordinary, although if Caprice really did want to make up for past wrongs against Nora, it made sense she would come to see what she could do. Still, a lot of people don't operate quite that way. They prefer the annoyance of feeling guilty to the humiliation of making amends. I was anxious to see where Caprice fit on this scale. Maybe she was here for other reasons. Destroying evidence? Planting seeds of distrust? Gloating? Although gloating seemed unlikely, given their history. She'd had plenty to gloat about when she destroyed Nora's marriage. Unless for some reason, she just needed another round.

Junie saw me, and I pointed to the cookhouse. She nodded and continued her conversation with a long-haired man in cutoffs and tattoos. I'd seen her with two men, but the second one was gone now. I debated whether I should drag her away, but the man was laughing, and they looked happy enough that I suspected Junie was just making a friend and not learning the ins and outs of fire-eating.

The cookhouse was across a stretch of open ground. I could hear the hum as people went about their normal activities. Children ran in and out of the RVs parked neatly on the grass. Two women cradling a pair of dachshund puppies strolled by and greeted me as they passed. To my right and just ahead, a trio of elephants was being bathed at the edge of a diminishing pond, and to my left, a man riding a camel was talking on a cell phone. As I passed them I saw that beyond the camel four teenagers were doing what looked like advanced acrobatics. I hoped Deena, alias Sporty Price, didn't get wind of this and abandon the parsonage to find more compatible parents and lodging.

The clearing past the pond was new. I vaguely remembered patches of woods here, but now what trees there had been were neatly sawed into eight-foot logs and lying in piles beside the road. I stopped to investigate, and when I heard someone behind me, I saw Junie not far away.

The road behind her was now empty. I waited until she joined me.

"Biosphere?" I asked. "Or housing. Which do you think?"

"Ajax says this is where the biosphere will be."

"Ajax?"

"The young man I was talking to. The biosphere's going to be huge. They've only just begun. It's all so exciting. Imagine having something like this right here in Emerald Springs."

I honestly couldn't. I didn't know exactly how rich Henry Cinch might be, but the kind of project they were envisioning would cost the moon. A few more billionaire converts were probably in order.

We turned to head across the road on a diagonal path to the cookhouse when I heard three loud pops, then the roar of thunder. For a moment I forgot that the sun was blistering everything in sight, and there wasn't a cloud in the sky. I actually thought we were about to have rain at last. Then a cloud of dust appeared not far from where we were standing, and began to sweep closer and closer. I heard a wild trumpeting, and the shouts of people in the distance. Another moment passed before I realized exactly what was in the center of the cloud.

"Elephants!" I grabbed Junie's arm and looked for a place to run. But the elephants were nearly upon us now, stampeding wildly and coming right for us.

With only seconds, I saw one chance. I shoved Junie toward the side of the road and a concrete culvert in a narrow drainage ditch just behind us that ran beneath it. Unfortunately it wasn't big enough for both of us.

She resisted, but only long enough to figure out there was no time to argue. She sprang down to the culvert, and I leaped forward, frantically searching for another solution, this time for me. Now the cloud had begun to envelop me, and I could swear I smelled elephant breath and hide. With the trumpeting growing loud enough to make me think I was nearing the pearly gates, I dove for what seemed like inches of space between two of the logs along the roadside, praying the gap would be wide enough to shelter me. I clawed my way in and down.

Just as the elephants arrived.

14

"He's gone." Yank draped a damp towel around my neck before he dropped to the log beside me. He took my hand and rubbed it hard between his to restore circulation. I was delighted to have circulation to restore. I'd come too close to perishing by pachyderm to take any bodily function for granted.

"We've got men looking for him, but he took off right after he stampeded the herd," Yank said.

"He" was Danny, one of the two young men that Yank had expressed concerns about earlier. The other, Ajax, who had regaled Junie with tales of the biosphere, had nearly been overtaken by the elephant storm, too, swinging up into the branches of one of the few remaining trees as the elephants roared by. Ajax was as shaken as I was, but he'd been perfectly clear about one thing. He had been looking in the direction of the elephants when Danny raised a flare gun and fired three shots toward the sky. Maybe Danny had been trying to move the elephants out of the pond after their baths; maybe he'd felt he was in danger by the way they were behaving and had fired to scare them away. Whatever had happened, we might never know, because right after the elephants took off down the road, Danny took off, too.

Junie hadn't been harmed. Now she was up at Nora's house getting a scraped hand washed and treated. As it roared by, an elephant had kicked one of the two logs that cradled me, sending it rolling toward the other and squeezing me even tighter between them. Consequently, I was bruised, and the wind had been knocked out of me, but I was lucky, I thought, to be alive and merely reviewing the memory.

"Why was Danny alone with the elephants?" I asked. My voice was nearly back to normal. For minutes after I'd pried myself from between the logs and gone in search of my mother, my vocal cords hadn't worked worth a darn, still knotted to suppress a scream, I guess. "If he's new here, why was he in charge of three elephants?"

"Normally he wouldn't be. But Levin, he's their trainer, said things were quiet and Danny had shown real aptitude, so when Danny said he'd be fine for a few minutes if Levin wanted to get out of the sun, he took him up on it. He was just going to get something cool to drink and come right back." Yank paused, and I could tell he wasn't finished by the way he dropped my hand, got to his feet, and began to pace.

"Thing is," he said, walking back and forth in front of me, "when Levin got just far enough away that he couldn't do anything to make a difference, he heard Danny shouting, then the shots."

"Maybe it's all a coincidence."

"Or maybe Danny wanted Levin to leave him alone with the elephants so he could wreak a little havoc. Maybe Danny had something to do with leaving the tiger's cage unlatched, too, the night I left the house without locking the door behind me."

This had occurred to me, as I'd sat here trying to remember how to breathe. "How often is a cage left unlatched?"

"Rarely to never."

I'd asked myself the next question, too, about twenty times. Now I asked it out loud. "We know what happened when the cage was unlocked. What was supposed to happen today? Three elephants got loose, but your folks will round them up, right? Before they get to town?"

"Here's hoping. They have one already."

"Danny must have known they'd be captured quickly."

"One would think."

"So what was this about?"

Yank didn't answer.

"There were three people directly in their path," I said. "What's the relationship between Ajax and Danny?"

"Apparently not much of one. Levin says they joined us about the same time, but he doesn't think they knew each other before that. They bunk together, and that's about it."

"No bad blood?"

"Not that Levin knows about. Of course I'll be asking the others. But you can imagine we don't encourage feuds. Our mission's to get along, not to engage in petty differences when there's vital work to do. Anyone who's having problems is helped, if possible. If not, they're asked to move on."

"So it's not likely Danny was trying to get even with Ajax?"

"We'll be questioning him."

I nodded slowly. "I doubt anybody was trying to scare or kill my mother."

"You would know better than I would."

"I don't think she has a real enemy in the world."

Yank cut to the chase. "That would leave you."

I'd already come to that conclusion. But why me? Yes, I was snooping around, refusing to accept that Nora was Grady Barber's murderer. But I was so far from answers it seemed inconceivable someone would try to stop me like this. I felt just a flicker of pride at the possibility before I squashed it like, well, a woman hiding from a stampede between two felled tree trunks. No, it *wasn't* good that somebody might be taking me seriously. Not if it meant they had sent three elephants to finish me off.

"It's so hot today," I said. "Maybe Danny was just trying to hurry the elephants along because they were sluggish."

"He wouldn't have learned that here. We don't treat animals that way. We would never use fear to move them along."

"God's creatures."

"Exactly."

The elephants hadn't exactly been sluggish when they charged out of nowhere, so I knew I was reaching for an explanation that didn't include me. "Maybe you'll find Danny and we can question him."

"He disappeared so fast, I have to think he had an escape route planned. But we'll see, I guess."

I saw Junie walking in our direction with two tall, graceful women beside her. My mother looked relatively unruffled. Once she had caught her breath and received assurances I was fine, she had fairly bubbled over at the excitement. Really, I don't think Junie's in any hurry to test her long-standing belief in reincarnation, but I do think that when the time comes, she's secretly hoping this life will end with a flourish. Elephants would have done the trick.

"You're about to get your wish," Yank said. "That's Caprice and Felice Zimboni with your mother."

I got to my feet, pleased to see my soles and heels remembered what to do. "Suspicious at all that this happened right after they got here?"

"Not one bit."

And why was I? What would have been the point? Hire Danny from afar, then arrive just in time to watch somebody they'd never met get stomped into the ground?

Junie was chatting with the women as if she'd known them forever—she has that gift. I examined the Zimbonis as they drew closer. Caprice was probably in her forties, but she looked younger. She carried herself like a queen, and her dark hair was wound like a coronet at the back of her head. She was slender and graceful, perfectly proportioned. Her features were less perfect but even more interesting. She wouldn't win beauty contests, but any artist would want to sketch her.

Felice was tall and slender, too. Her hair was lighter, her complexion more rosy than olive. She shared Caprice's long bones and natural grace, and anyone paying attention would see they were mother and daughter, even though Felice's features held more than a trace of Grady Barber.

Junie made the introductions. Both women expressed what seemed like genuine concern about my health, and I assured them that except for some interesting bruises in the next weeks, I was going to be fine.

"When I was a girl I saw an elephant kill a man," Caprice said. "I've never been afraid of them, but I've never taken them for granted, either."

Life in Italy hadn't affected her accent. She had the absence of accent I'd noted in Nora's speech. Felice's Italian roots were more audible, although her English was perfect.

"I always wished I could ride on one," she said. "Maybe not so much after today."

"I told them you're trying to help Nora," Junie said. "They want to help her, too."

"She was my friend," Caprice said. "We were like sisters."

I could hardly comment on the event that had destroyed that intimacy with the result of it standing beside her.

"I know she'd like to talk to you, too," I said instead. "She told me she would."

"We came back to the U.S., Felice and I, to set things right here. Felice thought it was time to meet her father. I wanted to see Nora, to try to explain things. After we arrived I was sure we had all the time in the world."

"I'm sorry about your father," I told Felice.

Felice nodded gravely. "I didn't know him, and I'm afraid to ask what you might know."

I suspected she'd heard plenty already, although maybe not that I was the one who had found him. I wondered if Veronica would be willing to tell Felice some of Grady's finer points. Felice deserved that much.

"You know there's going to be a memorial service next week?" I asked.

"I'll be there, but he's really a stranger to me. Once we

got to Michigan I tried repeatedly to contact him. I wasn't successful."

"I'm sorry about that, too."

"If we'd been in the States last week, maybe we would have come to see the talent show, so Felice could meet him there," Caprice said. "Although in retrospect, it's better that we weren't."

I zeroed in on the important part. "You were overseas?"

"Felice and I work with inner-city children in Detroit. We have a small circus all our own. We took it to Italy to perform. Just for two weeks, but that might as well have been a century to the kids. They loved it, and everybody loved them. Then we came home to this terrible news."

Like so many other things, this would be simple to check. I imagined she was telling the truth. There was always the possibility that somebody in her family had done away with Grady, but those odds were diminishing.

After a moment Felice excused herself and started toward the cookhouse with Junie, but Caprice held back.

"I'm going to try to see Nora, if they'll let me," she said. "But this is a good example, isn't it, of waiting too long to put things right?"

"She's forgiven you. She told me she understood what drove you."

"Grady was so persuasive, and I was so foolish." She smiled a little. "He wouldn't care, of course, but he did give me the thing I value most in the world. My wonderful daughter. Of course I hated him after he left me with nothing except a swollen belly and a circus in ruins. But in the end I was grateful to him, although nothing but sorry about the way Felice came into the world."

"To my knowledge he doesn't have any other children."

"Felice may well be his legal heir. I don't know, and I don't know if there'll be anything to inherit. But she's already said that if there is, it will go to our circus. We help teenagers reach their potential and become more than they

ever thought they could. Performing for Life would be a
tribute to Grady Barber, wouldn't it? Whether he deserved
one or not."

+ + +

When I drove up to the parsonage Teddy was sitting
cross-legged in the shade. She had a book beside her, probably something relaxing and lightweight, like Tillich's
The Courage to Be, or maybe some of Ed's sermon research.
I was afraid he and Teddy would be the only people in
church on Sunday who would understand what he was talking about.

I parked and went over to sit beside her. She looked
glum and bedraggled. Her glasses had slipped to the end of
her nose, and her hair was pushed behind her ears.

"So what's up?" I asked, stretching my legs out and leaning back against my arms.

"Deena still won't talk to Daddy."

"That worries you?"

"What if she never talks to him again?"

"I think that's unlikely."

"If it's unlikely, that means it could still happen."

"I guess, but I'm pretty sure you don't have to worry."

"I told her she was being stupid, and she ought to just
get over it."

"And that didn't help, did it?"

Teddy shook her head. "Now she's not speaking to me,
either."

"Think of it as a club that you, Daddy, and I are members of. But let's not charge dues, okay?"

"Can't you make her start acting normal again?"

"I wish. Unfortunately you can't make somebody act exactly the way you want them to. I can make her do things. I
can even make her answer questions and be more or less
polite, but I can't make her initiate a conversation or tell us
what she's doing. That's up to Deena."

"Can't Daddy do something?"

I tried not to smile. Teddy, unlike her sister, still thought Ed could work miracles. "Not even Daddy."

"What's the point of church and ministers if people won't listen and be good?"

"Deena's still good. She just hasn't figured out how to move on after she gets angry. She will."

"Do I have to act like her when I get to middle school?"

"Nope."

"I don't want to make mistakes."

I gave her a hug. "You will. It's okay. That's how you learn."

"She sure learns slow!"

I left Teddy to contemplate the mysteries of the universe and her even more complicated big sister and went inside to start dinner. I figured that telling Ed about the stampede could wait a year or two—or maybe just until whoever had sicced elephants in my direction was no longer a threat.

We had Mexican beans and rice and something too close to silence at the dinner table. I was afraid to talk about what I'd done for fear I'd go too far. Ed was thinking about his sermon. Deena and Teddy were too busy trying to stare each other down to articulate.

Afterwards I tossed everybody out of the kitchen so I could clean up in a nicer kind of silence. But the silence didn't last. Junie trooped in carrying a notepad. "Still doing all right? You don't think any ribs are broken?" she asked.

I *shush*ed her. "I've more or less not told Ed about the stampede."

"More or less?"

"Okay, I didn't tell him at all. I didn't even start a sentence."

"And you'll explain your bruises how?"

It always surprises me that after being the oh-so-thoughtful mother of Teddy or Deena, I can instantly turn into a little girl again.

"He'll worry," I said.

"I'm sure you're right. And he won't worry when he

goes to hug you and you faint dead away." She took my hand and patted it. "But you know best, precious."

I turned back to my dishes. "You should have come for dinner. You know you have a standing invitation."

"You don't have to worry about me. I have a life here and friends. It's a good place to be. And guess what? I already talked to Sue Grossman."

"You're a wonder." And she was. I leaned over and kissed her cheek. "You're now officially my assistant."

"Here's what she said." Junie propped the notebook on the counter beside the sink. The page was filled with her scrawls.

She looked up after a moment. "She said they weren't there."

"All that writing, and that's all she said?" But my mind was flashing on the possibilities. Madison and Tammy had not been in the middle of a wardrobe malfunction at Sue's house when Grady Barber was murdered. So where had they been?

"The rest of this is notes about the class she wants to teach." Junie clapped the notebook shut. "But she was positive about Madison not being there the night Grady was killed. She didn't see them that day or evening. There was a problem with a costume, but it happened another night. She even checked her receipt."

I wondered if Tammy had banked on Sue being fuzzy about the dates. Or maybe she had hoped I would be hesitant to approach a stranger. Whatever her reasoning, she had lied to me. And lying, under the circumstances, made very little sense, unless she was desperate.

Junie went to find her granddaughters. I hoped she would work a miracle and convince Deena to have a conversation.

She hadn't been upstairs more than a minute when the doorbell rang and I had another visitor.

Esther was waiting on the front porch when I answered, and she held out a book as soon as I opened the door. "I told you'd I'd find it."

Grady Barber smiled up at me from the cover, as he would never smile again in real life.

I took it and put it under my arm. "You're a miracle worker. Where did you get it?"

"One of those bookstores that only sells remaindered books. Apparently nobody bought it after it came out. I was in Columbus for an afternoon concert. I stopped by the store on the way home."

"What do I owe you?"

"Tea and an explanation if you figure out that somebody else killed him."

I didn't remember mentioning I planned to solve another murder, but before I could protest, Esther winked.

"Aggie dear, your secret's safe with me." She lifted her hand in good-bye and headed back to her car.

I could hardly wait for bedtime. I finished the dishes, helped Teddy with a complicated jigsaw puzzle, ate popcorn with everyone except Deena, and painfully fended off my husband as we got ready for bed, finally admitting the truth so he wouldn't think my libido had gone farther north for the summer.

"Elephants?" he asked.

"Wouldn't that be hard to explain to the congregation?"

He shook his head. "They expect nothing less from you."

He turned over and went to sleep, and grateful he had suppressed everything else he wanted to say, I eased my sore body into bed and opened Grady's autobiography.

One thing's for sure. This publisher had missed a great marketing opportunity. Grady's book should have been shelved in drugstores next to the sleep aids. Five intensely boring pages later, I was sound asleep.

15

Here's the thing about towns the size of Emerald Springs. You really do have to watch what you say, and you really do have to watch what you do. No matter how hard you try to avoid somebody, you'll run into them at the grocery store, or while you're out walking the dog—which is at least part of the reason we have a cat. On Friday morning, despite that precaution, Moonpie, our silver tabby, flexed his kitty muscle and climbed the tree in our side yard, refusing to climb back down.

I wasn't one bit worried, and I told Teddy so. "He seems perfectly happy up there. And he'll come down when he gets tired of waiting for a bird to land."

"I think he's scared."

"Sorry, but I think I'd be more scared climbing up to get him."

"You could get the ladder."

"Let's compromise. If he's not down in an hour, then I'll get the ladder."

"Daddy would get the ladder *now*."

Teddy could say this since Ed was off visiting a parishioner and wouldn't be around to fall off the ladder himself until noon.

"I'll be back at"—I checked my Kermit the Frog watch, last year's birthday gift from my sister Sid—"ten thirty. Are you going to stay here and coax him?"

"Somebody has to." Teddy looked as if I'd suggested we tie stones to Moonpie's tail and throw him into Emerald Springs, the real springs for which our town is named.

Thoroughly chastened, I went back inside and tried to figure out my plan for the day. Now that I knew Tammy and Madison hadn't been with Sue Grossman when Grady died, I had to confront Tammy and tell her I knew she was lying. And if I didn't get a straight answer, I had to figure out where to go from there. Planning seemed wise, but at the moment I couldn't think of any way to tactfully introduce the subject.

The door banged and Teddy tramped in.

"Somebody's getting Moonpie. It's that policeman."

I was afraid I knew exactly which policeman she meant. To my knowledge Teddy knows only one who might be familiar enough with my family to take this kind of risk.

"Detective Roussos?"

"He climbed up like a monkey. I wish I could do that."

"I'm glad you can't." I followed her outside. A pair of jeans-clad legs swung from one of the branches halfway up the tree.

"Roussos, what are you doing in my tree?" I shouted.

Leaves rustled, and the tree shook. I watched as Roussos more or less shimmied down to a lower branch and set Moonpie in the crook against the trunk. The cat ran down as nimbly as a squirrel.

"Teddy, did you see how easily that cat got down once he knew he had to?" I demanded.

She caught up with Moonpie, grabbed him, and tucked him under one arm to haul back inside. "Because he had help!"

Roussos was not as nimble as Moonpie, but nearly. He swung down and landed with a jolt, dusted off his jeans, and straightened.

"I can't believe you did that, Tarzan. I told her he would come down on his own."

"She looked upset."

"Are you on cat patrol today?" I gave up and smiled. "Thanks for putting us on the list."

"I'm on elephant stampede patrol."

I sobered quickly. "No need to be. There's no evidence I was a target yesterday, or really, that anybody was."

"You weren't going to mention this?"

"Eventually. I was trying to figure out what to say. I didn't want to sound like a crazy lady."

He cocked a brow, and the point was taken. He was used to me sounding like a crazy lady.

"I have coffee. Come on in, it's the least I can do." I didn't wait to see if he followed. The lure of coffee would reel him in.

In the kitchen I poured him a mug as he settled into a chair at the table, but I didn't offer cream or sugar. I knew how Roussos took it. Then I poured myself some, and took a seat across from him.

I saluted him with my mug. "So who told you?"

"Jankiewicz. I got the whole story."

Jankiewicz had clearly been shortened to "Yank." I wondered if he had called to warn Roussos of more hanky-panky, or to prove, yet again, that Nora wasn't the murderer. After all, if she was the killer, why was somebody trying to stop me from my investigation?

Unless Yank himself had hired Danny and arranged the episode for just that reason. I didn't like that thought, but it was plausible.

"What were you doing there?" Roussos asked. "That's the part he didn't tell me."

"Talking to people."

"You didn't learn your lesson after the last time, did you? You're putting yourself on the line again."

"Not really, but I'll confess that avoiding elephants never really occurred to me. I just wasn't thinking ahead. Now they're on my list."

"You religious types stick together. That's what this is about."

I nearly sprayed a mouthful of coffee over the table. I hacked for a moment, trying to breathe normally. "Roussos, do you know anything about churches and religions?"

"Not any more than I have to."

"Quick course, then. Some religions believe in divine revelation, in modern-day prophecy and people talking directly to God. Sister Nora's firmly in that camp. Then there are others who are more focused on facts we can prove, along with listening to that still, small voice inside us and doing good while we're here. Our church is firmly in *that* camp."

Since his eyes hadn't glazed over, I finished with a flourish. "However, for the record, what Nora's hearing and what my still, small voice is trying to tell me aren't too far off, so sometimes we do come together quite nicely. Global warming's a threat to us all. Maybe I'm not into divinely inspired biospheres as a solution, and I see how odd the circus, tent revival thing probably looks to you, but I *am* into people doing whatever they can to make a difference."

"So you're involved for what reason?"

"Because you're railroading an innocent woman."

"And since you're not into revelation, you'd know this how?"

"Did you miss that part of the lecture? That still, small voice along with the facts?"

"Do the facts indicate somebody was trying to kill you yesterday?"

I considered, staring at our blue willow sugar bowl. "I guess it's possible. But it has to be somebody who doesn't know me very well if he thinks that wouldn't just make me more curious."

"There's my clue. It was somebody who didn't know you lack good sense about your safety. That should narrow it way down."

I looked up. "Are you going to check into this? Other than just talking to me?"

He gave a short nod.

"There's something else you could do while you're at it." I watched all expression leave his face, a short trip.

"Come on, Roussos. The more you check and discount, the better your case against Nora, right?"

"What?"

I told him about Rob Taylor from Zelienople, Pennsylvania, who had been following Grady from town to town, the very man I had seen backstage on Grady's final night on earth. I also told him I had crossed Fred off my suspect list, that he had, as he'd said, been meditating in Big Sur and unable to murder Grady himself, despite all inclinations.

"I'll see what I can find out," he said grudgingly.

"I think you're helping because you know Nora didn't do it."

"You'd be wrong there." He finished his coffee and stood. "I just like all my ends tied up. In exchange, I want you to be extra careful from here on in. I know you're not going to stop, no matter what I say. But pay close attention to what's going on around you, and carry your cell. If anything seems out of the ordinary, call me on mine."

"I promise. The next time elephants come roaring toward me, I'll stop and punch in your number."

"Put me on speed dial."

With Deena more or less out of the picture, I hoped Teddy was up to that task.

Like the gracious hostess I am, I followed him out. As I walked the few steps I wondered if I ought to come clean about Tammy and Madison while Roussos was being so accommodating. But how could I turn in church members without talking to them first? I told myself if I piled on the assignments, Roussos would flip me off anyway. Feeling better, I said good-bye, thanked him again for rescuing my perfectly contented cat, and watched him walk out to the street where his car was parked.

Roussos would probably be calling in the next day or so to tell me that Rob Taylor, like everyone else I'd suspected, had an alibi for the time of Grady's death. When he did, if I hadn't cleared the Sargents to my satisfaction, I would tell him about them then. Which meant I had to clear them fast.

By the time Ed was due home for lunch, I'd made sandwiches along with plans for my afternoon. I'd decided not to call Tammy and lose the element of surprise. I was going to track her down. That's the other thing about a town the size of ours. There aren't that many places to go. Unless she and Madison were off on vacation, I would probably be able to find them.

When she came down to get her grilled cheese, Deena presented me with her list of chores. She had checked off most of them. Some, I knew, had been done with more finesse than others, but I wasn't going to quibble. This wasn't about perfection. It was about making amends.

"The Meanies are all meeting at the pool this afternoon," she said.

"A sensible place to be if they stay underwater and use lots of sunscreen."

"I just have to weed the flower beds, and I'll be done with all this stuff. I could do that tomorrow morning when it's cooler."

"Uh huh, or you could have done it this morning for the same reason."

"This isn't fair. I'm the only one who won't be there! Even Shannon's going."

"How did this information come your way? Carrier pigeon? Smoke signals? I seem to remember you're not taking calls or e-mail for a while."

"I got a letter, okay? They had to send me a *letter*." She rolled her eyes.

I was encouraged that at least one of the Meanies had learned how to address an envelope and put a stamp in the right corner. I'd been afraid this was a dying art.

"Deena, you know what you have to do before you have your privileges restored . . ." I frowned. "Did you say Shannon's going to be there? Her mother's letting her out of the house?"

"Even Shannon's mother."

"I guess I'm the Wicked Witch of the West, then, kiddo. Or maybe Shannon's done everything her parents wanted her to."

"You're not going to let me go?"

"Nope. And it's not just the flower beds. It's the attitude thing. The silent treatment, the refusal to apologize."

"Well, you can't make me!"

I chewed my bottom lip. Then, with every ounce of self-control I could muster, I nodded. "Right. Not until you're ready. Which means you probably need more time to consider. Because I think you're still a logical, considerate girl who knows she's got some work left to do. I have faith you'll figure that out in your own good time."

"I wish you'd just yell at me or something and get this over with."

"If it makes you feel better, I've sure been tempted."

She grabbed her plate and a bag of chips and took them upstairs, brushing past Teddy, who was on the way down.

"Maybe Deena's sick," she said. "Maybe there's something eating her brain. Like a parasite."

I didn't want to know where Teddy had learned about brain-eating parasites. Maybe the boys starring in the video had suggested it as a plot element. I couldn't blame them. Parasites were much more exciting than the moral dilemmas of a bicycle thief.

"It's called adolescence," I said. "It's short-term and it's not fatal."

Ed came home, changed into jeans and a T-shirt, and went out back with Teddy for batting practice. I imagined that discussions of theology would zing back and forth as fast as the softball.

I took off soon afterwards, despite a strong urge to smuggle my oldest daughter out of the house and over to the pool. But as unhappy as this brief hiatus in Deena's life made everybody, I knew Ed and I had to follow through. We didn't have to like being grown-up meanies, though.

I started my search at the discount store where Tammy worked as a manager and learned she was off for the day. Then I moved on to Tammy's house. With no success I broadened my search to the library, and after that I swung by the pool and the jogging trail, parked downtown, and window-shopped to no avail. I hit pay dirt when I went into Give Me a Break, our town's flourishing answer to Starbucks. Tammy was sitting in the corner with a book, making notes. My chance had come.

I took my half-caf, mocha latte con panna with me and hoped for the best.

"Tammy."

She looked up. For a moment she seemed glad to see me, then memory intruded and her eyes narrowed. "Aggie."

"May I join you for a few minutes?"

I could see she wanted to say no, but that was far too rude. She nodded at the chair across from her.

"Can I get you a refill?" I asked. She was drinking plain old coffee, which meant she was far less creative but far more likely to keep the barista happy than I was.

"No, I'm okay."

"Are you studying?"

She closed the book just a tad too hard. "I've decided that when Madison goes off to Ohio State or OU, I'm going to enter the nursing program at Emerald College. I'm just boning up on chemistry so I'll be ready."

I'd never heard Tammy had other career aspirations. "I'd have to start all over again. I don't remember a thing, not even the periodic table."

"I've just been waiting until she gets through school," Tammy said. "I wanted to be home with her as much as I could while she was growing up. I couldn't work, go to school, too, and be any kind of mother."

"You'll make a great nurse."

"But you're not here to talk about that, are you?"

"I think you know why I'm here."

"Why do you always stick your nose into other people's business?"

How could I be hurt when this was oh, so true? "This particular time it's because a woman's sitting in jail for a murder she didn't commit."

"I didn't kill Grady Barber. Madison didn't kill him. Can't that be good enough for you?"

"It will be, if you tell me where you were that night."

She didn't repeat her lie. I was sure she knew I had checked her story.

"I am a good mother."

"That's a good place to start. Something we can agree on."

"I just wanted the best for her. I wanted Madison to have what I didn't. I wanted her to have the whole world open to her."

I nodded, afraid to break her train of thought with questions. She paused for so long I wasn't sure what to do, but in the end, silence was the best option.

The defiant expression disappeared. "I didn't want to believe Grady Barber was anything except what he seemed on the surface. Professional. Kind. Happy to find such a talented girl in the place he'd come from himself. I ignored all the warning signs, because I didn't want to believe them. I ignored you. I even ignored Madison the night of her party. I told myself it was the alcohol talking."

I put down my drink and covered her hand a moment in sympathy. "I'm so sorry. He made a habit of trying to seduce finalists. It turns out Madison wasn't alone. I wish I'd known that for sure when I warned you."

"She fell apart the afternoon of the finals and refused to go back. She said he'd made it clear that if she was going to win, she was going to have to do him some favors, too. I didn't raise her to be that kind of girl, no matter what you think."

"Stop saying that. What do I think? I think you were young when you had her. I think you two grew up together and you did it with next to no help. But she's great. You're great. Don't assume things that aren't true."

"I should have listened to everything she was saying and everything she couldn't say."

"I'm not finding this parenting thing easy, either. I probably make as many mistakes as I have successes, but all our kids seem to be turning out okay. In the end you did listen and I'm sure you did everything you could to prevent disaster."

Her eyes were glistening, but she tried to smile her thanks. "When I finally faced the truth, I took her to see May. The evening of the finals."

"May Frankel?"

"She knows Madison, from high school and church. She was the obvious person to help her figure out what to do, so we went to her house. After they talked Madison decided that she wasn't going to participate in the Idyll anymore. She said it was too much to handle, that she just wanted to be out from under the stress. She came out of May's study and told me, and I was devastated. But I understood. Madison was in over her head, and I just hadn't faced it in time. So we decided to call the auditorium and tell the stage manager she was sick. Then the next morning we were going to talk to Mrs. Hayworth and explain what was going on. Although I doubt she would have believed it. She was so high on Grady Barber."

"What happened next?"

"The phones were all tied up. We couldn't get through. And by the time we finally did, somebody, a ticket seller I guess, told us what had happened. We were still at May's house, and she was able to talk to Madison about the murder, too. She's been a big help."

May had also been as silent as any counselor concerned about confidentiality has to be. I had to give my friend credit.

"How's Madison doing now?" I asked.

"She's doing okay. Nobody knows she wasn't going to

appear in the finals, so she hasn't had to answer questions about it. That's part of the reason I didn't want you to know." Tammy gave a wry smile. "The other part is that I didn't want you to know you were right. I guess that was childish."

"I guess that was human."

"I'm sure you're going to check out our story. Tell May she's doing fine, okay?"

"I believe you, but I think I am going over to May's. I've got my own kid problem to talk to her about."

"When Madison was born my family tried to convince me to give her up for adoption. When I refused, they cut me loose. They thought I'd give up quickly, but of course, I never did. After that I've always had this feeling, I guess, that if I ask anybody for help, somebody will try to take her away from me."

"You can be proud of what you accomplished, Tammy."

I left her staring off into space, but I was sure that after a minute passed, she'd be hitting the chemistry text again. Tammy Sargent was one determined woman. She would succeed at anything she set her mind to.

The Frankels have a lovely Tudor cottage on a quiet street not far from the coffee shop, with a small pool and patio in the back for parties. May likes to garden and prefers flower borders and shrubs to grass. Today, like the rest of Emerald Springs, her front yard showed the effects of too much heat and not enough water.

May and her husband, Simon, are psychologists with private practices in a small office building downtown. They also teach conflict resolution at the high school and classes at Emerald College. Somehow, in between, they've managed to raise two bright, interesting children. I wasn't sure I'd find May at home on a Friday afternoon, but when I drove up she was outside weeding in the shade of a trio of redbud trees.

"Hey there." She got to her feet when she saw me. "Can you tell me why weeds do so well in this weather when nothing else does?"

"It's one of those universal mysteries. Try Ed."

She wiped her hands on her khaki shorts. "I'm ready for a break. Want some iced tea?"

"No, I just indulged in a million-calorie mocha, but if you have five minutes, I'd like a conversation."

"Let's go inside."

May's kitchen is dark and cool, with framed still lifes and curtains made from William Morris floral prints. She poured herself tea and gave me iced water while I told her about my conversation with Tammy.

"I'm glad she told you. So are you here because you're checking up on her?" May asked.

"Just nominally, because I believed her and she knew I'd be checking. But our conversation did make me think about how tough it is to be a mother, and how hard to figure out what to do. How much do you interfere and how much do you let kids make their own mistakes?"

"Maddie keeps me informed about what's going on with Deena. I gather she's the only Meanie who's not at the community pool today?"

"Is this too professional? Should I make an appointment? I don't want to abuse our relationship."

She smiled. "Ask as a friend and I'll answer as one."

"I keep wondering if I'm doing the right thing about Deena. Ed won't say so, but I know he's really hurt at the way she's treating him. He's apologized sincerely and promised never to make the same mistake again. But Deena's still treating him like a pariah, and it's rubbed off on the rest of us, too."

"And you want to fix it."

"Well, sure."

"As one friend to another, you can't. It's up to Deena and Ed."

Of course I knew she was right, but I'd been hoping for a magic solution. "That's it? I can't wave a wand and make this go away?"

"You're a fixer, Aggie. That's your biggest role on this

earth. Find solutions, fix things. Houses. People. Murders. You were the fix-it lady for the Emerald Springs Idyll. All a piece of the same cloth. Only this time you're not in charge of fixing your family, no matter how much you want to. You have to stay out of it."

She was right, and at least I knew that Teddy came by this tendency honestly. She had been born with a double genetic whammy, since Ed was a fixer, too.

"Easier said than done." I shook my head.

"Like most things."

"I'm pretty busy anyway, trying to fix things for Nora Nelson. I don't think she killed Grady Barber. I think the murderer is still out there."

"Why is fixing that up to you?"

"Nobody else is doing it."

"If you ignored it, I guess you'd be fighting your own inclinations for no good reason. So checking on things makes sense to me. But you can't fix everything. You have to figure out where to draw the line and not feel guilty."

"I wonder if the person who murdered Grady felt the way I do? That something was wrong, and he or she had to take care of it? Maybe he or she's a fixer, too. Maybe as far as they were concerned, the only way to set things right was to kill Grady."

"That could be a piece of the puzzle. Of course that logic could lead straight back to Nora Nelson. If she believes she talks to God, she may well think God told her to murder him herself."

"I really think if she did, she wouldn't lie about it."

"Your instincts are good. I believe you."

"I didn't think I'd get right into the middle of a murder investigation again. I was sure I wouldn't."

"You don't know yourself as well as you think, then."

"I'm pretty good about figuring out who murderers are, but last time I came awfully close to not living to tell the story."

"And you're afraid the same thing will happen again?"

"Every other time, somebody else had to jump in and save me."

"We all need help. No man is an island, and no woman."

That sounded like what I'd just told Tammy. I told May so. "But I'm not going to put myself in the same situation again," I added. "I'm not going to be helpless. I'm going to make sure I'm safe, that I have backup, that I'm not vulnerable. Heck, if I can avoid getting trampled by elephants—"

"What?"

Those darned elephants. Despite the best of intentions, despite every plan to stay safe, to be careful, I'd nearly been flattened.

Still, I hadn't been, had I? I'd found a safe place. I'd survived. On my own. Nobody'd had to rescue me.

"It's kind of a long story," I said. "But maybe my luck is changing."

May opened a cabinet and pulled down a box of Girl Scout cookies and held them up like a bribe. "Then I'm glad I have a large glass of tea and an unopened box of Thin Mints. Let's go sit on my sunporch."

16

Our weekend went something like this: Deena finished her chores. Ed and I had three long conversations about Deena finishing her chores. Ed considered the pros and cons of telling her she was no longer our prisoner. Teddy had another unsuccessful heart-to-heart talk with Deena to make her see the error of her ways. Deena told us that if she couldn't go anywhere else, she didn't see why she had to go to church, either. Deena went to church under protest. That took us to dinner on Sunday. We were living our own little reality show.

I made eggplant Parmesan for dinner, one of those time-intensive meals guaranteed to draw people into the kitchen to laugh and talk during the ten years or so it takes to dip multiple slimy slices of eggplant into an egg solution, then flop them back and forth in bread crumbs before broiling. This time nobody came to converse or laugh and share in the misery. When we sat down to eat, I thought the dish tasted flat, like I'd left out the most important ingredient.

We said grace, and passed the food around in silence. Ed was the one to break it. "Deena, you can use the phone and computer now, and you can make plans with your friends for the week. You did everything we asked you to, except maybe learn from your experience. And without any proof of that, I guess we'll just have to assume you did."

Deena brightened visibly, but that disappeared almost immediately. "I worked hard on that list," she said.

"You did."

"So what's wrong?" The challenge was clear in her tone.

"I trust you to know that, too."

"I don't understand why when a parent makes a mistake, nobody does anything, but when a kid makes one, all hell breaks loose."

Silence reigned. As it extended I remembered my conversation with May and repeated her advice to myself like a mantra. Ed's not easy to read. He keeps his emotions under wraps, which comes in handy when members of the church are trying their hardest to provoke him. It came in handy now, although I knew that despite his outward calm, he was feeling a number of things.

"Nobody had to do anything to me," he said at last. "I felt sad that I hurt you, and I apologized. That was my punishment. But let's face it, you've extended your anger as far as you can, by continuing to punish me. So never underestimate your power. The difference is that I've been trying to teach you something. You don't have anything to teach me. You know I'm sorry and I learned my lesson. You've just been trying to hurt me, and by extension, Teddy and your mom."

"Nobody else I know gets lectures like this."

Ed asked for the bread, and Moonpie jumped up on the table to steal a piece for himself. By the time we'd banished him to the other room, Deena was no longer the center of attention, and Teddy was telling Ed about the new plotline for the video. The boys and girls had come to a compromise. Bicycle theft and guilt were still in, but the theft was now— as I'd predicted—the result of a brain-eating parasite that caused good children to turn bad. Were it only that simple.

After we cleaned up, Ed took Teddy out for ice cream and politely invited Deena to come, but she refused. Politely enough, too, I'm happy to say, but I noticed she couldn't quite look her father in the eye. I was just gathering the bills to extend the joy of the evening, when the phone rang and Deena called down to tell me the caller wanted me. The fact that someone older than thirteen had gotten through, now that Deena was no longer barred from using the telephone, was proof of the goodness of the universe.

Roussos was on the other end.

"Taylor's coming in to talk to us tomorrow."

"You're kidding. Here in town?"

"His choice. I just happened to mention we could have his local police interview him instead. He wasn't keen on the idea."

"Thanks for finding him so quickly."

"Do you want to sit in on the conversation if he allows it?"

For a moment I thought Roussos had asked me if I wanted to be there. I pictured myself hitting the side of my head to knock loose whatever was distorting the sound waves.

"You heard me right," he said.

I was delighted. "I'd like that a lot."

"I'm just asking so you can be sure it's the same guy you saw the night Barber was murdered."

"I got you."

"You won't speak unless spoken to?"

"I'll be the model of a parochial school third-grader."

"You never went to parochial school. You wouldn't have lasted a day."

"But I wanted to. I yearned to wear those cute little pleated skirts."

"Tomorrow morning at ten."

I hung up and shouted upstairs to tell Deena the phone was free again.

Ed was bedraggled by the time he made it to bed. Too many questions without answers for Teddy, too many days of Deena's freezing wrath. I was no longer quite so sore from my log encounter, and I made sure our night ended on a more pleasant note.

By nine thirty the next morning Deena was on her way to Maddie's house, and Teddy and her crew were getting ready to film a major scene in our backyard involving parasites made from grocery bags stuffed with grass clippings. The parasites hung by the lowest branches of the same tree from which Moonpie had been rescued, and in a perfect Norman Rockwell moment the boys, two freckled, crew-cut specimens, were hanging upside down among them making faces. Ed had a good book and a glass of lemonade so he could watch their progress from the deepest shade in the yard and make sure there were no fights over who held the camera. I was off to make Rob Taylor confess to murder.

Okay, I was off to keep my mouth shut and hope for the best.

When I got to the station, Roussos was waiting in the lobby, and he led me back to what I supposed was an interrogation room, although not the lone lightbulb hanging over a dented table variety. This one was pleasant enough, with fresh paint and fluorescent fixtures. The table was something you'd expect to see in the conference room of an ambulance-chasing law firm; the chairs were comfortable.

"When he comes in and sits down, just nod if it's the same guy you saw the night Barber died, and shake your head if it's not. I'll wait for a signal before I begin."

"I'll shrug if I can't say one way or the other."

"You do that."

Roussos and me, planning our secret code. This was too cool for words. I yearned to teach him some of the cloak-and-dagger hand signs my sisters and I had indulged in throughout childhood, but I know how to quit when I'm ahead.

I recognized Rob Taylor the moment he came in carrying a manilla folder, but I waited until he was seated and Roussos glanced at me before I nodded. And some people think I have no patience.

Roussos made no sign he'd noticed the nod, but he angled his chair so he was looking more directly at Taylor. He started by thanking Taylor for coming, and he explained he was just tying up a few loose ends in the investigation of Grady Barber's murder.

"I'd like to hear about your connection to the victim in your own words, if you will. Mrs. Wilcox worked as Barber's assistant right before he died, so we've asked her to sit in and explain anything that might come up. You're okay with that?"

"Yeah, I don't care if the whole wide world knows the things I know. He was a sleazebag, plain and simple."

Today Rob Taylor wore a curry-colored polo shirt with fashionably faded jeans and hiking boots. His dark hair was shiny and longish, swept back from a high forehead, and he had a gold stud in his left earlobe. The bottom edge of a tattoo was just visible under his left sleeve. I guessed he was in his early forties, about Roussos's age.

Roussos sat back, like one friend listening to another. "Tell us how you met Mr. Barber."

"My wife, Kathy, was a contestant in a Pittsburgh fundraiser, a talent show kind of like your Emerald Springs Idyll. Grady Barber was the so-called celebrity judge. Kathy did well in the competition, but then she found out that if she wanted to win, she had to put some of her other talents to good use."

"You want to be more specific?"

"Yeah, he wanted sex. Any way and anyplace she was willing to give it to him."

"He told her that outright?"

"Not at first. But he kept coming on to her, and finally right before the finals, he laid it on the line. He would look on her act a lot more favorably if she also"—he glanced at me, and I think he rethought his ending—"showed him what she could do in bed. That's when she told me what was going on."

"What did you do?"

"I confronted him. I was furious. He claimed Kathy had come on to *him*, and that she'd said if she didn't win the competition, then she would tell the press what she'd told me. He said she was trying to blackmail him, and he wasn't going to put up with it."

"Apparently you didn't believe him."

"I know my wife. I know how upset she was when she finally told me what was going on. But, of course, we had no proof. It was too late to prove what he'd done to Kathy, because she'd already dropped out, but I figured it wasn't too late to retrace the guy's steps and see if other women had experienced the same thing in other competitions. So that's what I did." Taylor nudged the folder in front of him across the table.

"And this is what you found?"

"Names, statements, phone numbers. I don't have much use for it now, do I? You can have it all."

Roussos picked up the folder and thumbed through it. "Apparently you tried to crash the welcome party at the Hayworth residence when Mr. Barber got to town. Is that true?"

"It was the perfect opportunity to announce what kind of judge they'd hired, and to warn your town what was in store for their contestants."

"You wanted to make a splash."

Rob Taylor didn't smile. "I did."

"But you were tossed out."

"And later Mrs. Hayworth tossed me out when I tried to tell her privately what had been going on. I showed her the statements, told her she could call former contestants, and she just said I was trying to ruin a good man because my wife hadn't won in Pittsburgh. She said the statements weren't worth a thing, that unless I had irrefutable proof, like tapes of conversations with Grady or witnesses to the so-called blackmail, she wasn't going to listen to me."

I was tempted to hold out my hand, as if I expected Roussos to gift me with the folder so I could page through it. But I knew better. I was never going to see this folder, never going to get the list of women who had been angry enough at their treatment to tell their stories to a stranger, the perfect list of possible suspects in the murder of Grady Barber.

The tip, I was afraid, of an iceberg loaded with suspects.

"Apparently you wore out your welcome and somehow got backstage the night Mr. Barber was murdered?" Roussos asked.

"Yeah, I'm persistent. I wanted to tell him I was never going to quit until I took him down. Way, way down. And I wanted to find the two female finalists and warn them, although it was probably a little late for that. I didn't find them, by the way."

"You more or less made this your mission."

"I was still furious. Furious at what he'd done, furious nobody was listening."

"Furious enough to kill him?"

Rob Taylor didn't deny it. "Somebody else took matters into her hands before I ever got that far. But yes, I was nearly that angry, particularly right after I learned what he'd been up to. But after I calmed down a little, I figured that bringing Barber's behavior out in the open would be the best punishment. If I could ruin his reputation with the truth, that would be good enough."

"Why didn't you just go to the press? Let them break the story?"

"I tried. You know what they told me? It wasn't important enough. Grady Barber was yesterday's news, and nobody cared if some disgruntled contestants were upset with him. Too much time to ascertain the facts, too little payoff."

"Mrs. Wilcox saw you leave the auditorium through the side door after you confronted Barber. What did you do then?"

"I didn't go back in, if that's what you're getting at. There was a bar around the corner from the campus. Sweeney's. I saw it and went in."

"You're saying that's where you were?"

"After Barber was killed, I made sure to safeguard my credit card receipts, in case this came up. You've got copies there. I paid for a beer right after I left the auditorium. Afterwards I started to leave, but I realized that I'd better eat something before I drove home. So there's another charge about thirty minutes later at the same bar, when I finished and left, and later there's a charge on the Turnpike when I got gas. But the bartender will probably remember me. I spent my time there talking about Barber, and none of it was flattering. I didn't know he'd been killed until I got home and saw it the next morning on the news."

I knew where Sweeney's was located in relationship to the auditorium. Maybe Taylor could have ducked out, run back to the campus, and somehow gotten inside and backstage without being seen, murdered Grady, moved the body and traced *nor* on the wall, sprinted back to the bar, and ordered nachos or chicken wings. But that scenario was unlikely. By that time of evening, getting back into the auditorium without a ticket, much less getting backstage, would have been nearly impossible. And that would have meant at least twenty minutes away from the bar. More likely thirty, and all that running back and forth would have been noted. If he'd driven instead, he would still have had to find parking when Idyll goers were already streaming in, run from and to the lots, drive back to Sweeney's, park . . .

Taylor added the clincher. "There was a group of students watching a ball game on the flat screen, too. I made a bet with one of them on a couple of plays and had to buy him a beer. If you find him, he'll remember me, too. The bartender probably knows his name."

"We've got a suspect," Roussos said. "We just wanted to clear up the stuff about Barber's private life."

"I don't know if you got the right suspect, but I bet there were a lot of people who wanted the guy dead. If I'd wanted to kill him, I probably would have had to take a number."

"Well, somebody drew number one."

Taylor shrugged. "I'm not sorry. The world's a better place."

Roussos stood and so did Taylor. Reluctantly I got to my feet, too. I wished I had some scintillating question to ask, something that would break apart his alibi and scare him into a confession. But I didn't think that was going to happen. Unfortunately for Sister Nora, it looked as if Rob Taylor was probably not Grady's murderer.

We walked out together. Taylor left and Roussos stood in the parking lot with his arms crossed over his chest.

"I'll check with the bartender at Sweeney's," he said. "If he's lying, that's enough of a reason to haul him back in here. But I don't think he is."

"There are a lot of women in that folder of his. Women Grady abused."

"Did you or anybody else see any strange women backstage that night, besides Nora Nelson?"

"You're not going to go any further with this, are you?"

"We have our suspect." He glanced at me. "But *you* are, right? Even now, you're not going to leave it alone."

"Have you found out anything about Danny? Danny from the tent show?"

"We've been looking for him. He cleared out but good, which makes me think he knows how to clear out without leaving a trace. But that doesn't mean he tried to murder you or that he didn't. It just means he's gone."

"And I'm still here."

"Here trying to solve a murder that's already solved." Roussos's eyes met mine. "I don't know why I worry about you. Maybe I'd just hate not having you flash those dimples at me the next time somebody in town winds up dead in your vicinity and you want a favor. Maybe I'd hate not having to keep you out of places you don't belong. Or not having an excuse to rescue that cat of yours. Whatever it is, take some advice. Be careful. Investigating the death of a creep like Barber is bad enough. Don't make me investigate yours. Okay?"

As far as it went, this was an emotional speech, a swipe at admitting that despite everything, we really did enjoy each other's company. I was touched, but not enough to give him what he wanted.

"If Grady's murder is really solved, then you have nothing to worry about, right? Nobody will care if I snoop."

"You watch out for yourself. You have a bad habit of figuring this stuff out when the bad guy's breathing down your neck. Did you put me on speed dial?"

I suspected Deena would be asked that question a lot in a year or two. I had to flash the dimples. "I'll make sure that happens."

"You do that."

+ + +

Monday is Ed's day off, and normally he doesn't go to meetings. But tonight there was a city council session scheduled to deal with parking around the Oval, just across from our church. After dinner he left to represent the church's interests, along with some of our board of trustees. The girls and I ate salads and fresh rolls, and Teddy went to bed early, tired from a day of filmmaking. When I went to bed I could still hear the low buzz of Deena's voice on the telephone, making up for lost time. It was a good thing we'd finally invested in voice mail and call-waiting so Ed could continue to stay in touch with our congregation.

I was determined to get at least halfway through *Sailing toward a Rainbow*, even if I had to get up and pace between paragraphs to stay awake. My fears were unjustified. The thermometer had hit ninety-four at about three, and although the temperature had dropped low enough that I could almost breathe comfortably outside, not so inside. The house, even with fans stirring the air, was so uncomfortable that I got up and took another shower, just to cool off a degree or two. There was no chance I was going to fall asleep easily tonight.

The heat had a secondary effect. I certainly didn't want to sleep, but I had trouble concentrating. I read every single sentence, some more than once, but at no time did I feel as if I was really getting to know Grady any better. The Emerald Springs he described wasn't the one I knew. Since towns this size change slowly when they do change, it was hard to imagine that it could have been as different then as he made it seem. In Grady's hometown, everyone was kind. Everyone smiled at him, patted him on the head, lent his beleaguered single mother support and comfort. In Grady's town every door was open and every neighbor felt obliged to participate in the task of raising him. To his benefit, of course. There wasn't a cocker spaniel or Siamese cat anywhere in town who didn't love him and beg to be petted. Even the robins built nests where he could watch them feed smiling earthworms to their young.

"Oh, *puhleese!*" I got up for a glass of iced water, despite knowing I would pay for it about two AM. I'd discovered nothing of interest about Grady's early childhood, and now it was time to push on to his school years. As before, I read sentence by sentence, and at the end of that section, I still didn't feel as if I knew him any better.

"Our hero." I put the book on the bed beside me and closed my eyes. In every story about his adolescence, Grady was the victor. He was kind to kids who didn't easily make friends, befriending one boy with a limp and another whose family lived on handouts. His friendship, of course, had meant everything to them. In truth, I imagined that these were the only boys in town who had dared to cast their lot with his. Grady had been one of them, an outcast, too.

In high school his potential had been like a lone star beaming through a cloudy night sky. His teachers had realized his intelligence and talent and fought to work with him. He was more modest about his relationship with girls, hinting winsomely that shyness was his excuse for not having a serious relationship. Not until he kissed his costar in *Wayfarers*.

"Give me a break." I thought about everything Winona and Veronica had told me. Grady and Winona had been an item, so to speak. When he'd abandoned her to become a movie star, she had fallen apart. Falling apart was more likely to have been connected to a serious relationship than to a casual friendship. But not only didn't Grady's autobiography mention Winona, it completely denied her existence. According to Grady, he hadn't even kissed a girl in our fair city.

Ed chose that moment to appear. "You can be the minister, and I'll stay home and raise the kids," he said.

He's made this offer before. I was not impressed. "You have to flip houses, while you're at it. And bake brownies, and go on field trips, and attend the Women's Society meetings, and take messages during social hour from people who think I'm too important to be bothered directly. You have to listen to people criticize my sermons, just to be helpful, of course, and smile brightly when they ask if you think the tire swing on the willow tree really sends the right message about the parsonage. But if you're willing, I'll go to sermon-ary."

"They actually discussed the possibility of changing the parking meters on the Oval so people have to pay to park on Sundays during worship services."

I patted the bed beside me. "Poor baby."

"They decided against it."

"See? A victory. What would the church do without you? Think of all the quarters you saved from a fate worse than death."

He fell down beside me. "My very own cheering section."

"Ed, do you remember the first girl you kissed?"

"Sarah Buckley."

"That must have been a whopper to be so memorable. How old were you?"

"About ten."

"What would you think about a heterosexual male who claims he didn't kiss a girl until he was eighteen?"

"Either his lips were sewed together for some esoteric medical purpose, or he's a liar."

"And what would you think of a man who lies in print about his first girlfriend?" I told him about Winona, and Grady's autobiography.

"I don't know why Barber wouldn't tell the truth, except that we know the truth was more or less a foreign concept to him. Maybe he thought a little innocence made him look more appealing."

"Can you imagine how Winona must have felt to have been written out of his life that way? After he left her here and never looked back? Then he pretends in print that she never even existed?"

"Are elephants involved here? Does she keep a pack of Dobermans for company?"

"I doubt it. She's kind of a Doberman herself."

"You'll be careful when you talk to her tomorrow?"

"How do you know I'm going to talk to her?"

He just looked at me and shook his head.

I kissed his nose. "If I was the minister, you'd have to go off and do all these scary investigations. Just be glad our roles really aren't reversed."

17

Discovering where Winona lived was as easy as opening the telephone book and looking up Unger. There was just one listing for a Jerry Unger, so I made a wild guess Winona was married to good ole Jer. Discovering they lived in the Village was the interesting part. Officially known as Essex Village, the Village is upscale and desirable enough to have its own nickname. Calling it the "Village" is our twist on the "Cape" or the "Vineyard." The houses are tastefully designed, well constructed, and shaded by towering trees and lilacs. I had no problem finding Winona's street or the adorable cottage that had a porcelain plaque with her house number to the right of a wisteria-adorned porch.

I'd stewed about this visit throughout the night. How would I feel if the boy I loved in high school ignored me completely in his autobiography, even pretended I never existed? And how would I feel if he had returned for a grand homecoming years later and viewed me only as the maid? Winona had gone into a tailspin when Grady left town without a backwards glance. She'd lost a good chance for a scholarship ticket out of poky little Emerald Springs. How could she not hold this against him?

Of course that was still a long way from murdering him to get even for the slight.

I had expected to find Winona in a less tony neighborhood, perhaps not Weezeltown, where she had grown up, but a street with older cars in driveways and battered bicycles chained to porch railings. Not so. If Winona lived here, she had done well for herself over the years. Even if the neighborhood hadn't told that story, the house itself would have. The exterior was charming right down to the last detail, and the flipper in me recognized the reason. Care, hard work, and a good eye had made a mildly cute house worthy of a spread in *Cottage Living* magazine.

I may have nerve, but not enough to walk up the flower-lined walkway to the front door and demand to know why Winona killed Grady Barber. I couldn't point my nonexistent magnifying glass at her, tell her I knew her motive and had irrefutable proof.

Nor could I give away the most significant clue to her guilt, one that had occurred to me the moment I'd first heard Veronica call her "Nonie." As he choked to death on his own blood, Grady had somehow managed to scrawl three letters on the wall, *nor*. But could he have died before he finished the last one? Could Grady have been trying to write *nonie*? With just a little more time, that lowercase *r* might have become an *n*.

Of course there was the small matter of that knife. I had no explanation for that, except that perhaps Winona had hired somebody, maybe Danny in particular, to steal it so she could pin the murder on somebody at the tent show. Why not point the police in the show's direction when Sister Nora's merry band were known to be the biggest kooks in town? Maybe Nora's arrival backstage, and the similarity to *nonie* were simply accidents.

Accidents do happen, despite what Freud insisted. I've rammed enough bumpers in my quest to parallel park to know this for a fact.

I wanted to know more about Winona, but I didn't feel up to inventing an excuse to confront her in her own house. Besides, she was probably at the Hayworths' cursing stainless steel appliances that are never, alas, less stained than plain old white ones.

I was contemplating my next move when a woman came out of a brick bungalow two doors down from Winona's cottage with a collie on a leash. The dog was already panting, and the woman's familiar face was turning pink from the sun. I recognized the cat's-eye glasses, the poorly dyed hair, the rotund middle. I couldn't believe my luck. The woman was Norma Beet, our church secretary. Since things slow down at church during the summer and attendance drops due to parishioners on vacation, Norma works only three afternoons a week until the middle of August. It looked to me as if she'd found a way to fill her mornings.

I got out of my car and hailed her. Norma was delighted to see me. The collie flopped down to the pavement and began to pant harder.

"What are you doing here?" she asked cheerfully. "Visiting friends? Taking a walk?" She went through a list of possibilities without slowing down to let me answer.

Norma has many strengths. Talking nonstop is not one of them. Used to this, I waited for her to breathe, then I jumped in. "I always enjoy a drive through this neighborhood. So what are you doing here?"

"Didn't you know? I finally talked my father into moving out of that monstrous house of his and into something easier to take care of. We bought this one because it's got a lovely garden in the back where he can putter whenever he feels like it. We moved in at the beginning of the summer." She regaled me with packing tales.

A few years ago Norma came to Emerald Springs from South Dakota to take care of her father, Alfred, a take-no-prisoners curmudgeon in his eighties who made everyone in church snap to his step until he was well into his seventies. When Alfred began to suffer health problems, Ed was instrumental in convincing him that Norma should move in, a decision that has suited them both. Now I was delighted she had talked Alfred into leaving a house that was big enough for a fraternity.

"Are you enjoying it here?" I asked, when there was another oxygen-depleted pause. "This really is the prettiest neighborhood in Emerald Springs."

"Oh, we love it! Even Dad. And the neighbors have

been so lovely. They're just the nicest people. I feel so wel-
comed."

I hoped the neighbors didn't run and hide whenever
Norma and the collie came out of the house. Norma takes
some getting used to, but I've learned to appreciate her, if
not her incessant chatter. She told me once that her childhood on a wheat farm had taught her to notice everything.
Living where big events rarely happened had taught her to
appreciate the smallest of changes. Consequently Norma
has almost total recall, and if she's around when an event
occurs, she can be relied on for the tiniest details. She's all
too willing to recount them, every one.

"Who's your friend?" I asked, squatting down to stroke
the collie's golden fur.

"This is Sammy. Dad and I rescued him from the pound.
Isn't he a beaut?"

He was that, but hot. I stood and volunteered to walk
with them around the block, and Norma was delighted. The
collie lumbered to his feet, and off we went.

"You must have moved while I was in Indiana, or I
would have heard. I could have helped," I told her.

"Don't worry. The Women's Society organized meals
while we were moving in, and some of the youth group
came over and helped us unload our smaller things. By the
time I separated the heirlooms from the junk, there was just
enough to furnish this house."

Before we even made the turn up the side street, Norma
told me about the changes they'd already made inside, and
what they still planned to do. When we had another block
under our belts I considered just edging into the subject of
Winona, but decided subtlety probably wasn't fair. When
Norma took another deep breath, I told her that I'd met
Winona at Veronica Hayworth's house and I was hoping to
learn a bit more about her.

"Because of Grady Barber's death," Norma said. "I figured you might be looking into that."

"Caught me."

"Well, I didn't realize you'd think there was anything special about the Ungers. They're just the nicest family. Winona's a top-notch mother. I never saw anybody work so hard. College, full-time job, starting her own business, running those children here and there once they get home from school.

"Wow. All that?"

"She's getting a degree at Emerald College, and she'll be starting her own business once she does. Meantime she's working for a woman over in Emerald Estates as a maid. The kids both need braces, and Jerry's a contractor, but times are slow right now. She says most of her paycheck goes to the orthodontist. She has a good job, though. Most of the time she's done working when the kids are out of school. A boy and a girl. Jessie and Jamie. Isn't that cute?"

The names showed a whimsical side to a woman who had never seemed to have one. "What kind of business?" If Winona was a freelancer for the Mob, I was on the track of something big.

"She told me she knows the service industry in Emerald Springs inside out. She's going to start a referral service. People can call her, and she'll find them the perfect employee for any job, then she'll make the contact and set up everything, check progress, and monitor quality. House repairs. Catering and party planning. Cleaning. Home care for the elderly. Pet sitting. She's been collecting lists and interviewing service providers for months now. She graduates in December, and she's already preparing to quit her job."

I suppose that a hit man might be considered a service provider, but somehow murder seemed at odds with Winona's work ethic and strong mothering skills.

Winona had gotten off to a difficult start, or rather, the episode with Grady had been a difficult detour in a life filled with promise. But it sounded as if Winona had recovered nicely and was once again determined to succeed.

Still, maybe she had secretly pined for Grady Barber since high school, hoping that if she saw him again, their love would be rekindled. Abandoned lovers can tell themselves a number of lies to buffer their pain. When the reunion finally occurred, could Grady's disdain have sent her into despair and ended with an uncontrollable need for revenge?

"I wonder if the marriage is happy," I said.

"Judging from what I see? Supremely so. They take every chance they can to do things as a family. And most evenings when Sammy and I walk by, Winona and Jerry are sitting together on the porch on the love seat, talking and laughing."

I heard a wistful note in Norma's voice. I think Norma has potential to be more attractive. A good salon, a diet, new glasses. It wouldn't take much more than that except a short course on active listening. She clearly has a lot of love to give. I wondered if I could help, and filed that away to reconsider after Grady's murderer was in jail. Matchmaker me.

We were nearly back to Norma's new house, and as we finished the walk, she told me about some of the other neighbors. "You've been a help," I said once we were standing on her sidewalk.

"There's Winona now." She nodded her head toward the cottage. "Her boss is away for a few days, and she's been home with the kids."

A late-model sedan, plain but impeccably clean, pulled into Winona's driveway. I was caught standing with Norma and gazing in Winona's direction. Winona got out, and two good-looking blond children followed through the rear doors. The kids streaked toward the house so fast I only had a blur to go on, but I was guessing middle school.

Winona came toward us. She smiled at Norma. "How are you?" Then she looked at me. "Mrs. Wilcox."

"Aggie was just driving through the neighborhood and saw me with Sammy," Norma explained. "We took him for a walk."

"Just driving through?" Winona sounded skeptical.

"I have to check on Dad," Norma said. "And I have to get Sammy some water. It's too hot for man or beast." She said good-bye and continued to talk to us until she was halfway up her sidewalk. The neighborhood seemed oddly quiet once she was inside.

"So . . . Norma was telling me all about her move," I said.

"That's our Norma."

"She seems happy. She loves the neighborhood."

"But you didn't come to see *her*, did you? Why are you here?"

I don't like to lie. I'm normally very good at telling a piece of the truth so I won't feel guilty about not telling every bit of it. Now I couldn't think of a piece that wouldn't give me away.

"I wanted to find out more about you," I said instead, giving her the whole darned thing in one gulp. "Veronica told me that you and Grady were more than just friends. She wasn't talking out of school, Winona. She was just telling me what she knew about him. She made me want to find out more."

Without the headband and gray uniform, Winona looked as pretty today as I'd guessed she might. She wore daffodil yellow shorts and a tank top, and her blond hair was parted on one side and waved along both cheeks. I was convinced her dangly sunflower earrings had been given to her by a child. Clearly she treasured them.

"We *were* more than that," she said. "But that was a long time ago. So I'm assuming you're not asking out of idle curiosity."

"I don't think Nora Nelson killed him."

"And you're hoping I did, so you can get her out of jail?"

"No. I'd much rather it was some evil psychopath who just got tired of hearing 'Sailing toward a Rainbow' in elevators, and wanted payback. But truthfully, I think it was somebody who knew him better than that."

"And I did and had a reason to hate him." Winona

smiled. Genuinely. "Truly, you know, I did hate him for a while. After I got over loving him, of course, which took some time. There's nothing quite like that first love. Anyway, I told myself he'd ruined my life. I was sure I'd never love anybody else or move on. For a while I pretty much made sure of that. Then I got a little help, started noticing it wasn't Grady who'd made me give up my other dreams or stop working on them. I'd done that part by myself. So I took a few classes, remembered how much I love to learn, got the job with Veronica so I'd have time to take more, met my husband . . ."

Her smile was relaxed and genuine. "Enough for you? I could go on. But the theme? I finally realized Grady did me a favor. I didn't need him. In fact through the years when I'd see an article about his failed marriages or his mediocre career, I felt nothing but gratitude. I learned a lot about myself. I learned to judge men on more than looks and empty words. I learned to work for myself and the people who really loved me. It's been a good, good life."

Why was my suspect list falling apart? Was I at fault for believing every good story they told me? Maybe Fred sent a twin brother to Big Sur while he doubled back to kill Grady. Maybe while May talked to Madison at her house the night of the finals, Tammy sneaked out and killed Grady, just for something to do while she waited. Maybe Rob Taylor paid off the whole staff at Sweeney's to claim he was there, and left his credit card so they could pretend to give him receipts. Maybe Winona Unger carried a torch into middle age for one Grady Barber and murdered him when he dismissed her as an unwelcome reminder of his unhappy past.

But truthfully, I didn't think so.

"Okay. You had almost no motive to kill him," I said. "I hear you."

"*No* motive, and no alibi—so you don't have to ask. Jerry took the kids to the movies that night, and I stayed home all alone and took a long bath and thought about the week. I hate to say this because it sounds so petty, but I enjoyed watching Grady make enemies here. I had no reason to want that to end precipitously. He was soiling his own nest with ill will and tantrums and slights. I'm ashamed to say I was enjoying the show. I am sorry he was killed, because nobody deserves to die the way he did. And I do feel sorry for Veronica. She worked so hard to bring him back here, and look what she got for her trouble. But that's the sum total of my emotion."

"Apparently from what Veronica told me, Grady had a history of putting both you *and* her to a lot of trouble."

"Yeah, high school. She and I had that in common, if not much else. She tried to make him a star. I just tried to help him pass his classes. Especially English. It's hard for me to figure out how Grady managed to write those lovely songs. He could hardly string four words together and write them down. Mrs. Wilkinson despaired of him. She worked harder than any of the rest of us combined, but a time or two she just gave up and passed him, even when he didn't deserve it."

"Mrs. Wilkinson?"

"Our junior English teacher. She was a character. Still is. But a truly dedicated teacher. A lot of people in Emerald Springs owe her everything. After Grady left, she propped me up and got me through graduation, although barely."

"Would that be *Daisy* Wilkinson?"

"It would. You know her?"

"I've only met her. My husband knows her well." Daisy Wilkinson was a member of our church, but too infirm to attend Sunday services very often. She lived in an assisted living facility near the police station, Old Mill Manor. Ed visited regularly, as did members of our Women's Society.

"I bring her here for Sunday dinner whenever she's feeling up to it," Winona said. "She's a little slip of a thing, and Jerry lifts her in and out of our car. The kids love to push her wheelchair."

"Maybe she'd like some company today."

"If you still want to know more about Grady, she'll enjoy talking about him, although she was quite upset when he was killed. Do you know, after everything she did for him, he couldn't find the time to go and visit her when he came back? I made sure he knew where to find her, but he couldn't be bothered." She shook her head, not as if she was angry, but just amazed anyone could be that selfish.

"I won't upset her more?"

"No, she forgets a lot of what's happening now, but she enjoys recounting her days as his English teacher."

I liked Winona. I told her so and wished her well.

"Then you've crossed me off your list of suspects?"

"You're free to move about your life."

"I hope you figure this out, but honestly? There are just too many things that point to Nora Nelson."

"You aren't the first person to say so."

She went inside, and I went back to my van. I wasn't sure a trip to Old Mill Manor would be helpful, but I was about to find out. I had enough time before I needed to go home and check on my girls to make a trip out there. I wondered what they were having for lunch.

+ + +

They were having cold turkey sandwiches, as it turned out. And fruit salad to go with it. Residents could choose between a selection with melons and another made with bananas and grapes. Daisy Wilkinson was a cantaloupe fiend and I managed to sneak her a second helping right before I carried her tray out to the shady patio where she wanted to have lunch.

Old Mill Manor was a facility with several levels of care. Some of the residents cooked their own meals and came and went as they pleased. Others, like Daisy, needed more help and took meals together. I noted a calendar filled with activities and hallways filled with smiling personnel. The building was clean and cheerful, and Daisy said she guessed it was an okay place to live if you had to get old and couldn't remember when to take your medicine or turn off the stove.

"My memory's about this long," she said, snapping her fingers. "What did you say your name is?"

I told her again.

"Oh, that's right. I know who you are." She waved a hand at me. "That husband of yours comes in pretty often to see how I'm doing. I was on the board of trustees back in my heyday, and I ran the religious education program for a year or two. Did some other jobs, too, but I don't remember what. Maybe I'm just forgetting the ones that weren't fun."

Daisy was only about five feet tall, and I could see how Winona's husband or any strong man could simply pick her up to move her around. She had tightly curled white hair and bright pink cheeks. Despite her age and slight stature, she still had a commanding presence. I imagined she'd had to develop one to survive teaching high school.

We settled at a small table in the corner, although we had our pick of seats. Most people were inside taking advantage of the air-conditioning, but Daisy had told me she was always cold and liked to be outdoors when she could.

"I'll share my sandwich, dear," she said. "But not my cantaloupe."

"I promised my girls I'd head home and make lunch in a little while," I said. "So I'd better save my appetite."

"Good, turkey's my favorite." She dug right in and seemed to enjoy every bite. After a swallow or two she looked at me. "Tell me again why you're here?"

When I arrived I had explained my presence, but I explained once more. "Winona Unger told me you worked with Grady Barber, and I'm trying to learn about his years in Emerald Springs."

"Are you going to write his biography? He wrote one

himself, you know, only it was filled with the most dreadful lies. And, of course, he didn't really write it, although that's what it said on the cover. He couldn't have. That boy couldn't write a sentence without outside help."

That boy hadn't been a boy for a very long time. I approached her information with caution. "I know Winona said he needed a lot of your help to get through English class."

"Grady Barber's problem was his birth date."

I was beginning to wonder how smart it had been to come here for information. Daisy Wilkinson was delightful, but I didn't think I was going to discover anything about Grady I could count on.

"What was wrong with his birth date?" I asked.

"Much too early." She took another bite of her sandwich and chewed thoughtfully. "You see, a decade later, we knew a lot more about how to help somebody like Grady. We knew about learning disabilities back then, of course. I did my homework. How to diagnose. How to treat. But what we understood was only a drop compared to what came later. Of course these days teachers are so busy filling out forms when they have a special student, they don't have much time to use what they know. But at least they know what they're up against."

"What are they up against?"

"In Grady's case it was probably dyseidetic dyslexia. Poor visual memory, you see. His symptoms were classic. He would learn a word and then not recognize it later in the same sentence. Letters got popped in anywhere they seemed to fit, and certainly not in places you or I would put them. He told me once that when he looked at a page, the letters jumped all around, and he just couldn't make them behave."

My mind was twirling back to the man I'd known. Grady had refused to do any of his paperwork. After Fred left he'd insisted Veronica find him an assistant or else.

Now I understood the real reason. Not because he was lazy or too important to do his own dirty work—although that might have been true as well—but because the tasks of reading and writing were so difficult he preferred not to do them. Or worse, he *couldn't* do them.

I wondered if Grady had ever really overcome his disability.

"How did he get through school?" I asked.

She was smiling now, and had even put down her sandwich. This was something she remembered.

"Well, he could read a little, although it took him five times as long to finish a paragraph as it would you or me. But he had a fabulous memory. So we worked on listening in class and paying attention. When he did that, and he was tested on what was said in lectures, he was okay if the written questions weren't too long or complex. Of course complicated essay questions were next to impossible. I talked to most of his teachers and explained, and they would read questions out loud to give him a head start, and not take off as many points for grammar or spelling. Some of them would even question him in private and score his tests on verbal information. At least the good teachers would do it that way. Some thought all this was nonsense, of course, and that he just had to work harder and adjust."

"How difficult for him. He was lucky he had your help."

"My help. Yes. And Nonie. Have you met dear Nonie? She did everything she could to help him pass. You really should look her up and listen to what she has to say about him."

There was no point in reminding Daisy that Nonie had sent me here. "I do know her, and she does have interesting things to say."

"I can't imagine anyone murdering a boy like Grady. Such a nice boy, although not everybody thought so. I always understood that when he acted out, he was just trying to cope with his disability and home life. It wasn't easy being Grady Barber. Of course later, it must have been much easier." She frowned and cocked her head. "Wasn't it?"

"He certainly did make a success of himself."

"I like to think I helped with that. But Nonie and Ronnie and of course Sandy Billings, the choir teacher, all did their share. Sandy was convinced that with his abilities he could get a scholarship to some little college looking for a tenor. She worked and worked with him to improve his voice and help him sing with confidence. Yes, he wasn't a popular boy, but he did have his own cheering section."

"Ronnie?"

"One of his little friends."

I wondered if Ronnie was the boy with the limp, or maybe the one from the poorest home in town. Apparently I hadn't paid enough attention to their names. Maybe Grady hadn't even used them in the book. "Can you tell me more about him?"

She looked confused. "No . . . Him? I don't remember, I guess. I've forgotten so much."

I wondered if Grady's choir teacher might have more helpful information, although at this point, I knew I was grasping at straws. I really didn't think Winona had killed Grady, and no one else here seemed to have a motive. So many years had gone by since Grady had lived in Emerald Springs. Was I really planning to interview every single person he'd ever talked to?

I grasped anyway. "Does Mrs. Billings still live in Emerald Springs?"

"Oh, I can answer that one. She moved away right after she retired. Somewhere warm. Florida, maybe, although I don't really know. We were never close." She leaned toward me. "She had a man on the side. Her husband, poor fellow, never suspected."

"Yikes."

She nodded, then she winked. "Imagine that? Two men! I couldn't hold on to one. My husband left me, but he was such a rascal I was better off without him. I had a fine life anyway. Do you know I once taught Grady Barber? The star of that movie about Noah and his family?"

I took her hand and squeezed it. "He was lucky to have you."

She smiled. "Indeed he was."

18

I do my best thinking in the middle of the night when the house is quiet and Ed is breathing deeply beside me. That's when I remember where I put my favorite recipe for mushroom stroganoff, and why I circled yesterday's date on the calendar. By then it's too late to get up and saute mushrooms or call the friend whose birthday I missed, but at least I no longer have to probe the darkest recesses of my mind.

Tonight I lay awake sweating out the details of my conversations with Winona and Daisy. I hadn't had time before this. After lunch I'd taken the girls to the pool, where I paid bills and caught up with the family paperwork. Next we made a trip to the pediatrician for their annual physicals, a stop for doughnuts to console them for being poked and prodded, then a visit to the grocery store. We'd had dinner; I'd helped Teddy with a crossword puzzle; I'd sneaked a quick look at Grady's autobiography to see if he had happened to mention the names of his two childhood friends.

He hadn't.

I was beginning to look forward to tearing out linoleum and choosing paint colors again.

"Go back to sleep," Ed mumbled.

"If I do, I might not solve Grady's murder."

"It'll keep." He turned over, and in a moment he was dead to the world again, as if to demonstrate how it was done.

I tried to breathe evenly, in case some part of him was still aware. My interview with Daisy had been far from perfect. When I'd told Ed about our conversation, I learned that Daisy had suffered a mild stroke in the spring and her short-term memory had suffered. Still, from what I could tell, her long-term memory was good. The lecture on dyslexia had sounded like a pro's. She'd remembered names, what she had done to help Grady, and so much about her past.

She had mentioned somebody named . . . Ronnie.

Of course with nobody pulling at me and no errands to run, the answer slapped me on the head.

I sat up. "Veronica."

"Aggie . . . make yourself . . . warm milk . . . Anything . . ."

"He called Winona, Nonie. I bet he called Veronica, Ronnie."

"Go 'way."

I went downstairs and made myself comfortable on the sofa. It was too hot to warm up anything, and anyway, before I thought about sleep, I wanted to think this through. Winona wasn't the only girl whom Grady hadn't mentioned in his autobiography. Veronica had been absent, as well. Knowing Grady, this made a certain kind of sense. He'd wanted the world to believe he'd earned his success with no help along the way. In his book he was the one who helped others . . .

Nobody was there to hear it, but I made the customary gagging sound to show what I thought of that.

None of the people who had helped him get through his classes, who had spent special time with him and supported him, had made it to his pages. Not Winona. Not Daisy Wilkinson, who clearly should have been there. Not Veronica.

Maybe there was a slightly less hostile explanation. Maybe one of Grady's disabilities was a poor memory. Maybe all these people really had faded out of his mind. He was a classic narcissist, after all. The world revolved around him, so why should he remember anybody else? Just existing in the shadow of his great light had been enough of a boon to bestow.

That triggered a memory of my own. Something that had been said about him . . . no, *to* him. Somebody had made a joke that really wasn't a joke. Somebody who had seemed unhappy not to be remembered.

For some reason I started to hum, then softly I sang the words to Grady's biggest hit.

Sailing toward a rainbow
Stretching overhead . . .
Colors flaming in the sky
Violet, gold, and red.

And then I knew.

"Lisa Lee."

On the night of the debut party less than two weeks ago—was that possible?—Lisa had sat down at the piano, played a few rippling chords, and begun the intro to "Sailing toward a Rainbow." Grady had made a dramatic entrance, and the party had been launched. But after he'd finished the song, he'd said something to her. What was it? Where was Norma Beet when I needed her?

My own memory wasn't that bad. I tried the words. "Where did you find a pianist like this?"

That wasn't perfect, but it was the gist of what he'd said.

What Lisa had replied was closer to exact, because at the time I'd thought it was odd enough, I'd more or less filed it away.

"I've just been hanging around waiting for you to come back . . ."

I paused. "Yikes."

She'd added something. What was it? I almost called Lucy to see if she remembered, but even Lucy's not that keen on a two AM phone call. I got up and started to pace, humming furiously as I walked back and forth across the room, to jog my memory.

"Waiting for you . . . come back . . ." What? "Waiting

for you to come back . . . so I could play for you?" That was it. But had she added "again"? I was pretty sure I had it right, as far as it went. But I had to give up trying to re-create her comeback word for word. I just wasn't going to be able to.

No matter what she'd said exactly, the meaning was clear to me now. Lisa Lee had played for Grady before, and the fact that he didn't remember and didn't recognize her had rankled.

I hadn't connected Lisa with Grady's past. She appeared to be older than Veronica or Winona, and she had none of Grady's youthful charm. Still, she could have been in school with them. The extra weight, the generally dumpy appear-ance? Both could age a woman at least a decade if she wasn't careful. And why else would she have seemed annoyed when he'd given her what appeared to be a compli-ment? He hadn't recognized her, and he should have. She had played the piano for him while he lived here. Probably for something *memorable*.

Could it have been his tryout for the role of Idan in *Way-farers of the Ark*?

Satisfied I'd plumbed the depths of this, I curled up on the sofa again and closed my eyes. Suddenly I was sleepy, and the thought of making the trip upstairs was daunting. I would just rest a little and see if anything else occurred to me. But tomorrow I would find Lisa Lee and see if she had anything or anyone to add to my narrowing list of suspects. I had a feeling there was something here that I hadn't quite put my finger on.

That was the last thought I had until somebody shook my shoulder.

I sat up and my eyes flew open. Sunlight was pouring in the windows, and Deena was standing over me.

"Mom? What are you doing down here?"

For a moment I couldn't remember, and all I could man-age was a frown.

"You and Daddy had a fight, didn't you?" Deena plopped down next to me. "It's my fault, isn't it?"

"*Ummm . . .*" I licked my lips. "What time is it?"

"Seven thirty."

"I . . . coffee." I got up and staggered toward the kitchen. As my legs warmed up, so did my brain. By the time I'd scooped out coffee and added water to the coffeemaker, I had remembered my previous night's escapade.

Deena was in boxers and a flowered tank top, her hair hanging like a cape over her shoulders. She looked adorable, something I'd never be allowed to say to her again. I got juice out of the refrigerator and held it out. She shook her head.

"You can have coffee if you put lots of milk in it," I said.

"Okay."

I got cups, good ones, not the assorted everyday mugs from advertising insurance companies and vacation spots where we hadn't been able to resist a souvenir. These were Great Aunt Martha's willowware, and I put them on saucers and brought them to the table, going back for a sugar bowl and a cream pitcher to fill with milk.

When the coffee was ready, I brought it to the table and poured her a dollop, as if we were once again having a childhood tea party.

"Your father kicked me out of the bedroom because I was tossing and turning. I came downstairs to get it out of my system and fell asleep on the sofa. We aren't having a fight. He just wanted some sleep."

Deena filled her cup to the brim with milk. "Really?"

"Uh huh. Daddy can sleep through almost anything, just not me whacking him with my elbows and knees."

"Why couldn't you sleep?"

"Just a lot on my mind, I guess."

"Is it my fault?"

This was getting interesting. We had worried that Deena didn't care one bit if she'd hurt anybody in the family, but here was proof that having faith in her best instincts had been the right course.

"Not your fault, sweetie," I said. "But let's just say it was. Why exactly would that be?"

She didn't answer for a while. I suspected she didn't know how.

"I made a big fuss," she said at last.

"That pretty well describes it, I guess."

"I just felt so humiliated."

"I know you did. But from our perspective it was a pretty extreme reaction for something everybody has already forgotten."

She looked up and almost smiled. "You're saying Daddy's sermons are forgettable?"

That she could joke about this was the best sign I could imagine. "Only the occasional teensy-weensy word or example. And don't ever tell him I said so."

This time she did smile. "I felt betrayed, you know? I mean, if I can't trust Daddy, who can I trust?"

She was entering a time in her life when that question would be crucial, and both of us knew it. No wonder she had been so disturbed. I tried to think of a way to help.

"You have to make allowances for everybody, Deena. Nobody's perfect. You have to look at all the times a person has been there for you, and measure that against the occasional mistakes. Some mistakes are too huge to overlook, of course. But this one wasn't."

"I guess."

I wish Ed had been there to hear that. It was as close to an apology as he might get.

But Deena was more mature than I gave her credit for. She'd done some thinking, because now she went on. "I don't know what to say to him. To Daddy, I mean. I don't know how to do it. It's just gone on so long."

"Just say what's in your heart, honey. That's all he wants to hear. You know how much he loves you."

Her eyes were suddenly shiny with tears. "Would you come with me?"

I was so surprised, I didn't know what to say. "Me?"

"You're the mom, right? Don't you, like, do this stuff? Isn't it in the set of instructions they gave you at the hospital or something?"

"Well, sure. I just didn't think you'd want me there."

"Well, if I screw up, you could help me out."

I nearly laughed. Luckily, she smiled, then she wiped her eyes with the back of her hand.

"Okay, when?" I asked. "I'll put it on my schedule. The Big Apology."

"I don't know. I'll think about it, okay?"

I reached over and covered her hand. "You bet."

She looked wistful. "Remember when we used to have tea with my dolls?"

"I do."

"I kind of miss it."

+ + +

Obviously houses mean a lot to me. Maybe this is because Ed and I have yet to own one. Plus, as a child, the closest my little family ever came to our own place was the RV we slept in when we traveled the craft show circuit. So by default I've become a connoisseur of other people's homes, and I've learned a few things along the way.

Homeowners come in several varieties. Some have set requirements and buy the first house that meets them, with little or no emotional attachment. Some have no idea what they need but buy as large and expensive as they think they can afford. If they're attached, it's usually to the prestige or the investment potential, not to the house itself.

Some are drawn to a house despite its size, what it offers or lacks, what it costs. I had a feeling Lisa Lee might be one of these. I imagined her house would be an expression of who she was and what she loved. I was correct.

Lisa's house was in a neighborhood that, unlike the Village, has no name, much less a nickname. Whenever I visit I'm convinced that the original developer was verging on retirement and built himself a house smack in the middle of his winding warren of trails, courts, rambles, and paths. I'm sure he designed his porch so he could sit outside in his dotage and watch drivers circling helplessly. Had anyone asked me, I would have named the neighborhood Cul-de-sac Catastrophe.

Lisa's address was Whaler's Walk. The house itself was a small cedar contemporary, very Frank Lloyd Wright on a budget. The windows were slits that reminded me of the arrow holes in a medieval castle. Each section of the house seemed to shelter under a different roof. The yard and exterior were adorned with stone sculptures, an assortment of wind chimes, and too many evergreens trimmed into geometric shapes.

"Artsy, a freethinker, not all that interested in conforming." Now all Lisa needed was a warm heart, and we might be friends.

The last was not to be. Lisa came to the door, graying hair flowing over a 1970s-style granny dress and a white Persian cat draped over one arm. Although we'd met several times, she didn't remember me, nor did she invite me inside after I introduced myself again.

"This is the time each day when I work on my poetry," she said.

And this was the time of day when I solved murders, but I really didn't think she'd appreciate hearing that.

"I'm sorry. I would have called but I couldn't find your number."

"It's unlisted. How did you find *me*?"

How did I find her? Well, I found her rude and unhelpful, but I didn't think that was what she was asking. "My friend Lucy Jacobs remembered your house," I said instead.

"Oh, yes, the realtor." She sighed, and I was nearly blown off the porch. Then she stepped aside and gestured me in.

The smell of unchanged cat litter hit me like a tidal wave.

The outside of the house was artistically cluttered. The inside was simply cluttered. Clothes, newspapers, books everywhere, and none of it where it ought to be. I glimpsed modern art on smudged walls, handmade afghans covered with fur, plates with food that was growing medically significant mold colonies. I wondered if Lisa was really working on her poetry, or if she just didn't want me to see how she lived.

And could this housekeeping disaster have been caused by Grady's death? Had Lisa been sent into an emotional decline? More interesting, was she suffering paroxysms of guilt? Somehow I found that hard to believe. A woman who couldn't deposit her own plates in the sink was unlikely to have the energy to stab a man with the force and fury Grady's murder had necessitated.

"Why did you need to see me?" she asked, gesturing to the sofa, although sitting would have meant digging out a place to park my bottom, and thoughts of fleas in the cushions kept me on my feet.

"I'll come straight to the point, so you can get back to your poetry. I'm not convinced Nora Nelson killed Grady Barber, and I'm doing some investigation on my own."

She bent to put the cat down, and it scurried out of the room to go about its work of distributing fur throughout the house. "Why do you care?"

"I like Nora. I can't imagine her stabbing anybody."

"She's crazy."

"She's committed to saving the planet. Most murderers don't think that far ahead."

"So why are you here? In my house?"

Not for the ambience, that was for sure. My nose itched, and the possibilities were so rich, it was a toss-up what was causing it. I tried to be succinct.

"Last night I remembered that when Grady complimented you at the welcome party, you seemed miffed. It occurred to me that maybe you had known him in high school, and he just didn't remember you."

"That's Grady for you. He left here and left everybody behind. Then he comes back like a hero and pretends he doesn't know a one of us."

"So you did know him."

"Know him?" She gave an ugly little laugh. "I was his accompanist all through high school. I went to his voice lessons with Mrs. Billings, our choir teacher. He went to *my* lessons so my piano teacher could give us pointers. I practiced with him. I taught him the scales, sang lines to him so he could learn them, because he couldn't read music worth a damn. Half the time he was reading right to left. I spent hours helping him get ready for the big audition."

Now I knew which of Esther's students had been Grady's personal pianist and made a mental note to tell her. "Did you play for him? For the *Wayfarers* audition, I mean?"

"Exactly why does any of this matter? I didn't kill him. I certainly wasn't fond of him, but his being here was a good thing for me. It put me center stage for a while. I have some new piano students because of the Idyll."

Maybe she went to *their* homes. My fingers were crossed.

I managed a soothing smile. "I'm sure you didn't kill him. Forgetting you wasn't a capital offense. But I hoped you could tell me more about high school. How he got his start. You know."

She made a sound of disgust. "There's not that much to tell. We worked our tails off helping him. He sat back and let us. Then he left us high and dry. Veronica, most of all, of course. And that Nonie person, although I never did understand what Grady saw in her. Look where she ended up. Waiting on Veronica."

I wanted to defend Nonie, who had everything going for her, while this woman probably needed her cat just to keep the rat infestation at manageable levels. There was a lot I *wasn't* saying this morning. I plunged on.

"How did the *Wayfarers* audition come about? It's pretty extraordinary, isn't it, that he would write such a gorgeous song, one that was so perfect for the film that they actually used it? And him, to boot."

"The moment I heard it I knew it would be a hit, if they could just get it into the right hands."

I nearly missed the important word there, then it penetrated. "They?"

"Yes, he and Veronica."

"What did Veronica have to do with it?"

"Oh, she helped him write it. I'm sure she was more or less his scribe. Like I said, he had his problems reading music, much less putting it down on paper, but he was the talented one. Of course you'd think they were Lerner and Loewe or something, the way Veronica acted about it. She's nearly as good at claiming credit for things as Grady is."

My brain was spinning. "A team, huh?"

"Between us, I wasn't one bit surprised when he decided to try out for *Wayfarers* without her. Of course it threw her for a loop, but that's showbiz."

"Of course." I had no idea what she was talking about, but I was afraid if I asked, she would clam up. I made *tsk*-ing noises. "But poor Veronica."

"She had a nice enough voice, a little weak, but it went well enough with Grady's. They practiced and practiced. I got so sick of playing for them, but that comes with the territory of any artist."

"So they rehearsed together?"

"Oh yes. I remember the day Veronica told us she'd managed to get them an audition time in the afternoon. Spots were hard to come by, but she pulled strings. She had plenty to pull. She was so excited. She was convinced they would both get roles in the movie. I never figured out why that meant so much to her. She already had everything. I could see how it would change Grady's life, though. He wanted to get out of here."

"But they didn't try out together after all." I made it a statement.

"No, he called me that morning at the crack of dawn and told me he'd gotten an earlier time. He begged me to come and play for him, so I dragged myself out of bed and went down to the room at the college where they were having the auditions. Veronica wasn't there. Grady told me she'd decided not to come, and he'd be singing alone. I didn't question it. I figured he'd finally wised up and realized she would drag him down."

I was putting all this together at the speed of light, trying to stay one jump ahead, but I was pretty sure Lisa had hit the fingernail on the ivory key with that last observation. Grady was loyal to Grady and nobody else. That had been established. The moment he realized he would do better at the audition without Veronica was the moment he'd made other arrangements.

"I imagine Veronica was miffed when you showed up that afternoon and Grady didn't," I said.

"Oh, I didn't go. I had no idea Veronica was still going to try out. Grady led me to think she had decided not to bother. But apparently she came, and when neither Grady or I was there, she got completely shook up. They had another pianist, but, of course, she didn't have a copy of the song with her. She thought I'd be there, and I had it memorized. So she had to try out alone, a capella." Lisa's eyes lit up, as if she was enjoying this. "And I hear they stopped her about a third of the way into it and sent her on her way."

"Poor Veronica."

"Yes, well, poor Veronica had to learn she couldn't have everything, didn't she? Life's just filled with difficult lessons."

Why hadn't I heard any of this before? Veronica had helped write "Sailing toward a Rainbow," yet she'd never mentioned it? Was she just embarrassed that she'd been taken in by the boy she'd risked her own popularity to help? Then Veronica had been cruelly surprised and humiliated when Grady abandoned her at the *Wayfarers* audition without even telling her his change of plans.

"Apparently she forgave him," I said carefully. "Or else why would she have invited him back to judge the Idyll?"

"Oh, well, they were both grown-ups by then, weren't they? Knowing Ronnie—Veronica—she probably reminded Grady that he owed her for the way he'd treated her as a teenager. She probably saw his coming here as payment for what he put her through. She could bask in a little reflected glory and use him to turn those old events to her advantage. She's a schemer, our Veronica. I wouldn't put it past her to threaten him, either. Playfully, of course, but real nonetheless."

"Threaten him?"

"Right, threaten to get the word out that she helped him write the song. Although, of course, there was no proof and who would care now anyway? But if Veronica wanted Grady for the Idyll, of course, she would find a way. That's the kind of person she is. And she certainly did, didn't she? Too bad for him."

✦ ✦ ✦

I parked in front of Camille Beauregard's house and wondered how my theory of house ownership applied here. Unlike Lisa's, this one was old, brick, and substantial. It was a graciously constructed original and not a flimsy imitation like most of those in Emerald Estates, although judging by the acre of land it sat on, the sheer height and breadth, it had cost the moon. The neighborhood was not in-your-face prestigious, but subtler, with more variety in size and age of the homes. I saw touches of Camille. No-nonsense good taste, and great bones with nothing padding them. I decided Camille had bought the house because it represented the woman she was, and not because of the attached prestige.

Okay, I was wasting time on pop psych, but I sat there a moment longer anyway. When I called Camille after my trip to Lisa Lee's, she invited me to come over, but only if I was willing to work out with her in her home gym. She did a second workout every day from eleven to twelve, and she thought I might want to join her.

About as much as I wanted to yank out my toenails.

I dragged myself out of the car and pulled down the coral tank top Vel had given me last Christmas. Complete with shelf bra and enough spandex to string a slingshot, it matched my black V-waist shorts with a coral stripe up the side. Vel had been on a fitness kick at the time, and she'd wished the same for me. When Camille had warned me not to wear anything that could get caught in the machinery, I'd thought of this outfit, still in the gift box in a drawer.

"The things I do because I'm nosy," I muttered, as I walked up the sidewalk.

Camille was jogging in place when she answered the door, two yapping Yorkies at her feet. I glimpsed contemporary furnishings, neutral-colored walls, everything spare and clean and not a whiff of cat urine. I breathed deeply. I was afraid I'd need the oxygen.

"Downstairs," she said, trotting off. I followed her, pumping my arms as I went to try to get into the mood. Wisely the Yorkies stayed behind.

We jolted down a set of stairs into the basement. We ran by a media room, and what looked like a home office, before Camille flung open a set of French doors into a torture chamber worthy of the Inquisition.

"Good Lord!" I stopped dead and stared at the piece of equipment in the center of the room. "I swear I'll tell you anything you want to know. And the earth *is* the center of the universe. It is, it is."

"Don't be a wuss."

"Oh please, can't I?"

Camille was still jogging in place, and she hadn't even broken a sweat. "Isn't it gorgeous?"

Gorgeous was hardly the word. The "thing" was almost as tall as Camille's ceiling, and with the seat that jutted out from one side, considerably wider. It was crammed with barbells, pulleys, and levers. I was almost sure it could stretch a man thin as a pancake in less than a minute.

"It looks lethal."

She, foolish girl, thought I was kidding. "Don't you love my gym?" she cooed.

Did I? I would have loved more exits, that's for sure. Right now Camille was standing between me and escape. I looked around. The place was huge. I saw a punching bag in one corner, a stationary bike and stair-climber in another. There was a treelike thingie holding a series of round disks, and a rack with even more barbells. The floor was some sort of foam jigsaw puzzle. Mirrors lined the walls, and "Gonna Fly Now" from *Rocky* was being piped in through giant stereo speakers.

"I've already done my stint on Godzilla there," Camille said, nodding toward the apparatus in the middle. "I'll set you up, then I'll ride the bike while you work, and we can chat."

"Chat?" I was fairly certain my responses would be limited to "*oomph*" and "*ouch*."

Didn't matter. In a few minutes I was lying at an incline on the seat, my feet resting on foot plates. Camille had taken pity on me and only added wuss weights to start me off. My job was to slowly extend my leg almost to its length and hold it, then bend that knee again and try the other leg.

"Do ten on each leg, then I'll add more." Camille trotted off to the bike and began to pedal to Beijing.

I pushed and nothing moved. I tried a little harder and my leg inched along. I was already panting.

"I think I need less weight," I said between puffs.

"You are such a cutup."

"Nope, I'm serious."

Camille jumped off the bike, came over, and made the adjustment. "You're *serious*, all right. You're in serious need of help, Aggie. We're going to have to set up a schedule for you to come and work out with me."

"You can call me at the hospital once I'm ambulatory again."

"So what was your great idea?" Camille was back on the bike, pedaling so fast I was afraid the whole thing was going to lift off the ground.

Camille and Veronica were friends. Camille and I were friends, but Veronica had been in her life longer. So it had made little sense for me to call Camille and tell her I had questions about Veronica that I'd rather she didn't mention to anyone else. I wasn't sure Camille would answer them, and I was darned sure she wouldn't keep them to herself.

So I'd come up with a little "shades of gray" lie to tell Camille. Now I justified it to myself by thinking about Sister Nora.

"I had a fund-raising idea, nothing on the scale of the Idyll, but something to bring in money for the pediatric wing. I thought maybe Veronica would consent to have a small concert of her songs, you know, the ones she's written herself. And we could dedicate it to Grady, because the two of them used to sing together. I think people would come just to honor them both."

"Veronica must really like you. Hardly anybody knows about her songs."

My foot almost slipped off the plate. I had guessed correctly. I took a moment to make sure my sole was solidly back on before I spoke. "Actually, it wasn't Veronica. Somebody else told me. I guess I'd better not say who, if it's supposed to be a secret."

"Oh, Veronica's just a private kind of gal. She has this face she shows the world, the perfect society matron, you know? But underneath she's very sensitive and creative. Weird, isn't it, that she chose the life she did?"

I could almost see Veronica sitting at my kitchen table, and hear her talking about her own mother, and the fluffy little life she hadn't wanted. How badly hadn't she wanted it? Badly enough to try to hang on to Grady's coattails and pretend she'd helped him write a song that became a world-wide hit?

Somehow, I didn't think so.

"Do you think she has enough songs for a concert?" I asked.

"Oh, she has oodles. And they're good, at least the few she's shared with me. She's very talented. The problem, I think, is that they're not what people are looking for now. Not edgy enough. Not rock, not hip-hop. More Barry Manilow and Neil Diamond stuff."

"I'm not sure what you mean by a problem." I was sweating now, and my legs were shaking from the unaccustomed activity.

"A problem selling them. From what she says, a song-writer really needs a performer who'll get excited about her work and record it. That's how they make their way to the top."

I knew I had to be careful, very careful now, and not with my feet. "With Veronica's people skills and contacts, it seems like she'd have luck approaching some appropriate performers, doesn't it? She's so good one-on-one."

"She's done that on her trips to California, you know, for that board she's on. I guess it's a lot harder than it sounds to meet the right people, although she did have a near miss a while ago."

"Did she?"

"She wouldn't tell me much about it. Just that she thought she'd worked out something, and she was so excited. Then I guess it fell through. She was really depressed for a few months, not like herself at all. And she stopped writing, although I think she started again recently."

"A while ago?"

"A year maybe. Almost two? Anyway, I think she's back on track."

My heart was pounding now, and I wasn't sure whether it was from the exercise, or Camille's revelation. "Well, that's good news."

"I don't think she'd be willing to expose herself that way in public, though, Aggie. With the songs, I mean, even though your idea's very nice. But she told me once that a long time ago she sang one of her songs in an audition and was completely humiliated when the judges sent her away. So she doesn't perform, and she doesn't show her songs to just anybody."

I was almost sure I knew one person she had showed them to. "Except when she's trying to sell them," I said.

"I bet even that's hard for her." Camille got off the bike and came over to show me the next exercise, which involved using my toes to push the same footrest and strengthen my calves.

"We're almost done, right?" I smiled brightly. "Once my legs are all toned and perfect?"

Camille laughed, much the way the Inquisition judges must have laughed at Galileo.

"When do you think we will be finished?" I asked as she added weights.

"Maybe an hour. I have some great exercises with the medicine ball. And I thought we could finish you up with the punching bag."

I hoped that in an hour I would still have the breath for a phone call. Because the moment I was finished here, if I was still alive, I was going to punch all right. I was going to punch in Fred's number on my speed dial for one final heart-to-heart. It was a good thing I had never learned how to delete it.

19

I was tired of making mistakes, of putting myself in danger, of waiting until a killer was practically standing in front of me before all the clues came together in my head. I was tired of depending on other people to happen along when things looked particularly gruesome. This time I was going to get everything right.

Of course, I'm not stupid. "Right" and even "best" would have been to tell Detective Roussos what I'd figured out, and let him do the dirty work. Unfortunately I didn't have enough proof to lift even one of his bushy eyebrows, much less send him to investigate. My phone call with Fred had confirmed my theory. Now I was pretty sure what had taken place, and why Grady had ended up dead on the green room floor. I just needed proof.

With Lucy's help, I was going to get it.

Unlike my mother, I'm not into costumes, but when I got up on Friday morning I dressed carefully. Care was good, since every muscle in my body was still screaming from the workout at Camille's. We were scheduled for the same time next week. I figured if my plans today went awry and I ended up with angel wings, missing the date with Godzilla would be a silver lining.

In case I needed to move quickly, I put on comfortable, loose-fitting clothing, although not so loose the fabric would be easy to grab. I debated running shoes or something with a harder heel and went for flats with enough of a heel to do damage if necessary.

I'm not my father's daughter for nothing.

I had debated and rejected telling Ed my plan. I knew what he would say, and could I blame him? But I had to do this. Whatever I thought of the idea, Nora Nelson deserved to build her biosphere. Grady Barber, as obnoxious as he had been, deserved to have his real killer apprehended. I deserved to get back to my normal life.

Emerald Springs deserved a good thunderstorm, but that was the one item I couldn't do anything about.

I took a couple of deep breaths and groaned my way through a series of stretching exercises, then I went downstairs. Ed was making breakfast. My stomach was tied in knots, and I didn't think I could hold a full cup of coffee without spilling it, but I had to make a stab at eating. I needed to leave the house at nine this morning, but not a minute after. That meant I still had time to kill.

I wish I hadn't thought about it in quite those words.

"Morning, sleepyhead," he said.

I gave him a good-morning kiss. We did our morning exchange about how we'd slept and our craziest dreams, then Ed recounted the news headlines, which are a lot more interesting coming from him than teasing them out of the *Flow*. A disaster somewhere other than Emerald Springs will be relegated to our back pages, while a significant local event, like cows escaping a pasture, or a city council discussion on trash pickup, will be front headlines.

"Yum," I said, as my stomach turned over at the sight of blueberry-splattered whole wheat pancakes. Even one of those babies was going to sink like a stone.

"Get yourself some coffee."

I was careful to fill my mug only halfway. I got out the butter and syrup and kept my eye on the kitchen clock. Once the table was set and the girls arrived, we sat down to eat together, although luckily, nobody was feeling chatty. The minute hand was moving slowly. My jaw was moving even more slowly, but I managed to finish every bite on my plate and most of my coffee.

"Isn't Grady Barber's memorial service this afternoon?" Ed asked.

"It is." I nodded, as if this meant nothing.

"You're planning to go, I take it?"

"Yep. You don't have to be there, though. You do enough yourself without attending this one."

"It'll probably be a media circus."

If the service actually went forward, the *Flow* and possibly the wire services would cover the event, but if things went as planned this morning, in the next few days there would be more interesting news to write about.

Nine o'clock had almost arrived. I got up and put my dishes in the sink, then I snapped my fingers. "You know, I just remembered where I left my cell phone."

"You lost your cell phone?"

"I was afraid I did, but I just realized I had it out when I was in the church yesterday talking to Esther. I think I laid it on one of the pews."

"January will find it when he cleans this afternoon."

January was our sexton, and I was pretty sure he wasn't going to find it, since I'd hidden it so well. "Maybe, but I think I'll run over and get it. I don't want to leave it to chance. Do you mind?"

"I'm hanging around here until noon. I'll be at the church after that."

"While I'm over there maybe I'll do a little cleanup on those leftover wedding flowers. Esther and I both thought they needed freshening before Sunday."

"Since when is that your job?"

"Since I realized that nobody else was going to do it."

He looked skeptical, but he didn't grab me by the collar and demand to know what was going on.

Teddy began to tell her father about the latest installment of the movie. "Do brain parasites worry about right and wrong?" she asked in finale.

Teddy to the rescue. I kissed Ed's cheek before I got the church keys out of our basket. Now I knew he wasn't going to think about me for some time. Deena looked like she was chewing on something other than pancakes, and I hoped that while I was gone, she would finally tell her dad she was sorry. That would take up some time, too.

I got out of the house right at nine and cut through the yard, crossed a small road, then wove my way through the parish house parking lot. So far, so good.

Lucy was not waiting in front of the church. This was *not* good. We had set this up carefully. She was supposed to be here right now, if not a few minutes ago. But a scan of the street and the sidewalks wasn't encouraging. No Lucy on the way, either.

"Lucy! You have some 'splaining to do!"

I unlocked the church and left the door ajar behind me so Lucy would come in the moment she arrived. I checked my watch. It was five minutes after. I was guessing that in about ten minutes, all hell might break loose.

"C'mon, Luce!" I went down to the front, pulled my cell phone from between cushions on the front pew, and punched in her number. I got voice mail and told her to get moving. Yesterday when I had hidden the phone, I hadn't just been here talking to Esther. I'd also been upstairs making sure a fresh ninety-minute tape was in the recorder in the choir loft. Our audio guy tapes Ed's sermons through our sound system every Sunday so they can be delivered to shut-ins or people who sleep in on Sunday and still want to know what's been said from the pulpit. Lucy was supposed to be up in the loft right now, hidden but ready to start the recorder when it was needed.

I debated what to do. I could call this off and find another way to get the information I needed. Or I could run upstairs, turn on the tape and still have plenty of time left for what I needed to do. The tape would still catch what I hoped it might. The only difference was that I wouldn't have immediate backup if things got tough.

I ran up to the choir loft. Even I knew how to punch Play and Record at the same time to get it started, plus there were neatly typed directions for the weeks a different volunteer took on the task. I made sure the tape was running, then ran back downstairs and turned on the microphone. Lucy still hadn't arrived, but one glance at my watch told me somebody else would probably be here shortly. Once I was no longer alone, Lucy would be too smart to come into the church, but I hoped she would wait in the foyer.

I had just enough time to make the phone call I'd been planning.

I pulled out the business card in my pocket and punched in a number. Unfortunately I got voice mail. Since my first message late last night had been pointed enough, I was almost sure the recipient would be here on time, unless he was out of town.

I know who murdered Grady Barber, and I can prove it.

Now there was nothing for me to do except look busy.

I was pulling wilting flowers out of one of two arrangements when I heard footsteps in the aisle beyond me. For a moment I didn't react, as if I were so absorbed I hadn't heard anyone. Then, after a few seconds, I stopped and glanced up. Casual all the way.

"Veronica." I checked my watch, as if her unexpected appearance had rattled me. "I thought you were coming to my house. I was just getting ready to meet you over there."

"I got there a little early. Your husband said I'd find you here."

After working so closely with her, I knew a few things for sure about Veronica Hayworth. One was that she was always early. I'd banked on this result, and I hadn't been wrong. I would have patted myself on the back had it been anatomically possible to do it gracefully, and if it wouldn't have been such a giveaway.

I put the discarded flowers to one side and started down to meet her. She wore wide-leg white pants and a short-sleeved black jacket buttoned to the neck. A fringed white purse was strung over one shoulder. She looked crisp, cool, and unruffled. I hoped that would change.

"Shall we go back to my house?" I tried to look worried, and I'm sure I succeeded, since that part, at least, was true. "We could sit, have a cup of coffee."

"I'm in kind of a hurry. I'd better say no."

We joined up at the piano, again exactly what I'd hoped for. She stood with her back to the pews, facing the piano and me. I was angled a bit so I could see down the aisles if I had dared a glance. I didn't. I had to focus on Veronica, and I didn't want her to think I was expecting anyone else.

"How was your trip?" I asked.

"Blessedly short. Now I have a lot to do for the service this afternoon."

"It's going to be an emotional day. I'm sorry you're having to do all the work, when you were so close to Grady."

"Yes. Well. Somebody had to organize it. Your message said you had something we might want to add? Readings maybe?" She looked just the tiniest bit skeptical.

"Not readings, exactly. Just an idea." I sat on the bench. I'd made sure the fallboard was flipped up so the keys were exposed. Now, without saying anything else, I started to pick out a tune. Not exactly one-fingered. I'm no musician, but I did have that one intensive summer of piano lessons. Although no one will ever ask me to sing in the church choir, my ear's not too bad. I only made the occasional mistake.

"It's such a wonderful song," I said, plunking keys. " 'Sailing toward a Rainbow.' Whose idea was the title? Yours or Grady's?"

"Aggie, I've got a million things to do before the service."

"Okay. Here's my idea. I think *you* should sing this song today. After all, you helped Grady write it. Nobody could do it with more feeling, Veronica. Even if the last time you sang it, things didn't exactly work out."

Her expression didn't change. I had to give Veronica credit. She was a good actress. I wondered how many years it had taken to learn how to hide her feelings this well. How many people had she fooled in the course of those years? Had she ever trusted anybody enough to bare her soul? I doubted it.

"I'm not going to sing anything," she said evenly. "We have everything worked out already."

"Then maybe one of the other songs you wrote? Did you write any of the rest of them *with* Grady? Or were they all just your own creation, even 'Rainbow'? Or this . . ." I began to pick out the melody to "Remember Me in April."

"I don't think he had a hand in this one," I said. "Not in writing it, although, of course, he took full credit again."

Her tone was polite, even if the words were not. "I really don't have time for games. What point are you trying to make?"

I was warmed up now, and the butterflies in my stomach had settled. Now that I'd started, all I could do was forge ahead.

"You're very good at hiding things, aren't you? And really good at planning and executing a strategy once you have all the details in place. Of course *execute*'s a bad word, isn't it? I'm not trying to mock you. I know you killed Grady, and I know why. But I don't think you executed him. Not exactly. You were ready to kill him if you had to. You'd set everything up perfectly, although I really doubt you meant to do it the night of the finals."

She was silent, but her expression still didn't change.

"I'll tell you how I see it." I continued to pick out the song for a moment while I gathered my thoughts, then I stopped playing.

"I know about the *Wayfarers* tryout. I know he abandoned you, humiliated you, then took credit for a song that you'd written. He didn't have much, if anything, to do with writing it, did he? It was your song all along, but you knew he was the one to really do it justice at the audition. So you were willing to share the credit, and you hoped it would be a ticket out of Emerald Springs for both of you. You wanted something more than the fluffy little life your mother had led. You were ready to reach for it."

"And that leads to murder how?" She sounded genuinely interested.

"It wouldn't have, I suppose, if it had ended there. But it didn't. He pulled a fast one on you, and by the time that was over, you knew that nobody would believe the song was really yours. I think you probably imagined getting even with him for years. Most people would have. It was such a betrayal, it cried out for revenge. But after a while you grew up, you made a life here, you married a big shot in Emerald Springs, and you probably didn't want to lose what you could count on. You're the proverbial big frog in a small pond, Veronica. There are people who would give a lot to be you."

"What a lovely way to put it."

I shrugged. "You probably told yourself to let the whole thing go. For a while. You promised yourself you'd learned your lesson, that nobody could ever take advantage of you that way again. Then Grady did it once more."

"Aggie, this is all very interesting, but it sounds like a half-baked theory you came up with because you don't want to believe Nora Nelson murdered Grady. Unfortunately I think you're the only person besides those crazy performers out at the farm who thinks she's innocent. Now, I'm sorr—"

I ignored my mother's teachings and interrupted. "See, the one thing you were *never* able to give up was your songwriting. And the songs kept you connected to that high school dream, even though everything in your real life said it was time for that to be over with. So you kept writing, and when you went to California for your board meetings, you always spent a couple of extra days in Los Angeles trying to interest agents or, really, anybody who would meet with you, in your growing body of work."

"That would be pretty pathetic, wouldn't it?"

"Really? I don't think so. It shows initiative, which we

know you have in abundance. And I imagine charm plays a part in who's successful and who isn't. I'm sure some people just met with you because you were so easy on the eye, so intelligent, so talented at making them feel good about themselves."

"Please. Compliments given in the name of pinning a murder on me?"

"Then you ran into Grady. Or maybe you set up an appointment with him. I'm not sure. I do know you met with him. Fred Handlemann—you remember Fred—told me yesterday that he'd met you in Los Angeles himself. Grady introduced you as an old friend."

"Ran into Grady? Do you think I'm that ineffectual?"

I had hit a sore spot. Encouraged, I tried for the same place again.

"Maybe not ineffectual, Veronica. Maybe just scared to face him after everything, afraid you might look like a fool."

"Absolutely not. I managed to get his number, and I called him. I told him he owed me dinner for stealing 'Rainbow' from me."

I was more encouraged. I was also hoping the tape recorder was picking this up, and that Lucy was now standing in the foyer, although if she was, she was awfully good at not making any noise.

"I imagine Grady wasn't very enthused about meeting with you," I said. "I'd guess you sweetened the pot to get him there."

She was silent and wide-eyed a moment. Surprised at herself for responding? Surprised at my insights? Wondering what to say next? I couldn't tell.

She pulled herself together. "There are people in town who know I once claimed that I helped Grady write 'Rainbow.' You haven't discovered anything new. And meeting with an old friend on a business trip is nothing but a big yawn."

"But do they know you also wrote 'Remember Me in April'?"

"Why are you harping on that?"

"I think, Veronica, that when the police search your home, they'll find your hand-notated score, the original. Or maybe you sent it to your lawyer with instructions not to open it. If it was sealed and postmarked, the date you wrote it would be clear. You see, I believe that when you met Grady for dinner that night in L.A., you took a copy of 'Remember Me in April' with you, because you were so tired of dealing with people who didn't know you, you decided to deal with somebody who did. Grady was a rat, but he was a known quantity. And you thought that because he owed you, he would at least take a look at 'April' and let you play it for him."

"You have quite an imagination."

"So do you, because although I haven't heard your other songs, these two are good. Imaginative, evocative, perfect for Grady's voice. And obviously written by the same person. Now that we know that person wasn't *Grady*, it leads right back to you."

"I suppose you're an expert on the subject of songwriting as well as so many other things?"

"I'm guessing you went to his house, where there was a piano you could play it on. I also imagine that the moment he heard it, Grady realized how perfect it would be for him. I saw a lot of different sides to Grady Barber while we were working so closely, and I know that when he needed to, he could charm the socks off almost anybody. I think that night he charmed *you*. I think he told you how sorry he was for what he'd done, that he'd been thinking about you for years, that he hadn't known how to approach you. Maybe he even sang the song's chorus along with you. Under the circumstances it would have had particular meaning."

I picked out the notes and sang the words as best I could.

I tried to stay
I didn't want to leave you when the air was soft and
  gray

I didn't want to leave you, not then or any day
But, you see, I had no choice
I had to go away.

Veronica looked pained, either at the message, or more likely my voice. "If any of this crazy tale you're spinning is true, why on earth would I have just given him another song? I'm sure you checked. My name isn't on 'April.'"

"Oh, I think you were so wary at first, understandably so, that you wanted to keep it strictly business."

And now I was at the place where I went straight out on a limb. I just hoped that like Moonpie, I was really going to be okay.

I closed the fallboard and stood so we were eye to eye. "But I don't think you kept that night strictly business, Veronica. I'm guessing he wined and dined you, that he complimented you, not just on the song, but on everything. Maybe you'd never been his girlfriend in high school, but this wasn't the same scruffy Grady, the outcast that your in crowd made fun of. This was Grady Barber the film star, the Vegas entertainer, the man who left Emerald Springs, the way *you'd* wanted to, and made a new, exciting life for himself. I think you went to bed with him. And I'm afraid I know what Grady liked to do when he was in bed with a woman. He liked to make videotapes. He liked to film his activities, then he liked to hold the tapes over his lovers' heads for whatever he needed from them. Our Grady was an *A* number one blackmailer. And he used that tape to blackmail you and make you give up another song."

"How did you come up with this?"

The words weren't an admission, but I thought Veronica sounded more interested in knowing how I'd arrived at my conclusion than in proving her innocence.

"I know how savvy you are," I explained. "All along you were willing to just let him have the song, because, of course, this was never about money. But you probably wanted the credit, right? And I know you wouldn't have walked into this blindly. I believe this was all about getting the respect you deserved. So you must have gone to Grady with a plan to protect yourself. And the *only* thing I can think of that might have derailed that plan is sex. You don't want the life you have, but you've never quite been able to leave it. You made one attempt as a teenager and lived with that humiliation for too long. So when you had to choose whether to give Grady another song or to let Grady give your husband the videotape, you made the safest choice. You chose what you already had and handed over 'Remember Me in April.' "

Veronica looked off into the distance, almost as if she were watching that scene in L.A. unfold again. "He called it tit for tat. Do you know, he actually said that? He thought he was so funny. And that's the moment when I knew I wanted him dead."

Not yet an admission of guilt, but oh, so close. Of course my elation was tempered by that eternal question "Why?" I had hoped she would be so overcome by emotion she would blurt out the truth, but Veronica still seemed collected and sure of herself. Was she simply ready for this to be over with? To let the world know what she had done and take her punishment?

I doubted I could count on that.

"How did you come up with your plan to kill him?" I asked.

She looked back at me and smiled, but she didn't speak.

"I'll tell you what I think," I said. "Your anger built once you came home, didn't it? You kept trying to figure out ways to get even, this time for real. Then, your husband told you about Sister Nora and the real estate deal he was trying to finalize. Lucy told me only a few realtors knew about their search for property, and I'm sure Farley was one of them. When he found out Lucy Jacobs had sold Nora the perfect farm, he was furious. I'm sure he told you all about it. And you knew who Nora was. You probably knew everything about Grady's life, about all his marriages—"

"The day I heard Nora Nelson was coming to Emerald Springs to live, I felt like God was talking to *me*. I felt like He had stepped down from heaven and put his hand on my shoulder and told me to go ahead and bring Grady here. Nora Nelson's crazy. She hears voices. She thinks God's speaking to her and telling her to save the world. She deserves to be locked up."

I made sure my jaw wasn't hanging open, but it was an effort. Who was the real maniac here? Nora, who heard God telling her to do good works and save the earth? Or this woman, who heard God telling her to kill a man who had wronged her and frame someone else? I didn't even know what to say, but it didn't matter, because Veronica filled the silence.

"And you know what? The day, the very day after I heard Nora was moving here, the judge we'd hoped to get for the Emerald Springs Idyll backed out. And I knew then what I was going to do, what I was *supposed* to do."

"Everything just fell together?" I asked this as gently as I could.

"Like it was meant to be."

"*Umm* . . . Maybe so, but how did you get Grady to come? Why would he show his face in town knowing you had proof that 'Remember Me in April' was your composition? Wasn't he afraid you'd tell people, even if it ruined your marriage? That you were setting him up so he'd be here when you did?"

"He knew better. After all, I'd given him the song, hadn't I?"

She wanted me to work it out, but my brain had stretched as far as it would go. At no point in my hypothesis had I figured on Veronica's conviction that she was meant to murder Grady, that somehow she had divine permission, even help. That gave everything a new twist. People who are misguided enough to use God as an excuse for violence are people with no problems repeating themselves. I had been banking on Veronica's innate good sense to

keep this conversation in bounds, good sense that had been
distorted by her fury at Grady the night of the Idyll finals,
but good sense that could still be appealed to. Now I knew
better.

"So you're not quite as adept at this as you think you
are," Veronica said when I didn't, couldn't, respond. "I'll
just tell you, so you won't have to strain so hard. I told
Grady I had *another* song for him. One that was better than
the other two put together. I told him I would give it to him
free and clear if he came to Emerald Springs and gave me
the tape."

"You thought that would end it?"

"Of course, I knew he could make a million copies first,
but I told him that like before, I'd have proof this song belonged to me. If a tape of us together ever showed up anywhere, I'd bring out the heavy guns, because by then I'd
have nothing to lose. But unless that happened, this would be
the end. He would come and judge the Idyll, which would
make up for a lot of the bad things he'd done. After all, raising that money for the new pediatric wing would make me
look like the town savior. At least I'd have that. Grady would
have a wonderful new song, and I would have the tape and
my place in Emerald Springs history. And all our business
would be completed."

I remembered that right from the beginning, Fred had
said Grady was behaving much worse than usual now
that he was home again. So greed had brought him to our
fair city, but even Grady had realized he might be walking
into trouble.

"And he bought that?" I asked

She shrugged one slender shoulder. "He was hungry for
another hit. I'd given him the only two he'd ever had. He
was willing."

He was a fool. But hadn't we all been fools? Hadn't we
underestimated this woman? Luckily, I hadn't underestimated her so much that I hadn't gotten backup. And now, I
was almost sure my backup had arrived. As Veronica had

given her explanation, I had heard the front doors of the church open, and the faintest whisper of footsteps.

Saved. And in a Unitarian-Universalist church, too, where such things are almost never discussed.

I didn't look up. I ignored the subtle creaking of the floorboards and spoke louder. "And then, you killed him," I said, hoping to get this over with. She hadn't really admitted to murder yet, just the desire.

She still didn't. "Of course I didn't kill him. Yes, I wanted him dead, but it's a long way from wanting to doing. Then things took a turn I would never have believed. Nora went backstage the night of the finals and murdered him herself. And Grady managed to scrawl *nor* on the wall before he died. A trooper, our Grady. Right up until the end. See what I mean? It was all meant to be."

"Only it wasn't Nora's name he was scrawling, Veronica. It was *yours.* Grady was dyslexic. Lisa Lee told me in high school, he even tried to read music right to left. In those last moments, when he only had seconds to live, he scrawled the name he had known you by in high school. Ronnie. He could only manage *ron*, the first three letters, before he died. Unfortunately for poor Nora, he was printing your name, as he had so often printed others."

I paused for effect. "Backwards."

She stared at me, and for the first time I saw anger flickering in her eyes. "I didn't go there that night with murder in mind."

Man, oh man, I was hoping, yes, praying, that this last sentence had been caught on tape. I wanted so badly to see who was coming down the aisle, but as she continued, I was scared to look away.

"Yes, I set up everything just in case. I hired a boy from that ridiculous tent show to steal something from Nora's house I could use as a weapon. I had no idea she was shacking up with a knife thrower. Another piece of divine collaboration, wouldn't you say?"

"Or simply a coincidence."